Passing into Light

"To me, [Sharon Ewell Foster] is one of America's best kept secrets—but not for long! Sharon writes for those of us who want more than just words on a page, but pictures painted on the canvases of our minds. She has proven to be 'the Picasso of the pen!'"

BISHOP T. D. JAKES

"I could not put the book down. I am normally not a fiction reader, but as I read, I was hungry for more chapters and found myself being pulled into Shirley's world. As a psychotherapist and personal development coach, I thought the book gave the reader a vivid account of one woman's journey back through the personal pain of the past only to emerge victoriously into the light of her future. There was so much wisdom and courage in the book."

DR. FREDA JONES, PSYCHOTHERAPIST

"Sharon Ewell Foster is an author who allows God to use her through her novels. Her love for Him is the blueprint for the incredible stories she weaves. With every page, readers are left feeling inspired and hopeful with the knowledge that through God, all things are possible. Sharon Ewell Foster's books are smoothly written and definitely a must-read for those of us who are still seeking God's plan for our lives."

LISA R. HAMMACK, EBONY EYES BOOK CLUB

"When you read the writings of Sharon Ewell Foster, you will find that the very essence of God is being unveiled before you. Her words suggest a knowing that delves deep into the core of God's loving nature. To have read a book written by Sharon Ewell Foster is to have had an inside look at the heart and mind of God."

REGINA GAIL MALLOY, READING CLUB HOST, HEAVEN 600 RADIO

"*Passing into Light* is a story that mixes mother wit, suspense, twists and turns, and a little romance. Sharon Ewell Foster even manages to throw some angels into the mix and serves up a dish that is as full of substance as it is sweet. Enjoy it with a glass of 'sweet ice tea.' It's a book that sticks to the ribs and satisfies the heart."

EMMA RODGERS, CO-OWNER, BLACK IMAGES BOOK BAZAAR, DALLAS

"In Sharon Ewell Foster we have a literary gem. A writer with the rare ability to craft memorable characters amidst compelling plots spun with graceful prose, Foster's contributions continue to raise the bar for quality literature. Foster is, very clearly, God's instrument; the melody is beautiful."

JAMELLAH ELLIS, AUTHOR OF *THAT FAITH, THAT TRUST, THAT LOVE*
AND "CHASING HORIZONS," A SHORT STORY IN THE ANTHOLOGY
PROVERBS FOR THE PEOPLE.

"A prolific writer, Sharon Ewell Foster manages to serve up literary cuisine with the seasoned insight of Iyanla Vanzant. Can a story get any better? Sharon Ewell Foster makes certain it does."

PAT G'ORGE-WALKER, AUTHOR OF *SISTER BETTY! GOD'S CALLING YOU,*
AGAIN! AND CHRISTIAN COMEDIAN, WWW.SISTERBETTY.COM

Sharon Foster's stories are a magnificent portrayal of the awesomeness of God in a world hungry for life-saving answers to life-threatening situations.

ANGELA BENSON, AUTHOR OF *AWAKENING MERCY*

Riding Through Shadows

"Foster's book offers important spiritual lessons about the power of the tongue, the effect of praise and prayer as a spiritual weapon, and the importance of spiritual deliverance."

CBA MARKETPLACE

"Foster's gift of imagination and description is evident throughout, as she paints graphic pictures of the spirit realm, including behind-the-scenes spiritual warfare."

CHRISTIAN RETAILING

Ain't No River

"An entertaining story about family and relationships that incorporates the wisdom of Bible verses throughout…a well-written story."
BOOKLIST

"Ms. Foster has exceptional talent in creating a wonderful book. And in preaching the Word without being preachy. I eagerly look forward to more of her work."
SCRIBES WORLD REVIEWS

"*Ain't No River* is beautifully written and reaffirms Ms. Foster's place among the literary elite."
PAMELA WALKER-WILLIAMS, PAGETURNER.NET

"A must-read, inspirational, and spirit-filled account of human struggle that transcends generations, gender, economic status, and cultural differences."
RHONDA K. SUTTLE, NATIONAL DIRECTOR, NAACP ACT-SO

"*Ain't No River* will capture your heart and soul."
VANESSA WOODWARD, FOUNDER AND CEO, JOURNEY'S END

Passing by Samaria

"A rhapsody in prose. It is an intriguing look back that also speaks loudly to the times we live in. For a religious novel to simmer in the African-American religious tradition yet carry a universal message is a rarity. Readers will be thankful for this rare and splendid work of love, faith, and art."
BARBARA A. REYNOLDS, PRESIDENT, REYNOLDS NEWS SERVICE; AUTHOR, RADIO TALK SHOW/TELEVISION NEWS COMMENTATOR, SYNDICATED COLUMNIST

"*Passing by Samaria* takes a sensitive and thoughtful look at a revolutionary time in American history. Foster's characters are unforgettable; full of life and unhesitatingly charming, they drive this powerful book."
KWEISI MFUME, PRESIDENT AND CEO, NAACP

Sharon Ewell Foster

Passing into Light

Multnomah®Publishers *Sisters, Oregon*

PASSING INTO LIGHT
published by Multnomah Publishers, Inc.
Published in association with the literary agency of Sara A. Fortenberry,
1001 Halcyon Ave., Nashville, TN 37204

© 2002 by Sharon Ewell Foster
International Standard Book Number: 1-59052-066-1

Cover image by Photonica / Karen Beard
Cover design by Chris Gilbert—UDG/DesignWorks

Unless otherwise noted, all Scripture references are from:
The Holy Bible, King James Version (KJV).
Other Scripture is from:
The Holy Bible, New King James Version (NKJV)
© 1984 by Thomas Nelson, Inc.

The Holy Bible, New International Version (NIV)
© 1973, 1984 by International Bible Society,
used by permission of Zondervan Publishing House.

Multnomah is a trademark of Multnomah Publishers, Inc.,
and is registered in the U.S. Patent and Trademark Office.
The colophon is a trademark of Multnomah Publishers, Inc.

Printed in the United States of America

For information:
MULTNOMAH PUBLISHERS, INC. • P.O. BOX 1720 • SISTERS, OR 97759

Library of Congress Cataloging-in-Publication Data

Foster, Sharon Ewell.
  Passing into light / by Sharon Ewell Foster.
      p. cm.
  ISBN 1-59052-066-1 (pbk.)
  1. Single parents—Fiction. 2. Grief—Fiction. I. Title.
PS3556.O7724 P374 2003
813'.54—dc21

                          2002154749

03 04 05 06 07 08 09—10 9 8 7 6 5 4 3 2 1 0

Dedication

This book is dedicated to the women and children who have called Holy Angels Homeless Shelter, in East Saint Louis, Illinois, home. They are living miracles and symbols of hope. Their courageous stories, and their willingness to share them, inspired a story ending beyond my hopes.

Passing into Light is also dedicated to the director of the shelter, Ms. Patricia Lewis, to social worker Paulyn Snyder, minister Anthony Vinson, and to all those of all colors and all denominations who serve and make Holy Angels a house of light and a symbol of God's love—even for those struggling to find their way through the darkest of times.

Finally, the book is dedicated to God, who hides us under the shelter of His wings.

ACKNOWLEDGMENTS

A man's gift maketh room for him,
and bringeth him before great men.
PROVERBS 18:16

*T*hank you to all the great people in my life. I cannot name you all, but please know that I thank you, appreciate you, and am honored by who you are.

Thank you to all my faithful readers. Your notes, e-mails, prayers, and words of encouragement held me up and covered me.

Thank you to my family and loved ones whose hope and prayers are reflected on every page. Thank you Lanea, Chase, Ervin, LaJuana, Kytti, Clarence, Mama, Daddy, my brothers, Mama and Daddy Starks and the Starks family (we still have papers), Jan, Freda, Regina Gail, Lisa, Carol, Edie, Glenda, Venus, Candy, Sandra, Pat, Angela, and Cheryl.

Thank you to Sara Fortenberry, Karen Ball, and the entire team at Multnomah Publishers.

Thank you to the members of the God Chasers discipleship class, Deaconess Adelaide Dargan, Minister Allan Gray, and Minister Darlene Gilbert and the Morning Glory Intercessors, Sister Angela Smith and the Kingdom Women.

Thank you to Mother Davis and Sister Doretha Brown, who inspired the wise women in my stories.

Thank you to the people whose words minister to me: Joyce Meyer; Rev. G. E. Patterson, Evangelist Jackie

McCullough, and Rev. Valerie Wells. Thank you to Rev. Dr. Walter Scott Thomas, pastor of New Psalmist Baptist Church and to lovely First Lady Patricia Thomas. Thank you for the push. Thank you to Bishop Howard Oby, pastor of Beloved Tabernacle of God, at whose knee, studying, I began to fully understand the beauty of the Truth set before us. Love to you and Miss Portia.

Thank you to April Kihlstrom and the BIAW challenge issued at RWA. Thanks also to Nora Roberts for issuing the salvo. Thanks also to Tia Shabazz and the Black Writer's Alliance.

Thank you to Bishop T. D. Jakes and First Lady Serita Jakes. Your kindness, graciousness, wisdom, and encouragement exhorted me to do the impossible and to finish this book. Thank you both for your generosity and for the sacrificial love you give.

Finally, thank You, God, for reminding me through the Holy Spirit that I can do all things through Christ, which strengtheneth me. Thank You for hope and joy unspeakable. Thank You for happy endings.

As Jesus was getting into the boat,
the man who had been demon-possessed
begged to go with him. Jesus did not let him, but said,
"Go home to your family and tell them how
much the Lord has done for you,
and how he has had mercy on you."
So the man went away and began to tell
in the Decapolis [the Ten Cities] how much
Jesus had done for him.
And all the people were amazed.

MARK 5:18–20, NIV

ONE

HUNTSVILLE, ALABAMA, 1986

*I*t was stupid to run, but it was stupid to stay.

The silver Toyota Corolla clipped down the road past dried brown grass, wooden fences, and green leafed trees. Shirley was making good time and had long since kissed Highway 55 good-bye. Her kids were curled up in each other's arms—at least as much as the seat belts would allow—sleeping and drooling. She glanced at them in the rearview mirror.

Mika's hot-pink leg warmers matched her pink spandex, knee-length shorts and her pink sleeveless T-shirt, all topped by a gray sweatshirt that hung off one shoulder. A hot-pink and day-glo-green headband held most of her hair out of her face, except for the thick upturned bangs that had escaped. Honey-colored Mika looked like the actress from *Flashdance* had collided with Cyndi Lauper. Girls just want to have fun. Shirley shook her head. She didn't remember fashion being such a big deal when she was in the fourth grade.

Lex, a deeper brown than his sister, had one Adidas tennis shoe on, the other was in the rear window next to an empty juice box. His head full of curly-kinky hair was smashed flat

11

on one side where he had been lying. One leg of his bright blue nylon tracksuit had crept up over his bony knee. Slobber had made a dark trail on the yellow, blue, and green panels of his lightweight jacket. And the collar was up; even in his sleep, little Lexington managed to keep his collar up. How could a little kid know so much about collars and stuff? Shirley let herself smile. Fashion sense must run in the family—she looked briefly at her gray sweatpants and plain red cotton T-shirt—just not on her side.

They would cross through Tuscaloosa soon, and Shirley's plan was to drive straight across Texas.

California was going to mean a brand new life. She patted the brown envelope on the seat next to her. *Thank you, God.* It was their seed money to get settled in the New World. Alabama was behind them. The money was all they had. That and too many memories tied with pink ribbon.

The ribbon-tied bundle was full of letters, papers, and pictures. There were pictures of the kids, of Danny, of the whole family together. There was a letter from her uncles, and tied in the same bundle were discharge papers, even an envelope from her husband's memorial service—some things the guys thought she should have—that she had never been able to open. All of it was tied together with pink ribbon. And the funny thing was, she didn't own anything else that was pink.

It was time to move forward.

Mother Johnson had never seen the kids. And Shirley knew Mika and Lex would love her. Mother had been on Shirley's mind, but Tyler, Texas, was the doorway to too many memories.

It was the best thing for them—for her and the kids—to go to California. Mika and Lex would be happy there. They could get a new start in a place where no one knew them, where there wouldn't be any questions. Maybe she could go to nursing school at UC Davis. There was no one there to pry, they would be able to heal. She would be able to pull her family—to pull herself—back together.

There had been too many dreams. Shirley lived days where she and the children seemed happy—days where she appeared to be content—but there were also the dreams.

Sometimes the dreams were just about her husband. Everyday dreams, where they walked and talked or rode to the grocery store. Dreams where he played his guitar and sang to her. Dreams that brought Danny back to life. She could touch him, taste him, smell him. She could even make love to him so that she awakened flushed and blushing. Those were the good dreams.

Broken yellow lines on the highway whizzed by. Shirley searched through radio stations looking for a song. She stopped when she heard Patti Labelle and Michael McDonald singing "On My Own." It was probably the wrong song to listen to—it was already too clear to her and the kids, they were on their own. Danny wasn't going to be coming back.

Yes, there were good dreams. But then there were the other dreams, the ones that made her want to claw her way out of them. It was better to start over, to breathe again.

Start over. That was the plan...before the police car stopped her. Red and blue lights flashed behind her. The sound of the siren seemed to envelop the car.

"Where're you on your way to so fast, lady?" The policeman leaned into the window and looked closely at her, then at the children lying in the back. Shirley could see another policeman in the patrol car and assumed he was running her plates.

"You were going pretty fast. This one's going to cost you."

Her heart was thumping as though she had committed a crime—a greater crime than speeding. "We're on our way to California."

"California?" She heard the inquiry in the state trooper's voice but wasn't sure how to respond, so she just nodded.

A voice from the other side of the car startled her. It was the other trooper. "Well, it looks like your trip is going to be delayed a little. You're going to have to come with us."

"What's wrong? What did I do? What about my kids? What about my car?" She could feel her cool exterior falling apart.

"Just calm down, lady. The kids will come with us," the second officer said from behind his dark shades. "We'll just go to the station, check out what needs to be checked out, and we'll take it from there. We'll leave your car here." He tipped his glasses so that he could see over the rim. "We should be putting you in cuffs, ma'am—" Shirley's heart jumped—"but we won't, out of respect for the children and until we can get this cleared up. But if I were you, I would be thinking about who I could call to bail me out and to come and get my kids."

As they rode, Shirley thought of every story she had heard about criminals masquerading as cops. How stupid she had been to go along with these men! She was too scared to even ask why she was being taken to the station, why she would need to be bailed out, or why she would need someone to get her kids. How did she even know who they were? They might not be troopers—but imposters. She looked around the backseat. It was too late now. She and Mika and Lex were locked in.

Mika and Lex looked back and forth at each other, at her, at the policemen. They scrunched themselves down under her arms and close to her body. Their clothes and their faces were wrinkled with sleep. Shirley forced herself to smile at them. "Isn't this neat? I always wondered what the inside of a police car looked like," she lied. "Don't worry. Mommy's got every-thing under control. There's just some paperwork to complete. That's all." She hugged them until the car pulled into town.

The police station was small. Somehow it reminded her of Tyler. Everything outside was brown. A battered brown pickup truck pulled up beside them—it looked like a utility truck. A girl with very pale, dirty hair hopped out of the passenger's side. She looked dazed. There was a long, bleeding cut on her face. The man that got out of the driver's side door was also young, but he looked angry. His hair was almost the same color as the girl's, but he was balding prematurely on top. His features were brutish, and his skin was flushed red. He stomped around the side of the car, his stomach pulling against his pizza delivery shirt, grabbed the girl's arm and almost dragged her into the station.

"She's a thief!" He cursed at the two policemen. The girl said nothing in her own defense. She just stumbled along while the angry young man jerked at her arm. "I caught her red-handed. Stealing tips and money from the cash register. Hard-earned money—money *I* earned. I'm working hard for a living." He spit on the ground. "And she's stealing it."

The inside of the station was another shade, a lighter shade, of the brown exterior. "It always happens this way." The first trooper nodded at the young man. "We're quiet and noth-ing is going on—" he shook his hands in the air—"then it's a three-ring circus." He motioned to Shirley to sit on a dark brown, worn wooden bench, then motioned for the pale-haired girl to sit on a bench across from her. The girl's lip was starting to swell.

The two troopers and the young man walked to a desk and stood talking, looking occasionally in the direction of Shirley and the girl. The trooper who'd called in Shirley's plates had his shades perched on top of his head. He sat down and started making phone calls. In between murmurings, sometimes the three of them would explode with laughter, as though they were old friends.

Shirley kept her arms around Mika and Lex. She made small talk about where they were going tonight, what they would do when they got there.

After what seemed to be forever, the first trooper approached them. "Well, ladies. We're having trouble getting through to the folks we need to talk with to get things squared up. So we're just going to let the two of you cool off in the holding cell until we can get things cleared up."

Finally the girl protested. "Well, if you put me in, you need to put *him* in. Maybe I stole a few lousy bucks—I ain't sayin' I did and I ain't sayin' I didn't—but *he* beat me up. What about that? You see this blood running down my face, dontcha?"

The young man lumbered toward them, raging—his fists raised and his jaw muscles clenched. "She's a lyin' thief! I never laid a hand on her. She ran into a wall trying to get away."

"Right! And you're John Travolta!" The girl stuck her chin out.

"All right, miss." The cop with the shades called to them from the chair where he sat with his ear to the phone. "You just calm down!"

"She's the thief and now she's trying to ruin my reputation." The young man shrugged at the trooper on the phone, as though to show he had calmed down and it was no big deal.

Shirley wasn't sure if she should speak or not, if her talking might make things worse for her and the children. "What about my kids?" she whispered to the trooper who held her arm to pull her to her feet.

"They'll be okay. If we have to detain you much longer, we'll call social services. For right now, they'll be okay where they are."

Shirley held her breath as she spoke again. "What am I being detained for? Why can't I just pay the fine and go?"

He narrowed his eyes. "Don't get cute, lady. There's a car just like the one you're driving that's missing. We just need to get confirmation on the license plate number. So don't play innocent. Things will go better if you just stay quiet."

The cell he took them to was dark, with bars, just like the ones on television. The trooper unlocked the door. "You two girls play nice in here." He chuckled as he walked away.

"Oh, God, help me." Shirley whispered and closed her eyes.

She must have fallen asleep, because suddenly it was as though she could see Mika and Lex huddled on the bench outside in the police station lobby. Shirley had to be dreaming. She was enveloped by a warm light…a presence…and she heard a voice that spoke to her, but not in words.

"Don't fear. Where you go, you will not go alone," Shirley felt the presence say. "You will not be alone. Don't be afraid."

Shirley forced herself awake and opened her eyes. This was supposed to be about starting over, about new beginnings. There was no angel in front of her. She was in a dark, dirty jail cell. She didn't know why she was there or when she would be leaving. She couldn't see her children, all she could see in front of her was a strangely familiar girl. Right now, it didn't seem like a new start or a dream; it was feeling like more of a nightmare.

TWO

*I*t was another hot day in Texas. There was nothing unusual, then, about two old ladies sitting on a porch and fanning. There was nothing peculiar about them smiling at each other, or about their heads nodding as they spoke back and forth. It was expected that they would drink cool drinks and that they would find shelter under the shade of a tree.

"You ain't seen her in years, Mother. I want to believe, too. You know I love her, too." Ma Dear looked away. "But, I don't think she's thinking about you. It sure don't look like it." She turned to look into Mother Johnson's eyes. "You've been through enough. I just don't want to see you be hurt." A sorrowful smile crossed Ma Dear's lips.

"I know, Ma Dear. But, that don't matter. She's still on my mind. We can't stop doing right just because people don't have the strength to do right by us. I'm just going to keep on praying and believing…she's going to turn up. I'm just counting on God's grace." Mother Johnson touched a hand to one of her thin, dark knees and then reached to touch her dollop of white hair.

"Mother, you are good woman, a strong woman."

"Honey, anything I am is because of God's grace. You know that, Ma Dear. You've known me all my life. I've had my time being a little rough around the edges."

Ma Dear laughed. "Hush, girl." She was still more like a schoolgirl inside a plump, aged body. Ma Dear slapped her leg. "I tell you what, you don't tell nobody about me, and I won't tell nobody about you! And that ain't just because I might have a little bit more to tell." She shook her head and her chest bobbed up and down a little when she giggled. "You're right about grace, though, Mother. It's because of that grace that we can believe that God hears us."

Mother nodded and fanned herself. "Sure, it's about grace. And I've been thinking, Ma Dear. It's a wonder that with all we do, all the times we keep falling down and breaking the Lord's heart, that He keeps taking us back. It's a miracle that He keeps loving us. He just keeps on loving us. He keeps forgiving us and taking us back."

Ma Dear's foot started patting. "Just like that Scripture that says, 'If my people, which are called by my name, shall humble themselves, and pray, and seek my face, and turn from their wicked ways; then will I hear from heaven, and will forgive their sin, and will heal their land.'"

Mother and Ma Dear sat in silence. They rocked slowly. Finally, Mother spoke. "The good thing is that I know He won't be angry with us forever. He won't ever let His children be lost too long. That's why I know He's going to send Shirley back. I know He is. I already got the rooms ready."

THREE

Shirley felt as though she were running out of air, as though she were in *The Twilight Zone,* as though she were lost behind the great rock that sat at the end of her street when she was a child. She looked at every corner of the cell trying to find meaning, to explain what was happening. Panic was overtaking her, and she wanted to scream. She closed her eyes, and it was as if she could see Mika and Lex huddled together on the police station bench.

Shirley looked at the girl across the cell from her. The girl reminded her of someone. Some of her hair had fallen onto her face, and she seemed to be playing a game, blowing it off. Shirley felt overwhelmed. "O God, help me." She closed her eyes again.

She was tired, so tired…but the last thing she wanted now was to sleep. She didn't need one of the other dreams—not while she sat in the dark, grimy cell. A dream about saying good-bye to her father, about him leaving for the war and never returning. Or a dream about Big Uncle and Little Uncle, who were once so close, but who now were far away. Dreams about her mother, and about Danny going away.

And still, after all these years, there were dreams about Sheri.

That was the thing about the dreams. There was no telling, when she drifted off to sleep, if they would be sweet or if they would be dark. So she fought sleep, fought the uncertainty of the dreams.

God, I've got to get out of here.

Shirley fought until Morpheus won and she surrendered to a dream about Danny.

Danny played his acoustic guitar and sang to her over the phone. There was something about the sound of his fingers whisking over the strings, sliding over the frets, that reminded her of something. Reminded her of something just out of her reach, something that made her lips part and brought the feeling of a cool breeze to the nape of her neck. Shirley pressed the phone close to her ear, closed her eyes, and imagined him not on his way overseas, but sitting on the stool in their bedroom near where she now sat on the side of the bed. His voice was soft and spoke tenderness to her.

"Danny…" She was drifting, and it was difficult to speak. "Danny, don't be a hero, okay?"

He continued to play and laughed within the mood of his accompaniment. "What else can I be, baby? I've pretty much messed up everything else I've tried to be…I'm not going to get any medals for fatherhood or being a husband." He chuckled again. "Maybe I can get this one thing right." The guitar strings squeaked softly as he pressed and fingered them.

"Don't say that. Okay, Danny? We've had tough times. Everybody does. But we're past that now. And every morning, I thank God for you in my life. So don't say that. Because of you, I understand what the word godsend means. You're already a hero in our lives—mine and the kids'."

There was still just the sound of his guitar, so she went on. "We need you to come home. So you don't have anything to prove, okay, Danny?" He seemed to be flowing in and out of songs, memories that pinched her cheeks, pulled at her ankles, and brushed her lips. "Okay, Danny?"

He played the bridge of something delicate and familiar. "Yeah, baby. No doubt about it. Not that there's anything to worry about. It's just Germany, not World War III." A few more strums. "Kiss the kids for me." He played some more. "Yeah, I've been praying, too."

He said it so softly she almost didn't hear. "What did you say, Danny? Did you say you prayed?"

"Yeah, no big deal. I just decided to stop running. Just one more thing in my life I needed to get right. I've been talking to the chaplain pretty regularly. He's a cool guy. No big deal, okay? We can talk about it when I get home. I gotta go, okay." He sang a few lines and stopped. "Oh yeah, remind me to tell you something when I get back."

"Tell me now."

"No, wait until I get back. It's going to blow your mind. It's something you never would have expected in a million years. It's about as unexpected as me saying yes to God."

Thank You, God. Thank You. It was Shirley's turn to sing to Danny. A few bars was all she could manage before her voice broke. As Danny began to play again, she cleared her throat and told him she loved him. She did not expect or wait for a reply. She started to count to ten, the ritual that ensured that they hung up the phone at the same time. "One, two, three—"

"Shirley?" He stopped playing. "Shirley, I love you." She wept as she replaced the phone in its cradle.

Someone shook her shoulder, and Shirley realized her head had been nodding. "Come on, lady. You need to get out of here before your car gets towed from out front. We won't be responsible if your car gets towed. We had it brought down here, but we're not responsible beyond that."

It was the policeman who had locked them in the cell, and he was holding the blond-haired girl by the arm. "Everything checked out on your car. We got a call about a robbery not far from here. You fit the description, but—" he shrugged his shoulders and then looked from Shirley to the pale-haired girl—"we've got work to do, so the two of you need to get out of here."

"That's it?" Shirley frowned.

He cocked his head. "You got something else you want to tell me, lady?"

She stood up quickly and walked out the door and into her children's arms. They left the station. Together they walked past the girl, who stood on the sidewalk, looking lost and confused.

"Just get out of town," Shirley had heard the policeman tell the girl. "If we see you here at daylight, we've got the perfect apartment just waiting for you."

Shirley, Mika, and Lex packed themselves into the car. She had enough excitement with an eight-year-old girl and a three-year-old boy. More jail she didn't need. Shirley couldn't wait to leave Texas behind her. Mother Johnson would have to wait until another time. Shirley and her children had had about all of Texas that they could bear.

"Miss?"

Shirley turned at the voice and the hand that tapped her on the shoulder.

"Miss, can you give me a lift out of town? I need—if I can just get back home. I never should have come here in the first place." The girl's eyes were a clear, almost crystal blue. Shirley felt again that there was something familiar about her. "Please," the girl begged. "I won't give you no trouble."

"Where is home?" *Why are you even talking to her? She's a thief. And you've got two kids in the car.* "How far away is your home?" Her mouth was speaking on its own, as though she had lost control.

"Tyler," the girl said. "I'm from Tyler, Texas. The rose capital of the world."

Shirley closed her eyes briefly and sighed. This was crazy. She knew better. *The plan was to get away, remember?*

She motioned to the passenger's side. "Get in."

FOUR

*I*t was crazy—carrying the girl with them—and Shirley knew it. She had two little kids in the car. It was crazy.

Windy, with an *i*, the girl said her name was, and she kept scratching her head.

The more Windy scratched her head, the more certain Shirley was that she knew her, or someone like her.

The girl slapped her bare feet up on the dashboard. Her toes were painted with purple glitter toenail polish.

"I sure appreciate this," Windy said like Shirley was giving her a ride home from the store instead of a jail cell. "I'll pay you back. You can count on it."

"Mm-hm." Shirley nodded and smiled like she'd seen people do a million times—like they did when they didn't want to be bothered. A sort of I'm-saying-okay-but-truth-be-told-I-really-wish-you-weren't-here-in-front-of-me kind of look. "Mm-hmm," she repeated.

"I bet you're wondering how I even got there, aren't you? And how I got to working for a jerk like that?" Windy's almost white-blond hair stuck around her face like some sort of corn silk and straw hybrid. "I was just trying to make me some quick money, was all. I was just trying to get out of the godfor-saken rat hole. I mean, working in a pizza joint is not what I want to do for the rest of my life."

The girl dug down into her pocket and pulled out a small can of hair mousse. Windy shook the can, then pressed down on the dispenser until a blob of white foam appeared in her free hand. She jabbed the can back into her pocket and then rubbed her hands together. She used her fingers to apply the mousse, pulling at her hair until it lifted in spikes inches from her head.

Shirley wondered, for the forty-sixth time, how she'd got-ten her family into this. Mika and Lex didn't seem to mind so much. They were staring at the girl.

"I know you don't know nothing about me, but I'm real smart. I am. And I come from a good family. My daddy's edu-cated and a preacher." Windy picked at the flaking polish on her right big toe.

The mousse didn't seem to be holding against the air blow-ing in the window. She brushed the clumped hair out of her face. "I know you may not believe me, but he is. That's part of why I had to get away. I ain't bad, but it's hard having a preacher for a daddy—expecting you to be good all the time. Folks expecting you to be like him and good all the time. I ain't good *all* the time. Nobody can be." She paused. "Actually, I'm not from Tyler, I'm from Oklahoma, but Tyler's where my grandmother is."

Shirley felt her shoulders tensing. It was probably time to pull over.

"I ain't bad, like I said. But what I am saying is that I have to live my own life. I can't live under my daddy's shadow, even if he is a powerful and good man. Did you ever deal with that?

26

I mean, trying not to be who your people are or who they want you to be?"

"Of course." Shirley shuddered when a state trooper pulled up alongside them in the right-hand lane. *Not again*. She spoke again when the cruiser pulled past. "We all do."

"Maybe so." Windy tugged at the sleeve of her T-shirt. She'd told Shirley she had to surrender the smock from the pizza place before she left the station. "All I ever really wanted was some kids. Some babies, and to live in a nice quiet house, maybe in some nice quiet little town." She tossed her hair out of her face again. "I would have stayed where I was, but it was too hard living in my daddy's shadow. That's why I had to leave. I been making my way ever since. And like I said, I stopped to help that pizza guy and earn a little quick money. But..."

She shrugged. "Of course, you know people always take kindness for weakness, and I can't help but be kind since my daddy's a preacher and all." Windy switched legs and began to pick the polish on her other big toe. "'For I knew it, that big jerk tried to make a move on me. When I told him no, as nice as you could imagine—" Shirley *couldn't* imagine—"the big galoot started manhandling me. So I picked up one of those things they use to slide the pizza out of the oven and walloped him." Windy slapped her leg and hooted. "You should have seen it! That big bear was coming down." She stopped picking her toenails and dug into her pockets, then produced a pack of gum. "Want some?"

"No thanks." Shirley glanced into the rearview mirror. She was glad the kids had fallen asleep so she wouldn't have to signal them not to take the toe-jammy offer.

"Anyways, I figured I better get out of there before he came to. You may not believe me because of what he said, but I was in the cash register just getting what was owed to me when the big fool woke up. He commenced to slamming and slapping me around."

Shirley caught a quick look at Windy. She was a funny girl—a lot different than she had appeared at the station. There she'd looked angry and hard. Here in the car, she looked and sounded like a tousle-haired teenager.

Her face looked as though she were recounting the action from a movie she had seen. "I tried to fight back, even though my daddy would have told me to turn the other cheek." She shook her head, then nodded at Shirley. "That's what I always tried to tell my daddy. There's a time for everything, and sometimes it's time to shake more than the Good Book at a guy. So, that's what I done. I knocked him 'cross the room with the back of one of them wood things, again."

Windy laughed at her own story. "I was about to get away clean, but he recovered somehow and got the best of me. Which wasn't hard to do seeing that I'm five-foot-one and he was about a thousand feet tall. I think he didn't know how he was going to explain all them bruises and cuts to everybody—especially to his wife. He's married, you know. So I think that's when he got the bright idea in his beady little head to drag me down to the law."

The girl's face turned hard again. She looked straight ahead. "You know you can't trust men. They use you and then leave you…or slam you around. But I told myself when I left home, I was not going to let any man get the best of me or bring me down or use me." She looked at Shirley, and then used her hands to part her hair. "See this?" There was a white scar. "I earned it. I let somebody plow into me, but not anymore. I would kill somebody before I would let myself be caged up and used again."

Shirley got a sick feeling in the pit of her stomach.

Windy dropped her hands and her face softened again. "So, like I said, I was getting out of there, whatever it took. When they got me down to the jail, I could have told them cops all that guy done to me. There's lots I could have said. I could have called my daddy. But sometimes, just like Jesus, the best thing to do is to say nothing. So that takes me right on up to meeting you—not under the best of circumstances, sorry to say. But, I sure do appreciate this ride. Sure do."

Windy pointed a finger—stubby with the nail painted glow-in-the-dark blue—between herself and Shirley. "We're just two women—" she turned and pointed toward the backseat, where Mika and her little brother were somehow managing to sleep through it all—"and a couple of kids, looking out for each other, watching each other's backs."

Windy dug into her pockets for the gum again and shoved another piece into her mouth so that one of her cheeks had a bulge. "So, now, tell me about you!"

FIVE

~~~~~~~~~~~~~~~~~~~~~~

Shirley tried to think of a way to say nothing to Windy in a way that would not be rude. "There's not much to tell."

"Was your daddy a preacher?"

Was she a Valley Girl or what? "No, he wasn't."

"So, what about him?"

What about *him?* Windy pressed as though she didn't know about decorum, as if she didn't know about tact. "My daddy was in the army."

"In the army? What did he do?"

"He flew helicopters."

"No way! If there was anything better than a preacher that a daddy could be, that just might be it. Wow!"

Shirley smiled in spite of herself, but she could feel her shoulders tightening—she did not want to talk.

Windy turned and looked over the seat at Mika and Lex. "Cute kids."

"Thanks."

"That's what I want. Babies. Lots of them." She turned back in the seat. "You on your way to pick up your husband?"

"He's…he's gone." Shirley fought not to react, not to let Windy—a stranger, a strange girl—see inside of her. She fought not to tell the girl too much, not to show her the open wound. "I don't have a husband."

Windy cocked her head. "You don't look like the type that wouldn't have a husband."

She was not going to tell this girl, this thief, anything about herself. "I said I don't…" Shirley could barely inhale enough air to speak. *This must be what it feels like to breathe in Denver, not enough oxygen, not enough air.* But she was not going to get worked up over this kid. "Look, I don't have a husband." She breathed. "Not anymore. He's gone. Not left me, I mean he was killed in Germany."

"I didn't know we were at war with Germany."

Shirley fought to keep her voice under control, to keep at bay the panic that she always felt when she talked about Danny and how he died. "There was no war. He was just in the wrong place at the wrong time. There was a car bomb outside of the base where he worked. It killed him and a woman." She shrugged and tried to sound casual. "It was just the luck of the draw. You know, he served his country faithfully—no news, no parades—and that was that." She was saying too much too fast. "Besides, I didn't know there was a certain look you had to have to be a woman who has a baby without a husband. All sorts of women are having babies alone—lawyers and movie stars. I didn't think there was any certain look required."

Shirley forced herself to change the subject from Danny, to try to laugh. "I mean, does your name have to be Tawanda or Shaneequa?" She forced herself to laugh again. "Or maybe you have to have cornrows or fake nails with designs painted on them." She was beginning to breathe. "I didn't know there was a certain type or that she had to look a certain way."

"A woman who's pregnant without a husband looks like me," Windy said.

"Look, Windy, we have to get past all those stereotypes. All kinds of women are having children and raising them by themselves. Some of them are choosing to have the children alone."

"I'm saying that a woman who is having a baby without a husband looks *just* like me."

"Sure, you're young." Shirley glanced at Windy. "And you don't look like some woman executive. You look like...you look like a teenager, a kid—" what Shirley didn't say was, *Sure, your hair is flying all over the place, your toenails don't look exactly like something out of* Young Miss, *and your shorts could be a little longer*—"but that's no reason."

"I'm saying I'm having a baby."

Shirley fought to keep the car on the road.

Windy turned in her seat and kept talking, as if she hadn't dropped a bomb. "Cute kids. They really and truly are. And they seem—from what I've seen—to mind really well. They just do whatever you tell them to do. They look like little angels sleeping." She smiled and, for the fiftieth time, brushed the hair out of her eyes. "And they seem to get along real well. Not like my little cousins—man, oh man, they can't be left alone together. Not even in a police station. Why, they would have had that joint torn apart in two seconds flat. The cops would have been begging us to leave just to take those brats with us."

She turned back in her seat and looked at Shirley. "Man, oh man. Cecile and Leslie is always fighting. Pulling each other's hair, scratching each other. But don't try to separate them. The two of them will holler loud enough to wake the dead. Gosh-amighty."

Windy was on a roll. "And Daddy hates that. He can't get no good sermon together to preach with them two going at it. But it's even worse, you know, when the two of them get to yelling. Them two scream loud enough that they ought to be the ones picked to announce Judgment Day!" She turned her body more in Shirley's direction. "You ever seen such a thing?"

"Yes, unfortunately, I have."

Her expression looked tender. "I ain't worried, though. I mean, I miss them two and I love them to death. But when I have kids, they're going to be like yours—behavior-wise anyway." She didn't stop. "I keep meaning to ask about you, then I get started talking a mile a minute. Go on, now, Shirley. Tell me about you."

Shirley stared straight ahead. This was way more than she had bargained for. *Black Widow Hauled in by Cops Hits the Road with Pregnant White Girl*. It sounded like a perfect title for an *Enquirer* feature, and like the last thing Shirley could ever have imagined. She knew better than to pick up this girl. She knew better. What was she going to do now? Something had to give.

SIX

Ma Dear glided back and forth in her rocker—
the one she always sat in on Mother
Johnson's porch—like she was trying to kill
cockroaches. In fact, it was less like a glide than it was like a
ramming. "If the same blood that spilled from Jesus' veins
didn't also cover me, I'd be tempted to call her a heifer!" She
eyed the third rocker, the one to the right of Mother Johnson's,
where the new woman usually sat.

Mother stopped gliding for a second. It usually took a lot
to make her stop gliding. "Ma Dear!"

"Yes, I would, Mother. I might have to go to the altar for it,
but, yes, I would. And you know, in the old days I would have
said a lot more than that!" Ma Dear squinted one eye and
glared at the empty rocker.

"Thank goodness these ain't the old days."

"Humph." Ma Dear pursed her lips and rolled her eyes at
the chair as though there was someone sitting in it to receive
what she was handing out. "What I want to know is—" Ma
Dear's chubby cheeks were flushed with anger—"why you ever
bought that third chair in the first place. The new porch was

fine. It was good enough. I always hated walking up that hill to get to the back, though I did like the swing. And I like these new gliders. Rocking chairs that glide—the world is a wonder." Ma Dear sat back in her chair for a moment. She snuggled into place and seemed to relax into the rhythm of the chair's movement.

Abruptly, Ma Dear leaned forward and her body was rigid again. "All of that is good, but why couldn't you just leave well enough alone, Mother? If you didn't buy it, she wouldn't be coming by here with her stiff-necked, holier-than-thou self. At least she wouldn't have nowhere to sit, so she wouldn't be tempted to stay long."

"Ma Dear, you know the Word says if you want a friend you have to show yourself friendly." Mother Johnson resumed her rocking. Where Ma Dear filled up her seat, Mother's little frame left enough room for at least a child or two.

"Maybe so, Mother. And no disrespect to the Lord," Ma Dear nodded reverently toward heaven, "but I don't ever remember saying I wanted that tight-lipped—"

"All right, Ma Dear, that's enough, now! I mean it, now. I'm not gone let you sit up on my porch and talk this way. We been friends since we were girls, but now—"

"No disrespect, Mother. But I know you see the way she looks at us—'specially at me—like she better than us. Like she doing us a favor to come by here and interrupt our conversation while she drinks up all the sweet ice tea. Since she's been coming by, I can't hardly get a cold glass." Ma Dear shook her head and waved her hands with almost every word. She meant what she was saying.

"Now, Ma Dear, you know I always got more ice tea. And you and me got so many conversations under our belts, we could stand to lose a few here and there." Mother Johnson reached over and patted her best friend's fat stomach. Love seemed to be all in her touch.

Ma Dear was too angry to give in to a little affection. "All right, Mother. You the one that know things, but that woman is going to bring trouble to this house. You mind my words."

"Well then, stop speaking those words. You know the power of life and death is in the tongue."

"It surely is." Ma Dear shook her head full of curly salt-and-pepper hair. "And that old biddy ain't got nothing good to say." If Mother Johnson had ever had a roach problem—which she didn't—she was never going to need an exterminator if Ma Dear kept rocking or gliding the way she was. She was going to wear a groove in the new porch. That is, if she didn't set it aflame.

"I hate the way she looks at us, like not only are we not the right color, but *I* ain't classy enough for her." Ma Dear slapped the arm of her glider. "Looking at me like she's Miss Manners or something. Putting on airs, starching her collars when she know it's hot as blue blazes this summer in Texas. She know good and well she sweating just like all the rest of us." Ma Dear began to mock Mildred's movements—not enough to get out of her seat, though. "And wearing that sun hat like she's Miss Scarlet O'Hara and Tyler is her plantation. Well, by the look of the wrinkles in her face, Rhett Butler been gone a long time—and I don't blame him!"

Mother Johnson stopped rocking, planted her little feet on the floor, and turn to face Ma Dear. "Now, Ma Dear, just what is it? My goodness, I have heard you go on before, especially after you been praying for healing." Mother slapped one of her knees. "Like, remember that time you went and prayed for that man who was 'bout to die? You know the one. The man's family came to get you." Mother cackled.

Ma Dear's face began to relax. "Oh, you talking about that man with the death rattle years back."

"Yes, honey. That's the one. He was at death's door, and you prayed and he came back."

"Sure enough, he did. Ain't Jesus wonderful? Thousands of years later, and His name still has miraculous power." Ma Dear's dimples kept getting deeper and deeper until she blushed like a young girl. She was still a pretty woman. "You should have seen that man pop back into the land of the living. Why, it almost scared me to death. But great God from Zion, it was something to behold."

"That's what you said, Ma Dear. That's what you said." Mother smiled. It was as though the two of them were school-girls again. "And I think you said everything was peaches and cream until the man's daughter got a little beside herself."

"Yes, she did! Beside herself! She got ahead of herself—carrying on like she was too good for the likes of me. I wasn't too good to pray. But when she had what she wanted, she wanted to wash her hands of me."

"That's what you said, Ma Dear."

"That's when I had to let her know that this sure enough is butter and not Parkay!" Ma Dear's rocking came to a halt and she started patting her foot. "I'll tell you, Mother. I made a believer out of her. I cussed up a blue streak." She hung her head slightly. "Though I'm still a little ashamed to say it."

"But not *too* ashamed."

"Well, Mother, I don't mean no harm, but that young woman's attitude crunched down on my nerves like a tight shoe on a foot full of corns, and I had to get her off of them.

But you're right, I cussed to shame the devil, right after I had prayed a prayer of healing and faith…and I ain't proud of that. I been praying about that, Mother. And you know the Lord is working with me. I been crying and praying for years for His help to stop my tongue, to tame it…"

Ma Dear's eyes squinted. "Wait a minute, Mother. You just wait one minute, Miss Mavis Johnson." Mavis was the name that Ma Dear—whose real name was Augusta Charles—called her friend when only a childhood name would do. It was the name that Ma Dear called Mother Johnson when she was especially excited or when she needed to remind Mother that she knew her long before she ever became a church mother or even the mother of two grown daughters. "I know you're awful fond of *Ironsides* and old Raymond Burr is your hero, but don't try any of that fast thinking on me. I may move more slowly than I used to, and these old hips may creak from time to time—" Ma Dear tapped a finger to the crown of her head—"but the brain is just as sharp and as quick as it ever was."

Mother Johnson tried to keep from laughing, but she knew her face said that she had been caught. "What are you talking about, Ma Dear?"

"You know what I'm talking about. Trying to get me feeling bad about my mouth so that I will lay off your new uppity friend. Well, you can't get up early enough in the morning to fool me into feeling guilty over your tired little friend."

"Oh, Ma Dear, what is it that upsets you so about her?"

"Well, for one thing, she is always trying to act important." Ma Dear mocked Mildred's voice. "'Why, we would never do *that* in St. Louis.'" Ma Dear waved her hands in the air like Mildred. She dropped her hands back to the arms of her chair. "St. Louis? When she knows good and well that she's from *East*

St. Louis, and East St. Louis is in Illinois, not Missouri."

"Yes, you and I know that. But what difference—"

"She's always saying *St. Louis* like East St. Louis ain't good enough for a fine lady like her. It just makes me think she's got something to hide. And I told you, it's the way she looks at me…at *us*…like she's some kind of glassy-eyed lizard looking at muddy water. You're a lot more forgiving than me, Mother. I just can't abide it."

"For goodness' sakes, Ma Dear. What are you talking about? Glassy-eyed lizard?"

"Oh, Mother, it ain't been that long since we were girls."

Mother frowned, lifted her arm, and swatted at the soft, sagging, lined skin that drooped from her forearm. "Ain't been that long? Who are we trying to kid?"

"All right, Mother. But what I mean is, remember how those lizards at the pond had two eyelids. The one was regular—the same color as their nasty brown or green skin. But the other one was clear. You had to really look to see it. Remember? Just scampering around, they kept both of those eyelids up. But as soon as something came that made that old lizard feel uncomfortable—like some muddy water—that old lizard put down that clear eyelid so he could pass through and see, but keep the dirty water out." Ma Dear moved her eyelids up and down as though she were the lizard. She shook her head and continued talking. "That's how she looks at us. At least that's how she looks at me, like dirty water, and she is using her clear eyelids to shut me out."

"Oh, Ma Dear, I just think the two of you are misjudging each other. And maybe it's too much judging going on, and you are not giving each other time or room enough to see if you like each other."

"Well, besides that, Mother, she looks down on me because she doesn't believe in healing."

"And you look down on her because she and the folks at her church are quiet."

"No, I'm happy they're quiet. Their singing is bad enough to kill a cow, and I like a little milk and cheese every now and then."

Mother fought with herself not to laugh at Ma Dear's caustic crack. "Oh, now, Ma Dear, you know we can get a little flat at my church sometimes, too."

"I ain't saying that ain't the truth. I guess God really does see beyond our faults."

"I'm just saying that's no way to start a friendship. That's all I'm saying, Ma Dear."

Ma Dear pushed her point further. "And she thinks I'm man crazy."

"Well, Ma Dear, you know you do have that wandering eye."

Ma Dear's face took a slight look of pleading. "But it's better, now, Mother." There was a kind of whining or pleading sound in her voice. "Don't you think? I mean I been with the same husband now since before Shirley graduated high school. And I love that man—though I do have to say I'm still upset about not having a church wedding. I don't look much at other men, no matter how good-looking they are...not anymore, Mother, and you know that's the truth. I've been trying real hard."

"Yes, that's the truth. I know you have. Old habits are hard to break." Mother Johnson moved slowly back and forth in her glider. "I just try to be nice to Mildred. She's new here with no friends to speak of and little family—just Mr. Jack and his people—"

"Not *Mister* Jack. Those days are over, Mother. That man is young enough to be your son. You don't have to call him that anymore. Jim Crow days are over. We don't ride the back of the bus anymore. Let the *Mister* go."

Mother nodded. "I know, Ma Dear." Mother kept gliding. "Old habits are hard to break."

Ma Dear nodded her agreement. "Like I said, Mother, though, your new friend acts like she's better than us. And I can't abide that."

Mother smiled. "Like *I* said, old habits are hard to break." She looked Ma Dear in the eye. "You and me go way back. Nothing's going to separate us, but death. So you don't have to worry about a new friendship."

Ma Dear sniffed and turned her head. She looked back at Mother Johnson. "I ain't worried."

"And you don't have to cloak that worry behind other things. You and me are good, deep friends. So I can tell you anything—right, wrong, or indifferent. Mildred is just learning me. I have to go slow with her, so she'll know she can trust me."

Mother Johnson shook her head. "No, I don't like the way she looks at us sometimes, but there's enough God in me not to let it upset me. In time, we'll be able to talk about it. And she'll probably tell me some things she doesn't like about me." She touched Ma Dear's hand. "But I've also been hoping that some- how the two of you would get past what's between you and become friends…for the Lord's sake."

Ma Dear frowned. "You always got to use your secret weapon, don't you? '*For the Lord's sake.*'" Ma Dear looked away and mumbled to herself. Finally, she turned back to Mother Johnson and said, "I ain't promising anything, Mother. But, we'll see."

The two old women sat quietly for a while, gliding back and forth. Then Mother cleared her throat. "It's been coming stronger, you know."

"What's been coming, Mother?"

"The feeling that Shirley's coming home."

SEVEN

Shirley kept hold of the wheel and tried to keep hold of her sanity. What was going on? How and what was she supposed to do with a pregnant teenager?

"That's why I'm on my way to Tyler." Windy sounded calm. She continued talking as though she wasn't aware that what she'd said was about enough to make Shirley pull the car over. "My grandmother wants me to come and stay with her. I was gonna have my baby and raise it on my own." She looked at Shirley and patted her stomach. "I could, too. We could make it just fine. But my grandmother's getting older and she's all excited about the baby. She can't wait to have a bundle of joy to bounce on her knee. It'll remind her of when I was a little towheaded, sucking baby. I thought, all right. It might be a good thing all around. So, I told her 'Hold on, Grandma, I'm coming.'" Windy smiled so big her eyes almost closed. "We're going to have such a good time."

How was that even possible? This whole thing was insane. How were they ever going to make it?

As though to rub it in or to erase any doubt Shirley might still have that all this had been planned just to push her over the edge, Amy Grant's sweet voice wafted from the car speakers. It was "Love Will Find a Way." Shirley didn't know the last time she'd heard that song. Love might find a way, but it sure wasn't clear right now. There was no need for Providence to be so cruel. Shirley rolled her shoulders forward, then rolled them backward. "So didn't your grandmother send a plane ticket or at least a bus ticket for you?"

Windy stopped talking. She blinked several times, looked out the window, looked back, took a quick breath, and began talking again. "Of course she did. What kind of grandma would she be if she didn't try to look out for me? I kept telling her, 'Granny, I don't need no ticket. I can make it on my own. I got a little money stashed away.' But she wouldn't hear of it." Windy waved the thought away with her hands. "She loves me just that much. She wanted to fly me into Tyler, because I'm her favorite grandchild. But I told her not to spend all the money on plane fare. I'd much rather take the bus, I told her. I like watching the scenery."

Shirley stared at the girl. She didn't know anyone else who would rather take a bus. Who would rather sit in a smoky, seedy bus station trying to avoid pickpockets and users while she waited for bus connection after bus connection?

Maybe it's just me. Or maybe it was just too many Trailways. Maybe it was the bus ride to Tyler with Mother Johnson, who though distant in relationship turned out to be the closest relative she had, after her father's death and her mother's breakdown. Maybe it was Tony Taylor and his brother picking her up from the train station the day Mother Johnson fell ill. Or maybe there was no real point in trying to figure it out.

"'No, Granny,' I said. 'Use the money, if you just have to spend it, to set up the nursery and get the crib and other things the baby's going to need.'" Windy shrugged her shoulders. "I mean, she's just like that. She's warm and cuddly—just plump enough to squeeze. She's got dimples and she's always saying something nice. But no matter what I said, I knew she was going to want to fix things up. You know, put up new wallpaper, get the baby bed and put one of those things over it—you know those things with the little animals that float over the bed and play music."

"A mobile?"

"Yeah, I guess that's right. So, I told her, don't spend money on the plane. The bus is good enough for me. I can see the scenery and meet people, I told her." Windy hugged her knees to her chest. "I love people. Most people are nice, you know? Not like that jerk at the pizza place. Most people are nice." As if all the air had gone out of her, Windy deflated and looked out the window, apparently deep in thought.

Just as suddenly, she turned to look briefly at Mika and Lex, was refilled and began to talk again. "I know I keep saying it, but they are such cute kids. Their dad must have been a real looker." She grimaced. "Sorry about how that sounded. I don't mean you're ugly or anything. I just…oh, never mind."

"No offense intended, Windy, and none taken." The kids did look a lot like Danny—that's what made forgetting so difficult.

"Thanks. So, anyway, like I said, I love people and she bought me a bus ticket." She stopped talking and then smiled a big smile as though everything were settled and perfect.

Shirley attempted to stretch the muscles in her neck without driving the car out of her lane. "So how did you end up in a jail outside of Tuscaloosa?"

Windy blinked, again. She bit her lip, turned and looked out the window, then turned and looked back.

"Mama?" It was Lex, waking in the backseat. He and Mika both had begun to stir.

Shirley glanced in the rearview mirror. "Lex and Mika, how are you guys? Need to make a pit stop?"

"Yes, ma'am. And we're hungry, Mommy."

"Okay, let me find a place." Shirley hunted billboards along the highway until she saw an ad for a HoJo's only one exit away. In a short time, they were pit-stopped, seated, and the waitress was delivering hamburgers and fries to everyone—except Mika, who preferred the hot dogs with baked beans.

"So, Mama, is Daddy going to be able to find us here?"

"Don't talk with your mouth full, boy!" Mika was always the boundary keeper. But Lexington kept asking the question that wore her out. He didn't understand—yet, at least—that his father's absence was permanent. Shirley knew she could have done more to help him understand, but the question sapped her strength, so she gave the only answer she could manage to give. "We don't have to worry about him finding us. Don't you worry about that, Lex. Just eat your burger, okay?"

She took comfort in the little silver pot that sat in front of her—the kind that carried hot water in restaurants all over the country day after day. There was solace for her in the scratched gray Formica counter and tabletops. The ketchup that refused to shake out of the bottle, just as it had all the years she could remember, gave her hope that one day things were going to return to normal.

Windy alternately sucked on a strawberry milkshake and pushed triplets of French fries in her mouth. "I thought you said your husband—"

"Not now, okay, Windy?" Shirley looked an apology. "Later, okay? Please?"

"No, problem." Windy's straw made that sucking sound that meant it had hit the bottom of the glass. "I think I'm gonna have another one of these." She pointed at her empty drink.

A waitress came and took the additional milkshake order.

"Not malt; I want the milkshake."

It was the same waitress who had seated them and given them their menus. "Three?" she had said, then, looking at Shirley, Mika, and Lex.

"No, four. We're all together," Shirley had said.

The waitress had looked confused, then, just as quickly, her face got tight. Now she looked just as displeased and suspicious about them all sitting together—about Windy sitting with them—as she had when she first seated them. No one else in the restaurant seemed bothered, but this waitress seemed to be sending Windy eye-messages to let her know she would have been much better off sitting with people more suitable, with people more her kind.

Windy didn't seem to be receiving the signals.

Shirley wiped her mouth and ignored the waitress. It wasn't that long ago when laws and customs kept her from going wherever she wanted to go. She wasn't about to let an *attitude* keep her away. Shirley picked up her water glass and took a drink. "So how was it again that you ended up outside of Tuscaloosa?"

The blinking started, and Windy bit her lip, turned and looked out the window that framed their booth. "Well, I—"

"Mama, how much longer do we have to go?"

Shirley looked at her son. "Lexington, can't you see that Mama is having an adult conversation? You know I told you, if it's an emergency, then you say 'excuse me,' right? Otherwise, just wait like a gentleman until we're finished."

"Yes, ma'am. Sorry, Mommy." Lex went back to his burger and feeding his sister his fries. They whispered to each other.

She looked at Windy. "Sorry about that."

"*Excuse me,* Mama."

"Yes, Lexington."

"May we go outside? We're finished."

"I don't think thats an emergency." Shirley looked at the bench just outside of the window. "Just for a few minutes. You have to stay on the bench where I can see you, okay? No running, or hitting, or anything else." Mika and Lex scrambled from the booth. Shirley watched them leave and didn't speak again until she saw them seated safely on the bench outside the window. "Sorry about that. So what were you saying, Windy?"

Windy used the back of her hand to wipe ketchup from the sides of her mouth. "You are so patient with them. Lots of mothers would have been whacking them and screaming their heads off—not in my family, I mean. But other people I know, they would be wailing and screaming, and the kids would be bawling their heads off."

"Thanks." Shirley sipped her tea and ate a couple of Lex's leftover fries. "So, tell me again how you got from the bus to the pizza place and then to jail."

Windy shrugged. "You know how bus stations are—all kinds of people lurking around. Well, this toothless old man in ratty clothes comes up and asks me if I can spare some money. I'm always happy to help, if I can. My grandmother sent me so much spending money—*pin money* she calls it, I don't know why—I just pulled a few dollars out of my pocket and handed them to him. Poor old thing, he walks off talking to himself. Pretty soon, this old bag lady comes to sit down near me. Some folks wouldn't have wanted her sitting near them, 'cause she was dirty and stinking. Her teeth were all rotted and she was talking to herself, too, just like the old man. But I thought nothing of it, she wasn't bothering me." Windy took a big pull from the straw in the shake that the disapproving waitress had just brought her. "That's cold! Brainfreeze!"

"Now, what about the old woman?"

Windy used her straw to stir the shake. "After a while, she gets up and she just walks away. Just good as you please. And I'm not complaining, 'cause like I said, she was a little gamy. The only thing is, when they call—you know, over the loud-speakers—to announce that my bus was ready and boarding, my ticket and all my money are gone and the bag lady has split. She's out of sight… Come to think of it, she and the old man could have been working together. You know I seen stuff like that on TV."

Shirley listened to Windy's story, but kept looking outside to keep an eye on Mika and Lex. "Did you call—"

Windy waved the idea away with her hand. "I thought about calling the cops, but I didn't want to get the old lady in trouble. 'Cause I figure I'll make it okay, even without the money and the ticket."

There was too much glass separating Shirley from her children, so she waved Mika and Lex back inside. "Well, why didn't you call your grandmother?"

A big, pleased smile spread across Windy's face. "I mean, come on. My grandmother's already done enough—inviting me to stay with her, wallpapering the walls with that flowered paper and all, getting the ticket and sending me the pin money and everything. So, I figured I wasn't that far away. People have been taking care of me all my life, but I can take care of myself, right? I wasn't that far away, so I figured I could get a quick job that paid a few bucks, make some fast money waiting on tables for tips and stuff." She shrugged. "Then—*Pow! Biff! Bam!*—I end up in the hands of the law."

Windy pressed a wrinkled napkin to her mouth. "So, you didn't tell me. Where are you guys on your way to?"

"California!" Lex arrived just in time and piped up, excited to have the answer to the question. It just wasn't the answer that Shirley wanted anyone to give.

EIGHT

I wonder where she is, where they are, right now."

There was nothing like a breeze on a hot, sunny day. Nothing, unless it was shade from a big, full, green tree. What topped it off was a cold glass of sweet tea, cold enough to almost make your head hurt, and sweet enough to set your teeth on edge—but not quite. Mother Johnson and Ma Dear had all three.

Mother sipped and nodded. "That's good tea, if I have to say so myself." She closed her eyes so she could feel it wash down her throat and then flow into her stomach. She opened her eyes and nodded toward the front bedroom window. "I got her room ready and I've made space for her chirren. Ain't it something to think about Shirley having chirren?"

"Sure is, Mother. I remember when she was just a child. Remember? I can still see her spinning in the leaves in the backyard. I guess that was long ago."

"Now she's all grown up."

Ma Dear took a big gulp of her tea. "I sure hope you got more of this?" She pressed the glass to her temple. "That child has sure been through a lot—Daddy dying in Vietnam. It's a shame about her uncles—it's a shame how things get all bound up. And her mama put away in the home."

Mother nodded. "Her mama's still in there, far as I know. Poor thing. Then Shirley's husband dying overseas. It would have been bad enough if it was a war, but to die that way, just in some explosion. Just some fool planting a bomb—"

"Just some fool trying to scare somebody by murdering people." Ma Dear frowned. "Just like that fool, or fools, that blew up the church with those four little black girls in it. People don't care nothing for other people's lives. Trying to scare people out of living." She shook her head.

"You know, Ma Dear, that's a lot for a young woman to take. It would be bad enough if it was a war, but just gone. Just one minute he's alive and the next minute he's gone. It's a lot for any woman to take. He wasn't my husband, and it hurt me. I just feel for her."

"I don't know what I'd do if something happened to my mister, Mother. You'd have to sweep me up off the floor. It took so long for me to even be ready to be a wife. Then it seemed like it took him forever to be ready to be a husband. I was 'bout to pull my hair out."

Mother laughed. "Oh, I remember that well. I thought for sure you'd be wearing a wig by now—or at least a weave. You know, I read in some magazine that Tina Turner wears a weave, but I got to give it to that child—she looks good."

Ma Dear nodded. "Thank the Lord Jesus I still got hair. Lots of us can't say that, but you're right about Miss Tina. But anyway, Mother, this waiting on the Lord for His timing about a husband and all—it wasn't no joke for me. Now, after all the waiting, I think I would just fall apart if something happened to him. I know I'm always fussing about us not having a proper wedding…but I sure wouldn't trade that for his sweetness in my life.

"I don't even like to think about what that poor child has been going through."

"Jesus knows."

"And for a while, it was like she was losing everything. Her uncles, just all her family. When she got married and had those children, I thought, now the baby finally has some peace."

Mother touched the glass to the side of her face, then took it down for a drink. "What I can tell her when she gets here, though, is that there is always joy on the other side of sorrow. When my husband left this world, I thought it would be the end of me. For a while, I just ghost-walked through it day by day. I guess I was waiting for my call to meet my husband on the other side. But God's got the time and the seasons in His hands. What I remember was that one day I was ghost-walking, then all of a sudden I wasn't. I was glad to be alive. When she gets here—and I'm as sure she's coming as I'm sure of my name—I'm going to hold her, then I'll tell her that joy really does come in the morning. Those that sow in tears really will reap in joy."

Ma Dear nodded. "Lord, keep them and get them here safe."

NINE

⁂

Shirley nodded for the check. The booth at the HoJo's was starting to feel way too small. Lex mentioning California to Windy just made things even more uncomfortable.

Windy's blue eyes—crinkled at the corners—were full of light. "California? Cool. I always wanted to go there." She was singing "California Girls" when the waitress brought the check to the table. She stopped singing and looked at Shirley. Her face was earnest, almost like she was in a confessional. "Thanks for this. I'll have to owe you." Windy shrugged. "You know, the bag lady and all."

Shirley willed her hands not to shake when she reached into her purse to pay the check. She fingered the brown envelope before she extracted the bills. It was just a burger and fries—and two shakes. There was no point in pitching a fit about it. The contents of the envelope was all they had, though, all that was going to get them to California.

She shook her head. They were going to make it. She had just signed on for getting the girl to Tyler. She would get Windy there, and that would be the end of it....and it would be good for her and the kids to see Mother Johnson. Then it was on to California. Tyler was a detour, but they would just have to be careful with money. That was all—just be careful. While Shirley paid and tipped, Windy tickled Mika and Lex and kept singing the Beach Boys' song.

Shirley closed her purse and looked at her son. "Lexington, didn't I tell you to stay out of grown people's conversations?"

Lex bowed his head. "Yes, ma'am."

She took a deep breath. "It's okay. Miss Windy asked me the question about where we were going. Next time, let me answer. You're excused, just be careful, okay?" Shirley watched Mika edge closer so that she could comfort her little brother. It was a good thing, their closeness.

Shirley looked at her watch. "Come on, we need to leave here if we're going to make it to Shreveport, Louisiana, before nightfall. And we have to find someplace to stay."

They drove all afternoon and most of the evening until they found a small hotel just outside of Monroe, some seventy or eighty miles from Shreveport. Down the street from the hotel, they bought a box of chicken with biscuits, mashed potatoes and gravy, coleslaw—along with a fried fish sandwich for Mika—before the four of them settled into the room.

When Shirley unlocked the door, Windy, who was the first in the room, flopped and bounced on one of the double beds. She rushed into the bathroom, then stood in the open doorway smelling the soap. "I can't wait to get to Tyler, and I know my grandma's going to be so happy to see me." Windy turned toward the room. "Granny's so excited about the baby." She inhaled the soap's commercial bouquet, then laid it back on the sink. "I bet she has sweet smelling stuff like this all over her house." She pointed at the nightstand between the beds.

"Somebody's even left us a paper."

Shirley looked at the stained, matted carpet and reminded herself that she wasn't trying to make a home. It was a temporary place to rest on the way to Tyler on the way to California. *Don't sweat the small stuff.* The bedspreads were the same nylon floral print spreads she had seen many times before. She smiled briefly—maybe there were only two of them in all the motels in the world and some elf had the job of moving them nationally from room to room.

She spoke to Mika and Lex. "Okay, you guys. Let's shake a leg. You've got to eat and get showered so you can get in the bed."

In less time than she anticipated, Lex and Mika were already fed, in the bed that the three of them would be sharing—Shirley sleeping lengthwise at the foot of the bed. Windy's bed was already turned down; she hadn't been able to resist trying it out.

Windy sat at the little table in the room and sucked the gristle off the bone of the last drumstick in the box and smacked her lips. "So tell me why you decided to go to Tyler instead of straight to California? I never would have done that—not in a million years."

"It's no big deal." It really was a big deal. She loved Mother Johnson and Ma Dear. She was grateful to them...but she hadn't called in years. She'd written letters and sent cards...until Danny. Then she'd written letters and never mailed them. Maybe she was afraid that she would hear a call to come home in Mother's voice, or maybe she was afraid that Mother would need her and it would call her away from her own life. Maybe there was no reason. It had been so long—so long she was afraid it was too long.

There had been some good things about Tyler. It was the

place that healed her. And there were good times, like with Tony Taylor. Funny that his name even came to mind…it had been years.

Tyler was also the place that held some of her most painful memories. It was the place where she had buried memories of her father, her mother, and her uncles. She did not want to breathe life back into them. It was the place where she had learned that racism not only swung from trees, but that it followed little girls into movie theaters. That was all over and done in her life, she didn't want to revive it.

But for weeks now, she had been seeing Mother Johnson's face and hearing her heavy rasping voice. Maybe it was time—briefly—to go home again.

Perhaps it was just coincidence that she had been mistakenly hauled to that backwater jail. Or just coincidence that Windy had come to her for help, and that the girl had been on her way to Tyler. Maybe it was coincidence, but it didn't feel like it. It felt like Providence; it felt like God's hand.

But it also felt like too much to try to explain to a pregnant teenager with purple toenails, cut-off shorts, and no money.

Was Windy kidding? Did she forget she had just asked for a ride? Shirley shrugged, "I just felt like we needed to make a brief stop by home on our way to California." She shook out the newspaper that she had been pretending to read.

It was funny to call Tyler, Texas, home. As long as she had been away, East St. Louis, Illinois, had felt like home. But now there was even less left of home there. Just even more painful memories.

Mother Johnson was now, at least physically, the closest thing she could touch to family.

Windy helped her throw away the empty chicken box and

the rest of the trash. Then Shirley—after she had washed up—crawled into bed, pulled the covers over her head, and waited to dream.

It must have been the long drive and eating chicken so late in the evening, combined with all the talk of Tyler. She dreamed that Mother Johnson was calling to her—calling her home, telling her not to be afraid, that she would be all right.

"The Lord's got joy for you, baby," Mother said. "Everything's going to be all right."

Then Shirley dreamed about Tony Taylor—about the cookies they shared on the playground, about the money he helped her save so that she could run away…run back to see her friend Sheri. She dreamed of Tony as a skinny little boy.

When she awoke the next morning, and all through the day, she wondered where he was now.

TEN

Tony Taylor pulled off the support belt he wore when he was working and threw it in the trunk of his car. The workday was over and it was time to unwind.

He knew about women and he knew about life; both had done him wrong. Both had taken more out of him than he knew he had to give. Tony was shut down, turned down, and burned out. He was through working for the man and playing the fool for women. Mostly now when he relaxed he relaxed in the company of men.

He had his own work thing. It was not what he had expected he would be doing, but it was honest, and he didn't have to look over his shoulder or watch his back. He called the shots. If he didn't work hard, he didn't eat; but no one could tell him when to eat or how high he could go.

As for women, limited contact was how he handled it. Lonely was much maligned and constant company was overrated. He just saw women when he couldn't stand not seeing them anymore. Keeping his self together, avoiding being used…that was worth the price of being alone. Tony had learned that he was good company.

He walked into the dark bar and appreciated the smell of wood, beer, and leather. While his eyes adjusted, he headed toward his favorite stool at the bar.

Tony knew from experience that there were all kinds of drunks. Some cursed, some laughed, and some cried in their beer while they told others about the wages of sin and cried out the name of the Lord. The man at the bar had to be the latter.

"I didn't think there was a God until I met Lucille. Lucille sure enough a picture of hell right here on earth, and she's got to be taking lessons from the devil…or else she's teaching him some things." The other men laughed.

"Here he goes again." One of the men nodded and laughed at Tony. "Pull up a chair, brother, this is going to be good."

The drunk man's mouth turned down at the corners. "For real. Listen to me. I'm trying to tell you something." The man finished the beer in his hand and knocked on the bar for the bartender to refill his glass. "My grandfather was a preacher. 'Don't let your nature get ahead of you, son.' That's what he used to tell me. My daddy used to tell me the same thing, but he hit the bottle every now and then—you see, we wasn't supposed to drink, but he would creep and do it."

The man hunched his shoulders as though he was sneaking. "I caught him one time, sloppy drunk—" he chopped his hand in the air—"and that was it, it was over. I wasn't listening to him no more. I still loved him, but he couldn't tell me nothing…'specially after I saw Lucille."

The man sitting next to Tony nudged him and laughed. He looked in the drunk man's direction. "I know what you mean about that, man." Tony nodded to the bartender and ordered his usual.

The drunk man shook his head. "My grandfather kept trying to talk to me, though. 'Don't let your nature lead you into doing things before you get married. The devil will ruin your life, son.'" He stuck his finger in his beer and looked at the bartender. "You know this is a shame, to expect a man to pay for a beer with this much head on it. Ain't nothing here but foam."

The man sitting next to Tony coaxed the drunk man back to his story. "Come on, now, man. I'll buy you another beer, man. Just tell the story."

The drunk man nodded. "All right, now. I'm going to hold you to your word." He nodded to the other men in the bar. "You heard him, now. You all heard. A man's word is his bond."

"Yeah, we heard," someone yelled. "Just finish the story, man." Lucille was popular in the bar.

The man, tottering back and forth on his seat, seemed pacified. "Anyway, my grandfather told me better. He put it to me plain."

The man next to Tony nodded. "Yeah, that sounds like old folks."

He shook his head. "I meant to listen, but then I saw Lucille. You talking about a good-looking woman, *that* was a good-looking woman. Still is—good stuff in all the right spots! But, I tell you young bloods something. Good looks don't cover up a spiky tongue. No sir. Good looks go away, but a spiky tongue is forever. If you going for good looks, make sure you check out the tongue first!"

One of the men in the back laughed. "Man, what you talking about?"

The drunk man took a big pull on his beer. Foam covered his moustache and chin. "There's a book in the Bible called Esther. If I heard it preached once, I heard it a hundred times. My grandfather, and every other preacher I know, pulls out

Esther on Mother's Day, Women's Day, whatever. See, they think it's a story to women telling them they need to beautify themselves if they want to marry a king…that if you're beautiful, God can use your beauty to do good.

"We always see what we been seeing all the time. For years, we been judging a woman's worth by her beauty. We still doing it, even preachers. That ain't what the book is really about. The book is a warning to men."

"*Preach* to us, Rev," one of the men hollered, and the other men laughed.

"Laugh if you want to, young blood, but you remember that what I'm saying is true. It's two main women in the story, and both of them is beautiful. In fact, my brothers, every woman in the story is beautiful. But the two most beautiful women is Vashti and Esther. Vashti is queen and she is beautiful, no doubt about it. But she is also rebellious and selfish and rude. She was greedy—the king had given her everything, and she wasn't even interested in trying to please him. She embarrassed her husband in front of the whole nation. I ain't gone go into detail, read the story for yourself. She embarrassed him so bad the other men were embarrassed *for* him, and you know that's bad."

"I seen Lucille do you that way, man!"

"Yeah, it's a pitiful thang, ain't it? That's why I'm trying to help you." The old man took a long drink from his mug, then wiped his mouth with the back of his hand. "So, anyway, the king gets rid of Vashti, but his heart is heavy—the man is lonely! So his boys set about trying to find a woman for him. But they kept doing and kept seeing what they had been doing and seeing all along. They keep just looking for outward beauty. They find all the beautiful women in the land…a fool's paradise.

"Only God steps in and uses a man to get the right woman

to the king—Esther. Now, Esther is beautiful, too. But Esther is different. She was kind to the king's servant—to a man that had nothing—that kindness got her the servant's favor so he was working to help her win. When it came time to get whatever gift she could get before she met with the king, Esther didn't take nothing—she was unselfish. Esther just took the servant's advice." The drunk man nodded. "And you know the servant's always got the skinny." He looked around the room and then continued telling his story. "And Esther was a praying woman.

"When all the beautiful women lined up—and you know after a while, all that beauty was *overwhelming* to that man— Esther stood out. She had beauty and more. What I'm trying to tell you, and I'll be happy if one person hears me, if you want to be a happy man—or a happy woman for that matter—it's the *more* that makes the difference. God knows beauty is a good thing, but it's the more that will make you smile when you think about going home."

Tony sipped his drink and looked at his hands. The old man was definitely a preaching drunk. It was a good lesson, just a little too late. But maybe, like the old man said, it would help someone that heard it. Tony just had a safer solution: just leave it all alone.

The man next to him nodded in his direction. "Hey, man. What you thinking about?" He pointed at the preaching drunk. "Lucille's old man is feeling so good, he done preached in the bar so hard, he's standing up for a round of drinks. He just about had altar call." He laughed. "And I think if he did, a lot of us would have come." He nodded at Tony's glass. "You looking kind of empty to me. Better get that thing full."

Tony nodded. He needed a drink. "Hit me, again, bartender. Another ginger ale on the rocks." A wife was the last thing on his mind.

ELEVEN

B y the time Shirley, Windy, Mika, and Lex pulled off of U.S. 271 and onto Gentry heading into Tyler, it was late in the afternoon. So much in the town, in the city, had changed; Shirley hardly knew where she was.

"I just need you to drop me off at this grocery store—a Jack something or other runs it. My granny's going to come by and pick me up there."

Shirley glanced at the girl. Windy was a strange girl, and she gave even stranger directions. There was only one store in town, that she recollected, that had an employee named Jack. "Windy, it's no problem. I can take you right to your grandmother's house."

"Oh no. I'm just doing what she told me to do. You know how old people are when they have a plan—you change one thing and they get all worked up. Just drop me off there. I'll just run inside and call. She'll be there in no time, believe me—" Windy patted her belly—"she can't hardly wait. Granny is so excited to see me and this baby."

She would start with the grocer that she remembered. When Shirley pulled into the store parking lot—which was now double the size it was when Shirley last was in town—there was a new, more professional sign and a new storefront. There was also a new name: Jack's Groceries. Obviously, Jack was no longer a clerk, and not even just a manager. He was now the owner.

Shirley pulled into a parking space near the front door—automatic doors. Windy stepped from the car and closed the car door. She smiled at Mika and Lex. "You two keep being good for your mama." She stooped down and looked at Shirley. "Thanks again for everything. I owe you big time. If you give me your address or number—"

"You don't owe me anything." Shirley put the car in reverse so that she could back out of the parking space and be on her way. "You were good company, Windy." She was surprised that she meant it. "Just do something nice for someone else…and take care of your baby."

Mika and Lex waved at the girl until they had driven out of sight.

Shirley wasn't sure how she made her way to the road that led her to Texas College, but soon afterward, she pulled onto Mother Johnson's street and, like some people do when they are almost home, she slowed her pace. Mika and Lex whispered to each other and bounced back and forth in the backseat. They pressed their faces against the backseat car door windows.

"Are we here, Mama?"

"Is this it? Is this our cousin's house?"

The street in front of Mother Johnson's house was fully paved now, but Shirley recognized the tree in the front yard. It was taller and thicker, but it leaned the same way it had when she was younger. The long slope of the driveway was familiar, but there was a new front porch that looked, unlike the rest of the house, professionally built. Shirley turned the car into the driveway, parked, and then got out of the car. "Come on," she told her kids.

She needed a moment before she saw Mother Johnson, before she tried to explain away the years that they had not spoken. So she walked the driveway and headed toward the backyard.

The side door of the house looked the same. She thought of all the visitors who had come to the door to seek Mother Johnson's wise counsel—unwed mothers, troubled men, and even Mother's best friend, Ma Dear. All of them coming, like Shirley, to feed on Mother Johnson's discernment, kindness, and strength. Mother Johnson loved all of them with the best kind of love—love that was unconditional and full of truth, even truth that sometimes inflicted necessary wounds. She loved them all and prayed them through their troubles. She rocked with them and held them until they were well enough to stand alone again.

"Ain't nothing magic or strange about it," Mother once told Shirley. "The Good Book say God give all His people gifts that we supposed to use in His Kingdom. I didn't make it up; it's plain in the Word of God. Right in 1 Corinthians it say some got the gift to heal, some got the gift of miracles, some can prophesy. God give me wisdom, and He give it to me to help His people.

"Some people get scared of it—it don't fit into they neat little picture they got of God. Some people get mad about it. I tells them I didn't write the Book; I just believe it. I believe in God and I believe in what He give me. The apostle Paul said we see as through a glass darkly. We just regular people; we can't see into heaven or into God's heart or mind. We can't see His plan. The gifts God give us, with all us working together, just give us a glimpse, a little light into the mind and heart of God. Just enough to hold us until we see Him face-to-face as He is. 'Course, none of it work if we ain't led by love, if we don't use all the gifts working together as one."

Shirley could imagine Mother's knotted fingers, her slightly stooped back, and she could hear the raspiness of Mother Johnson's voice. She could envision the light in Mother's eyes.

"The Word say He give me my gift before the world began, to prepare me to do good works for Him. Ain't that something? Before there was even a world, God bowed His head, full of hair like sheep's wool—" Shirley could still recall Mother Johnson patting at her own hair—"you know, that's why I smile every time I comb my hair. I think I got hair just like God."

Mother smiled. "Well, before time began, God smiled at the me that wasn't and was and picked me out from amongst all the souls and said, 'See that little one over there? We're going to send her into a world full of trouble. We're going to make her black in a world where people like white. We're going to make her a woman in a world where people only listen to the voices of men. We're going to make her poor in a world that prefers the rich. And after a while, we're going to make her old in a world of people that only want to be young.

"'Look like she ought to always be behind, but I'm gone give her this gift—wisdom. And I'm gone give her the faith to believe in the gift I give her. She gone help people. I'm making her part of My plan to make the crooked places straight, to bring water to parched land. And just when people count her out, she's gone shine, like perfected beauty out of Zion. She's going to read my Word and see that she is the head and not the tail, and she's gone believe what I say and not what she sees. She's gone remember, way deep down in her spirit, that I told her that some day the valleys would be exalted and the mountains would be made low. She's gone do the good work I'm preparing her to do, and she's gone make Me glad.'"

Shirley walked farther up the driveway and into the yard. She pointed out the fruit trees to Mika and Lex and told them that in the fall the pears on the trees were so heavy that they sweetened the air and made the branches sag.

"What's this little house, Mommy?" Lexington stood at the door of a little screened hut. The few pieces of wood that held it together were rough, gray, and cracked. The roof was made of mismatched tarpaper shingles. The prayer house was really no more than rusted, puckered screens that kept some flies and mosquitoes away. There were no walls on the house to separate its visitors' voices from God.

"It's a little house of prayer. And there is a mighty woman of God who lives in that house—" she pointed at Mother Johnson's house, then looked back at the prayer house—"who comes here to pray. She prays for those who are lonely and for those who are afraid. She prays for people who don't even know that she's praying for them—for people on drugs, on alcohol, for presidents and for kings, and for people who feel they have no place in this world.

"In this little place, she prays for those who are sick, but mostly Mother prays for children. For children in China, in Africa, in the cities, and in the country, for children all over the world. Right here in this hut, Mother Johnson prays and God hears."

Shirley put her arms around Mika and Lex and smiled. "And sometimes God sends other people to her, and she teaches *them* to pray." She closed her eyes so that she would not cry. She remembered being in the hut sitting at Mother's knee.

It was Wednesday, and, as was their habit, Shirley followed Mother Johnson to the prayer house. "Come on, Shirley. We got to make some noise today. We need the Lord to hear us."

As always there was no one around, but for some reason Shirley felt freer outside. She shook the tambourine and danced and sang. She prayed with Mother Johnson, or sat quietly when Mother said words she did not understand. Even the birds making their way further south seemed unusually quiet. "Amen," Mother said.

The prayer house was a fixture in her life while she lived with Mother Johnson. It was the place Shirley learned to pray, where she learned to become an intercessor. It was also the place where she stopped becoming and just was.

Shirley walked to the cabinet and took out a large saucepan. She opened the flatware drawer and grabbed a large metal spoon. She walked past the adults, out the door. Shirley walked with her head held high, taking careful steps until she reached the prayer house. She sat on the old worn pillow where Mother Johnson used to sit, and she began to sing.
Do Lord, do Lord,
Lord, remember me.
Do Lord, do Lord,
Lord, remember me.
Do Lord, do Lord,
Lord, remember me.
Do Lord remember me.
When I'm sick and can't get well,
Lord, remember me.

When I'm sick and can't get well,
Lord, remember me.
When I'm sick and can't get well,
Lord, remember me.
Do Lord, remember me.

I can't pray, but I can sing. I'm going to sing until she's well. *Shirley sang as loud as she could. Then she danced around in the prayer house while she beat the pot. She hollered the song. And then she cried. Cried because there was something stuck in her throat that made it hurt, that would not come out. She continued beating the pot, so that God would hear her, but she cried.* You can't let her die, Lord, *she thought.* You can't let her, die, Lord. Please. *But she was afraid to pray—something made her afraid to pray out loud. Shirley thought of Mother Johnson on the bed. She could see Mother, and it was almost as though she were being held down. Her lips began to move.*

And then she heard her voice. "Don't leave me alone, again, Lord." *She yelled in between gasps.* "Don't let her die. I love her. Please God. Please." *It was like fire in her throat. Shirley beat the pot while she prayed.* "Please, God. Please. Mother! Mother! I don't want you to die! Please, God." *She fought for words until she began to yell the verses she had memorized with Mother Johnson, the words she had recited over and over.* "Lift up your heads, O ye gates; and be ye lift up, ye everlasting doors; and the King of glory shall come in! Who is this King of glory? The LORD strong and mighty, the LORD mighty in battle. Lift up your heads, O ye gates; even lift them up, ye everlasting doors; and the King of glory shall come in." *She gasped for air.* "Come in, Lord! Come in, Lord! Please come in!"

Shirley remembered that when Ma Dear, Mother Johnson's best friend, told the story after that day, she said she ran from the house with some of the others when she heard. It was the strangest thing, Ma Dear always said. Shirley was crying and praying. Looking and acting more like Mother than Mother did herself, Ma Dear said. Sitting on the swing out back and retelling the story, she said Shirley shouted and danced, not like a young child at all, but more like an old woman. "I've never seen a child pray with such power before or since. My goodness, it was sure something to see. No doubt in my mind, Mother, the baby's prayers brought you back."

Mika tugged at Shirley's arm and brought her back to the present. "Mama, can we go inside?"

TWELVE

Shirley lifted her hand to the handle on the prayer house door. "All right, just for a minute. Then we need to let Mother Johnson know we're here." Shirley, Mika, and Lex stepped inside the small, screened space.

"What are all these pillows for, Mommy?" The stuffed cushions were red, green, yellow, all colors. Some were made from old quilts.

"To sit on or kneel on, when you pray."

"Pray outside?" Lex laughed. Lexington was right. Inside the prayer house was just like being outside. There were no real walls.

Mika joined him. "Everybody might hear you!"

Shirley smiled. "When I first came here, I felt the same way."

Mika picked up a tambourine. "Why is this out here, Mommy? And all these pots and pans?"

"Mother says some people pray silently, and God hears. They close their eyes, fold their hands, and God bows His ear to hear. Sometimes, though, like Jehoshaphat and David in the

Bible, people sing, shout, cry, and make all kinds of noise when they praise and pray. She says that sometimes people fight about it—about what's right and what's wrong—but loud or soft, God still hears.

"When Mother prays, she makes a mighty noise. She says she's got a lot to fight her way through in her prayers to God." Shirley crooked a finger at her children. "Come here, let me show you." She picked up a stick and began to scratch in the dust of the hut's dirt floor. "Mother says the Bible tells us to believe in what is unseen. She says we rely on friends, cars, houses, paychecks, and bank accounts—until they fall apart. Then when we hit rock bottom we call on what our spirits know is eternal. Mother says the unseen things have always been and will always be: God, Jesus, and the Holy Spirit."

She drew three horizontal lines on the ground. "Mother says God and His angels and all the heavenly host live up here on the top, what Paul called the Third Heaven." Shirley used the stick to point to the lowest level. "This is where we live, down here on earth. All we can see is what's on this level here with us. We have to have faith to believe the rest and to trust God that what His Word says about the rest is true."

Mika pointed to the middle area with her finger. "Well, what is this area, Mommy? Just the air?"

"That, it seems like, is the hardest part for us. Most people believe in Earth because we see it, and in heaven. It's the middle part that confuses most of us. God sees all of it, but the middle and heaven are a mystery to most of us." She looked at Mika and Lex. "Do you remember in Sunday school how the devil is sometimes called the prince of the air?"

Lex nodded. "Yes, ma'am. And we don't have to be afraid of him because he's already defeated."

"Well, my goodness. That's a big thought for such a little man. I think that child's going to be a preacher!"

The three turned at the voice. An old woman, dark and frail, stood smiling and looking at them through the screen door. "You all mind if Mother Johnson come in and sit with you?"

Shirley sat frozen.

Mika jumped to her feet and pushed open the screen door for Mother Johnson. Lexington jumped to his feet. "Are you Mother Johnson?"

"I sure am, baby. I'm your cousin."

Mika nodded. "Mommy talks about you all the time."

Lexington scratched his head. He looked at Mother Johnson from foot to head. His eyes settled on her gray hair. "You're *my* cousin?"

Mother Johnson chuckled. "Yes, I'm your cousin. I got a little wear and tear on me, but I'm still your cousin." She hugged Mika and then wrapped her arms around Lexington.

"I've been listening at you for a while, and you are two smart chirren. Blessed is what I would call you." Mother tugged Lexington's ear and then let him go.

Shirley couldn't speak. She couldn't tell if a great light had suddenly filled the prayer house, or if it was only in her heart.

"You chirren already know what much of the world is searching for. You don't have to be afraid of devils, or monsters, mean people, or anything else. Just look them in the eye and tell them, 'No matter what you do to me right now, the Word of God says evil is already defeated.' Hallelujah!"

It really was Mother Johnson standing there in the flesh. Shirley shook her head. How could she have ever thought of not coming this way? Thomas Wolfe was wrong.

Mother Johnson held out her hand to Mika. "Help an old lady ease down." She bent her knees and began a slow descent. "Move over there and share with me," she said to Lex. "That's a mighty big pillow and you're a mighty little fellow—little, but remember I called you mighty!" Mother Johnson winked at Lex. "Scootch on over there and make room for me and my bright and helpful friend." She smiled up at Mika. Finally, the two of them sank slowly onto the pillow. "Getting down is easy; the tricky part is getting up!" Mother laughed.

She looked between the children. "You two got yourselves a smart mother there, and it was an old woman's joy to have her here. She was a pretty girl just like you are." She looked at Mika. "A head full of hair—goodness, she had enough hair for two chirren. She sat right over there where you're sitting." She pointed in Lex's direction. "Lots of times, she was quiet, but she was listening, listening, listening to the mysteries of God. People going to fortune tellers and climbing up high mountains and missing that the greatest truth, the greatest love, the greatest power, the greatest mystery is God."

Shirley felt foolish, the way she was smiling. But she didn't care. She was home again.

"Your mother's right about that middle level and about the prince of the air. Here we are down here—" she pointed to the lowest level of the dust drawing—"sending prayers up and mad at God cause our answer is delayed 'cause we forgot all about the middle." Her dark eyes looked—from behind her new red frame glasses—from Mika to Lex. "Do you all know about Daniel?"

"Yes, ma'am." They nodded.

"Like Daniel in the lions' den." Lex began growling and rounded his hands into imaginary claws.

"And Daniel in the fiery furnace with the three Hebrew boys—Shadrach, Meshach, and Abednego."

Lex stopped growling and crowed. "That's my favorite! Abednego!"

Mother nodded. "Well, you might also know that Daniel was wise and he dreamed dreams and had visions from God that he could interpret."

"Yes, ma'am. I remember, he read the handwriting on the wall," Mika said.

"That's right. My goodness, two good-looking chirren and both of you are smart. God gone be able to use both of you. I believe that, yes sir." Mother Johnson smiled at both of them. "Well, one day Daniel was by this river just crying and bawling his heart out. You see he had been given a vision—a message from the Lord about something that was going to happen a long time later. Daniel was waiting for some more understanding, some more interpretation from the Lord, and it was taking a long time coming. So long that Daniel was just all worked up and crying about it."

Mother Johnson tapped Lex on the knee. "Did you ever have a promise from someone you loved and believed in, something they told you was going to happen, but the promise took a long time to come?"

Lex nodded. "Mommy promised me that one day we would get a puppy—a little black one with white feet."

"Lex, Mommy didn't say it was going to be black or have white feet. She just said a puppy."

"Well, that's what I saw in *my* vision! And I still don't have my puppy."

Shirley felt the parental twinge of guilt, but she kept quiet and let Mother Johnson finish her story.

"Well, that's all right, Lex. That's what people usually do all the time—add a little here and there to what God told them." She laughed at her own joke. "But that's good enough, honey. I bet it feels like it's taking too long for that puppy to get here."

"Yes, ma'am. It's taking forever!"

"It's not taking forever, Lexington. You're just being dramatic."

"No, I'm not, Mika. It feels like forever." Lexington reached around Mother Johnson as though he was going to hit his sister.

Shirley finally had to speak. "Lexington!"

Mother smiled at Shirley, nodded, and continued talking. "Well, Daniel felt just like you feel, Lex—it was taking forever. You got a word from your mother, and Daniel had a word from the Lord. Lots of folks, when things take a long time, just give up. They say it's hopeless, or that they must have missed God. But not Daniel. That boy kept crying and praying to the Lord. He even fasted—gave up some of the food and good stuff that he usually drank. That child Daniel would not give up."

"Don't ever give up!" Lex yelped.

Mika nodded at her brother, then at Mother Johnson. "That's what Mommy taught us—never give up."

"Well, you would have thought that Daniel took your mother's advice. God had shown him something and he wasn't going to quit until he had the whole thing." Mother pointed at the middle section again. "When we pray, we don't see that our words go from our lips to God's ears—we don't have to see it, but His Word tells us that's how it is. We don't see that He gives our answers to angels. We don't see that sometimes those angels have to fight hard past the prince of the air and his dark angels to get the answers to us. But that's what Daniel shows us—there's a war going on right here in the middle. We can't see it, but that don't mean that it ain't going on." She touched Lex's knee. "Before you get a puppy, your mama has to get a place, find the puppy, and get everything ready. Your mama has to fight through some circumstances to be able to keep her promise; it's hard, but it's what she promised she would do. Some of it you can't see, you're a child and she don't want you to see, but that don't mean it ain't going on."

"You mean I'm going to get the puppy?"

"That's what it means, baby. At just the right time, you're going to get that puppy. The same thing for Daniel—God promised and He's going to make sure that it gets there at just the appointed time. We can't see evil fighting to keep our promise away from us, but that's what's happening. We're children and we don't need to see everything, we just need to keep believing God. That's why we have to be like Daniel, we have to believe and pray. Even better, we got to fast and pray and sometimes—sad to say—we got to cry. The good news, when the devil is fighting, God got even more reinforcements He can send in to get the job done. We can't see it, but when we pray, God is listening. Just like your mama, or even better than your mama, it may take some time, but God is going to keep His promise.

"At the end of all that crying, praying, fasting, and angel fighting, Daniel got his promise—he got his word. Your mama is right; don't ever give up. Your answer is just a prayer, a fast, or maybe even a tear away."

Lex and Mika clapped their hands. "Never give up!"

THIRTEEN

Mika and Lex ran into the kitchen where their mother sat at the table. "Mommy, Mommy, we got our own room! It's all ready for us. Some of your old stuff is in the room, too."

"See I found this old cigar box." Mika held it out for her mother to see. It was covered with pasted-on pictures and cartoon cutouts.

Shirley nodded, looked at the shoebox, and then at Mother Johnson. It was the shoebox in which, years ago, she had saved money to run away—to escape Tyler and run back to East St. Louis, back to her friend Sheri. Shirley hoped her eyes conveyed to Mother Johnson the sorrow she still felt for running away that day, for the illness that almost killed Mother Johnson. She hoped that when she hugged Mother Johnson earlier Mother could feel her love and how much she had missed her.

Mother patted her hand. "Don't you worry none, baby. All that's under the bridge, thrown into the sea of forgetfulness. The devil thought he had me, but who would have thought I'd be rescued by a sweet little girl's prayers. You went out to that prayer house and opened up your mouth on *that* day. Yes sir!"

It was a pleasure to feel Mother Johnson's rough, bony, calloused hands rubbing hers. Their texture was craggy and familiar.

"I don't even feel like I've got a right to be here, Mother. I haven't been calling or keeping up with you. But…I…actually, I feel like that Willie Nelson song 'You Were Always on My Mind'."

Mother laughed. "I feel you, baby. What's a little time between true friends? Because you know we are more than relatives; we're friends."

Shirley nodded.

"So, did you ever find her? Did you ever find that child, your friend Sheri?"

Shirley shook her head. For some reason, she could not look Mother Johnson in the eye. "No, I mean, I've never been back to East St. Louis anyway. I've thought about it. But… Anyway, who knows? Maybe the doctors were right. Maybe there never was a Sheri. Maybe I made her up in my head. Since I've been away, I've thought about it a lot. And I've had lots of discussions with people about it—like with my psychology professors in college. One of them said, point-blank, that I made her up as a traumatic stress response. That explained why the names were so close—Sheri and Shirley. I mean, it's pretty obvious, isn't it?"

Mother Johnson kept rubbing Shirley's hands.

"My mother had a breakdown after my father died. My uncles disappeared. Maybe Sheri was part of my breakdown. Who knows? What I do know is that I don't let it torment me every day anymore. But there's lots I still don't know." She forced a smile; she felt tired. "I don't even know why I'm here."

Mother let go of Shirley's hand and got up from the table.

She lifted the kettle from the stove, filled it with water, replaced it, and ignited the flame. "Well, you don't have to figure it out in one day. I been feeling in my spirit that you were on the way. Whatever it is you can't figure out, it'll get figured before you leave. Your answer is on the way. It may have been a long time coming, but surely it's on the way."

Shirley sighed. "I'm glad you're optimistic, Mother. I feel like I'm in a fog, like nothing's clear. Like it's never going to be clear again. Since Danny's been gone…"

Mother Johnson sat back down. "I know about the fog, honey. I know about the widows' cry. I've seen some people even go through it when they get divorced. A kind of sadness, it feels like you're never going to shake it."

Shirley closed her eyes, but Mother kept talking. "Don't you worry, baby. Grief, sorrow, mourning is all just part of life. It's just a season. It don't last forever. When it's over, it will feel like it's just been a night. Your sorrow is just part of the natural cycle of life. You got to cry, the Bible calls it *travail*, before you give birth. Joy is coming."

She grabbed Shirley's hands. "Most folks might tell you to whitewash your troubles—cover them up with paint, or a little powder and lipstick, or with work. But I've got a whole lot of years behind me. When you need to cry, cry to the Lord. He listens and He keeps every one of your tears in a bottle. And even when you crying, you have to bless the Lord at all times through your tears. Sometimes when you praising Him, tears are going to be running down your face, the same way they ran down mine.

"Girl, I had so many tears, I thought they were going to cut into me like water on a rock. Sometimes when I was praising the Lord, it was hard. It was a sacrifice, but you do it anyhow.

But the good Lord don't mind you crying. While you crying, keep praying, keep believing that joy is coming. We don't like it. We don't want to hear about it, but we got to walk through the shadows before we can pass into the light. Joy is coming!"

Shirley opened her eyes and nodded. "Don't give up."

"Never give up." Mother squeezed Shirley's hands and then let go. She rose, went to the cupboards for cups and teabags, and brought them to the table. Using a potholder, she grabbed the boiling kettle to fill the cups. After replacing the kettle, she went back to the cupboard for one last thing. "Here's a little honey to help it go down."

That night, Shirley dreamed of her old house, of her father…and then of Sheri.

"You feel better now?"

Shirley nodded. "Yes, I'm okay."

"Bet I can beat you to the rock!" They ran hard, like young horses. The little bad girl got to the rock a few inches ahead of Shirley. They slammed their child bodies into the rock in a way that would have injured adults; then they slumped to the ground. The gray rock was so large that it hid them from the eyes of anyone who might have passed by the corner lot.

Shirley held out her candy necklace to the other girl again. "Want another bite?" The little bad girl leaned in and closed her mouth around the white, pink, orange, and yellow disks. "You can take a big bite," Shirley said.

They sat and settled, discussing the treasures they had found. They sat back to back with their heads leaning on each other. Shirley pressed the daylight as far as she could. "I got to go," she said.

"Okay. Next time bring some better candy or food," the little

bad girl said. "We might go somewhere more far."

They rose and parted, on their ways home. "Bye!" Shirley yelled. When Shirley passed by the first unlit street lamp, she started to pick up speed on her bike—she had to beat the lights home. "God, don't let me get home too late," she whispered. And it seemed to her that He held back dusk-dark in the sky a little longer so that she could make it home.

As she pumped the pedals, she heard the little bad girl yelling behind her. "Hey! Hey, little girl! My name—my name is Sheri!"

FOURTEEN

❧

Shirley stepped outside where Mother Johnson sat rocking—or more aptly, gliding—in her chair. "This front porch is a doozey, Mother."

"Hush, child. It takes Ma Dear to tell you about how she's been thanking the Lord that she doesn't have to walk up that steep driveway to the house."

"And what made you get these fancy gliding chairs?" More than a week had gone by since Shirley and the children arrived, but every day held something new.

"Oh, this blackberry's still got a little bit of juice left. Mario Andretti drives racing cars; I got my rocking glider-deluxe." She touched the light brown wooden arm of the chair. "Ain't this some kind of invention? A rocking chair that glides." Mother Johnson slapped her knee and laughed. "You know I'm pretty hot stuff. I'm moving on up, baby!"

She slowed her gliding. "Though when Ma Dear comes along, you'll think, instead of races, we're having rocking chair-iot wars." She pointed at the third rocker. "And if you go by Ma Dear, that's the culprit, right there."

Shirley walked to the steps, tucked the skirt of her dress

behind her, and sat down. "What's so special about that chair?"

Mother laughed as she told her about the third rocker and about Mildred. The old lady was new to town, Mother said, and was somehow related to Mr. Jack and his people.

Mother clapped her hands together and said she kept forgetting not to call Jack *Mister*. It had been so many years, and old habits die hard.

She told Shirley that Mildred was a little on the standoffish side. That she did sometimes look at them like she was better, like she was superior. "But, like I said, old habits die hard. And I ain't never decided who I was gone be based on what somebody said. If that was the case, I'd have been out of the race long ago. If you don't care what people think, they can't hurt you."

Of course, Mildred and Ma Dear were like oil and water. Ma Dear was working hard to be down to earth and not to be siddity. Mildred was working at putting on airs, and siddity seemed to be a good thing to her. "There's a whole lot of presuming and judging going on," Mother said. "They are trying to bring some kind of religious war right here to my front porch. Neither one of them will consider that the other one might have at least a little something right. Or that, heaven forbid, God might have room for both of them in His plan." Mother shook her head in mock worry. "A body might have thought that a new porch and these fine new chairs would be just a little bit of heaven. But instead of heaven, it's been... well, you know what I'm saying."

The two women sat and watched cars roll slowly by, their passengers—many of whom were strangers—waving in the free way that country people still do. Children rode past on bicycles, and teenaged boys wearing large, clunky shoes in bright colors that bore the names of famous athletes walked past bouncing basketballs. Girls giggled past wearing cornrows, pastel sundresses, and sandals. Mothers pushed babies in strollers and wiped perspiration from their brows with cloth diapers they wore over their shoulders.

Mother Johnson and Shirley fanned away flies and the years that had separated them. The sun made speckled patterns on their arms and faces, shining through the groupings of leaves from the tree overhead.

"I dreamed about him last night. About the last time we talked. Before…you know. Actually, I dream all the time. But last night I dreamed again about him." Sometimes it hurt to even say Danny's name.

A breeze blew between them. "That sure feels good," Mother said. "When my husband died, I dreamed about him almost every night…for a while anyway. Just regular stuff. We would be going to the grocery store, driving to the post office, talking about the chirren." She smiled like her thoughts were far way. "I guess it made it easier." Mother Johnson picked up the tail of her apron to fan herself. "Yes, I used to dream about him right regular. Not so much anymore."

They sat in silence. Shirley's mind drifted back to the dream, the one she'd had over and over. She could hear Danny's voice.

He played his guitar, sang a few lines and stopped. "Oh yeah, remind me to tell you something when I get back."

"Tell me now."

"No, wait until I get back. It's going to blow your mind. It's something you never would have expected in a million years."

Now, it was Shirley's turn to sing to Danny. A few bars was all she could manage before her voice broke. As Danny began to play again, she cleared her throat and told him she loved him, and did not expect or wait for a reply. She started to count to ten, the ritual that ensured that they hung up the phone at the same time. "One, two, three—"

"Shirley?" He stopped playing. "Shirley, I love you."

"Well, well! I'll be!" Ma Dear was standing at the gate, laughing. She nodded her head at Mother. "You still got the gift." She snapped her fingers. "No doubt about it. You said she was coming, and sure enough, here she is." Ma Dear giggled, hopping up and down in a way that was surprising for a woman her size. "Honey, get out the pie pans. Something good is gone be cooking tonight."

Time had been good to Ma Dear, just as it had to Mother. She still had the gift; her presence could brighten the darkest place. "The love of the good Lord and the love of a good man will keep you looking good. It will do it every time," Ma Dear was known to say. She was just as pretty as always, and her face was flushed with excitement. "If this don't beat all!" Ma Dear stood still and winked. "Except for the news I just heard about your new I'm-better-than-you-are friend! Wait until you hear what I get to tell you." She snapped her fingers. "Yes ma'am. Something good's gone be cooking tonight!"

FIFTEEN

Ma Dear wiggled her way into the seat of her glider. "It seems like the people that built these things would have had some consideration for the well-endowed woman. I like these chairs fine, but they could have give me a little more room for growth." She grinned at Shirley. "Look at you, all grown up." Ma Dear pointed at Shirley and looked at Mother Johnson. "Can you believe it? I know we've seen pictures and all, but it don't seem like that long ago this child was getting ready to go to the prom. Remember that?"

Mother nodded. "Yes, I remember."

"Remember, she had that big old Afro?" She looked at Shirley. "You sure did look pretty. And what was that boy's name? The little scrawny one. Well, I guess he wasn't so scrawny by the time the two of you were going to the prom. What was his name?" Ma Dear's eyes twinkled.

"Tony," Shirley said.

"That's right. Tony Taylor. His people were originally from down Frankston or Cuny way, ain't that right?"

Mother Johnson nodded. "Yes, Ma Dear. It was Frankston.

His grandfather lived hollering distance from Demosthenes, who was Shirley's grand or greatgrand. I can never get the relation stuff straight."

The two older women went to gliding and talking about other folks they knew who had left the country, people who had come to the city of Tyler looking for steadier work or just to escape the farm.

Ma Dear winked at Shirley. "You know he's back in town? Tony, that is. He's been gone for a while, too. I'm not sure if he was married or what, but he's home now…and he's single." Ma Dear was rocking at full glide. "I saw him. He turned out to be a pretty good-looking man. Not pretty, but a sturdy, steady-looking man." She touched Mother on the arm. "If it's anything I am, it's a good judge of men."

"You can bank on that," Mother said. "If anyone knows about a single man, Ma Dear knows. Or about any man for that matter." Mother laughed out loud.

"Oh, Mother, don't talk that way in front of the child. She'll think I'm man-crazy."

Mother Johnson tipped her eyeglasses and raised an eyebrow.

"Now, Mother, you know I'm a good girl now. Why I'm still married to the same man I was seeing and married to last time Shirley saw me. Me and Ely are still together. At least that's how things are today. I told him, though, he better play his cards or fold his hand." She leaned forward and peered at Shirley. "You know we didn't have a proper church wedding. We just stood before the justice of the peace." She eased back in her chair and kept talking. "I told him. Yes, I did. I've been telling this sweet church mother here—" she touched Mother's arm—"if a church wedding don't jump off here soon, I'm gone close this book and never look back."

Mother gave Shirley a look that said, *See? I told you so.*

Ma Dear glanced at Shirley. "Like I said, Tony looks like a good man going to waste."

Shirley forced herself to smile at Ma Dear. "That was a long time ago. Lots of years have passed since we went to the prom."

"That's what some folks say, but I say it's never too late for love."

Shirley mumbled a response and tried not to roll her eyes. "Gag me with a spoon."

Ma Dear raised an eyebrow. "What did you say?"

Shirley shook her head. "I didn't say anything…" Just then, Mika and Lex walked up the driveway dragging a large, scratched white plastic bucket full of fresh peaches. They came at the perfect moment to interrupt Ma Dear. Maybe they would distract the old woman from her matchmaking.

"Look, Mommy!"

"My, my, look at these babies!" Before long, Ma Dear had both children on her lap, laughing and tickling them. Their clothes were damp.

Shirley pointed between them. "Ma Dear, meet Mika and Lexington. We call him *Lex.*" She pointed at their clothes. "What were you guys doing back there?"

"We had to use the hose to wash off the fuzz," Mika said.

"We almost died from itching!"

"We weren't dying, Lexington."

"Well, *I* almost did!"

Ma Dear made them promise they would come spend the night at her house. "We'll make homemade potato chips."

"You can make potato chips?" Mika's eyes were wide.

"At home?" Lex tipped his head to look Ma Dear in the eye.

"Why sure. It ain't too much this old lady can't do." It was obvious that Ma Dear was thrilling the children. Her plump arms shook and she glided back and forth while she told them stories about young Shirley. "I remember seeing your mama picking pears and apples out back. Remember her playing in the leaves, Mother Johnson?"

"That I do."

Ma Dear winked at Mika and Lex. "If I ask that old lady over there, she'll say no to me. But I bet if the two of you ask her to turn those peaches into something, I bet we'll be eating pie tonight."

Shirley smiled at the children and watched as the two old friends argued over who was going to do the peeling. "You sent these two strong, brave chirren out to pick the peaches. They almost died from the itching, and now you trying to tell me you can't peel because you're scared of a little fuzz!"

Mother laughed. "Ma Dear, you take your brave, signifying, ain't-much-I-can't-do-self out of my chair, off my porch, and go make your own pie."

"Well, Mother, now that ain't friendly—" she smiled impishly—"it sure ain't Christian! What do you think Reverend Howard would say if he knew the mother of his church was acting this way? I don't think your pastor, the good reverend, would approve." Ma Dear paused and laid a hand across her breast with great dramatic flair. "And I *know* you wouldn't want me to leave without telling you the news I came here to tell you about your starch-collared new friend. *Whew!*" Ma Dear rolled her eyes and, using her hand, fanned herself in an exaggerated manner. The children lay on her bosom, playing with her curls, like black and white wisps, in front of her ears. "It sure is hot out here. If I had peach fuzz on me, I know where I'd want to be."

"Where, Miss Ma Dear?"

She laughed. "Mr. Lexington, Ma Dear is just fine—no *Miss* needed. *Miss* Ma Dear is way too much, even for me." She kissed Lex and Mika on their foreheads. "What I would do, if I was loaded down with peach fuzz, is take a bath—"

"A bath?" Lex frowned.

"Not just a regular bath. A bath in tepid water—just slightly warm, just warm enough not to be cool. And while the water was running, I would pour me some Mister Bubble in the bath, and then I would work it out!" Ma Dear wiggled in the chair and the children giggled.

Mother Johnson played along. "You know, Ma Dear, I just happen to have a couple boxes of Mister Bubble that I bought at the grocery store the other day."

"I thought I remembered you saying something about that. At Jack's grocery store?"

"That's the place. It was on sale. I got a couple of those boxes in the bathroom cabinet under the sink right now!"

"Oo-oo!" the children smiled and clapped their hands, then looked at their mother. "Can we, Mommy?"

"If it's all right with Mother Johnson."

"Sure, baby, you know it is."

Shirley forced herself to keep a no-nonsense expression on her face. "All right then, you guys. Mika you're in charge. Lexington, mind your sister. And don't you guys leave a mess."

"Yes, ma'am."

Shirley smiled, but not so much that it overrode her serious tone. "And what do you say?" The children thanked Mother Johnson and ran inside.

Ma Dear made a funny face, like she knew something that Mother Johnson and Shirley didn't know. "Mister Bubble, huh? That ain't all they're selling at Jack's grocery store." Ma Dear picked up the pace of her gliding. "No, sir. Something else was on special down there. And it involves your new friend, Miss Busybody." Ma Dear pretended to fan. "The shortage of sweet ice tea around here might have ended for a while to come."

Mother Johnson stopped gliding. "What are you talking about, Ma Dear?"

Shirley watched the two old women and smiled. It was good to see that some things had stayed the same. She was an adult, but it was good to get enjoyment out of the same thing that pleased her when she was a child: just listening.

"I mean what I said, Mother. Mildred won't be minding my business. She's going to have her *own* business to take care of— some unexpected business. It seems Miss Perfect had some dead bones laying around in her closet." Ma Dear shook her hands and arms like she was casting a magic spell. "And it seems those dead bones just got up and walked! In fact, they're dancing!" Ma Dear put a hand on her belly and laughed.

"What are you talking about?"

"It seems Miss I-Don't-Let-Dirt-Touch-Me has a little relative that just showed up from East St. Louis. That's *East* St. Louis, *Illinois;* not Saint Louis, Missouri, for anyone that might be asking."

"Ma Dear, you are wearing on my nerves."

"I'm just saying Shirley can sit on down in that third chair. Otherwise, it's going to be empty for a while."

"Ma Dear!"

"If you don't want me here, Mother, just let me know. I could be at home watching that girl, Oprah, on TV." Ma Dear batted her eyes at Mother Johnson, then went on talking.

"Well, it seems that this unexpected relative showed up at the grocery store and introduced herself to Jack...oh, that was after she had helped herself to a couple of free apples and a big bag of chips. One of the stock clerks saw her dining, or *borrowing* a few things, and thought she was stealing. He ran after her and chased her around the store.

"After they knocked down the cereal display—Cap'n Crunch it was, with Crunchberries...they just missed knocking over the King Vitaman—little miss was marched up to Jack's office. Of course, you know how filled up with himself he is, especially now that the store has his name on it." Ma Dear pursed her lips.

"I can just see him setting there with his too-tight white shirt and black tie, just sweating up a storm—it must run in the family. I can just see how pink his face must have been. Well, anyway, he grilled the child and lectured her. Of course, she couldn't get a word in edgewise.

"But when he stopped jerking his jaw so he could dial the police, that's when it all come out. That's when it all come out about your friend, Mildred." Ma Dear started fanning, again. "It sure is hot, ain't it? Mother, you got any of that sweet tea?"

SIXTEEN

⁓

*M*other jumped out of her rocking chair. "Ma Dear, if you don't finish telling this story, the only sweet ice tea you'll be drinking is the kind made with honey up in Heaven!"

Shirley put her hand over her mouth so that she wouldn't laugh out loud. Ma Dear feigned horror. "Mother, you're scaring me." She pretended to shrink back in fear. "Okay, okay, Mother! What is this world coming to when church mothers are threatening and attacking people on their own *new* front porches?" She held her hands outstretched to Shirley, as though pleading for help. Ma Dear then waved her hand frantically in the direction of a car that traveled down the street. "Ain't that Reverend Howard? Ain't that your pastor?" Ma Dear waved her hand and pretended to recoil in fear. "Help me, Reverend Howard! Save me from your wayward member!" The three women laughed.

Mother Johnson shook her head. "You know that's not him. But I tell you what, it's going to take more than Reverend Howard to get me off of you, if you don't finish telling this story."

Ma Dear looked back at Mother Johnson, dropped her head, and then dropped her hands in resignation. "Okay, I'll tell you."

Ma Dear said she got everything she knew from a reliable source—Miss Lootie Belle, who was the aunt of the mother of the store clerk who was right there to witness and hear it all. "You know, the store clerk that nabbed the girl," Ma Dear told Mother Johnson and Shirley.

According to Ma Dear, just as Jack was about to dial, the girl dropped the bomb. She was his relative, the girl said. So she assumed it would be okay to sample the produce. She was some kind of relative of his. "Her closest living relative, it seems, is our own starch-collared Mildred," Ma Dear said. "Well, you can just imagine that Jack went pale. Stead of calling the police, he ended up calling home and got Mildred on the phone. Sure enough the stealing whippersnapper belonged to her," Ma Dear said.

As Miss Lootie Belle had relayed the story to Ma Dear, Jack hit the roof, forgot all the customers downstairs, the clerks in the office, and even sweet Jesus up in heaven. "He put down a string of cussing so good all the little children stopped to take notes! He was using combinations that had never been heard."

Mother flopped back into her seat. "Oh, Ma Dear, stop exaggerating. It sounds bad enough without that."

"Oh, it's bad all right, and you ain't heard the half of it." Ma Dear went back to fanning herself. "You sure you can't get me a cold glass of sweet ice tea?"

Mother looked at Shirley and grabbed the arms of her glider. "You are going to have to pull me off of her. I'm about to beat her within an inch of her life!"

Shirley couldn't hold back the laughter. She brayed and her

sides heaved. And to think she had stopped by Jack's store on her way into town. "Don't get her just yet, Mother." Shirley worked hard to push air for the words. "Give her a chance."

Ma Dear nodded demurely. "Thank you, baby." Ma Dear got her glider in motion again. She whistled a tune that sounded vaguely like "Nearer My God to Thee." She craned her neck and pretended to be watching cars coming up and down the street, then she looked at Shirley. "You sure you don't want to see that boy?"

"What boy, Ma Dear?"

"You know, baby. Tony Taylor. You know Ma Dear wouldn't lie about a man—he really did turn out all right...and sure as I'm sitting here, I know he would come by if he knew you was here." It was too much to hope that Ma Dear would be distracted from matchmaking, even by a juicy story of grocery-store mayhem and intrigue. Ma Dear continued fanning. "My goodness gracious, it sure is a hot day!" She smiled solicitously as Shirley. "Baby, ain't you thirsty, too?"

Mother Johnson hopped from her seat and put her hands around Ma Dear's throat.

Shirley doubled over on the steps and began to make a funny sound—three or four hisses, followed by a squeak. Tears ran down her face. She began to hiccup.

Mother Johnson, small as she was, seemed to tower over her buxom friend. "I'm going to throttle you, Ma Dear!"

Ma Dear fought to catch her breath in between laughs. She pointed at Shirley. "Listen, the baby's got the hiccups." Mother Johnson stopped to listen, her hands still on Ma Dear's throat. Ma Dear tapped Mother on the hands. "She needs some sugar, Mother, to stop those hiccups...got any sweet ice tea?"

All three women started crying.

Mother let go, sat back down in her rocker, and wiped her eyes with the hem of her apron. "Ma Dear, you are too old to be keeping up this much foolishness. People passing by are gone think we've lost our minds."

Ma Dear reached out and touched her friend's arm. "Now, when did I ever care what people thought?"

"You ain't telling nothing but the truth." Mother Johnson chuckled and sighed.

"Besides that, Mother, you know that laughter is good medicine. The Bible says it strengthens the bones, or something like that." Ma Dear patted her hair like a young coquette. "That's why we old girls still looking good."

Shirley tried to catch her breath. It was good to be home, in the laughing presence of old friends.

Mother Johnson raised her hands in surrender. "Okay, Ma Dear, I give in. Finish the story, and I'll get you your tea."

"Well, if you had come to your senses sooner, I could have waited. But now I'm feeling right parched and I don't believe I can go on without..." Ma Dear pretended to dry cough.

Mother Johnson pushed to her feet. "You are just like a worrisome child. Hold on a minute." She walked to the door and went in the house. Shirley held her breath for as long as she could. Then she tried bending over. Nothing worked. Just when she thought they might have stopped, a hiccup pounded so hard in her chest that it echoed in her head.

After a few moments, Mother reappeared with three large glasses full of sweet tea and ice. Moisture frosted and condensed on the sides of the glass. "Now, if I don't get the rest of this story soon, somebody's going to die."

SEVENTEEN

I checked on the babies while I was inside," Mother Johnson said. "I got some tea for them, too." She passed the glasses to her friends. "They got the television on watching cartoons—*He-Man and She-Ra,* or something like that, they said."

"Thank you, Mother." Shirley drank deeply. It had been a long time since she had tasted Mother Johnson's sweet ice tea and she didn't know that she was so thirsty. "Mm-mm, it's good."

"Thank you, baby. And I put some in an ice tray in the freezer. I figured they might make good treats for the children."

Shirley nodded while she took another drink. The tea was made in a way that only folks in the South make it.

Mother Johnson sat down in her glider. "Okay, Ma Dear. At last, please finish the story."

Ma Dear took a long, savoring sip. "Now *that* is good tea. Nobody makes it like you, Mother." She drank again. "All right then. Where was I?"

Jack had called Mildred from his office at the store.

"That's right, Mother." Ma Dear's dimples deepened. "Oh

yeah. So, like I was saying, Jack hit the roof. He told your friend she better get herself on down there. And when your holier-than-thou friend stepped up in the store, she got the surprise of her life."

Ma Dear wiggled in her seat as though she were settling in for a long story. Lottie Belle said when Mildred came to the store, she almost fainted, Ma Dear said. Especially after she found out what her long-lost relative was packing with her.

It seemed that the child was indeed her granddaughter, though she barely knew her, Ma Dear said. Barely knew her because Mildred was on the outs—estranged from her son, who it turns out was touched in the head. He'd been involved in some foolishness having to do with overthrowing the United States government and was now on the lurk, who knows where, Ma Dear said.

Mother stopped gliding. "Ma Dear, *how* do you know all this?"

"I told you, Mother. I got good sources. If the FBI would hire me, there wouldn't be any Most Wanted List."

Shirley kept drinking, even as she was laughing—or hic-cupping. It was unbelievable that all this had happened when she was just at the grocery store the other day.

Ma Dear prattled on. "But like I said, what turned your friend's hair white—oh, I'm sorry, her hair's already white. Well, what made her stockings bunch up was what her little grand-daughter had with her." Ma Dear paused, eyes on her audience. "An undelivered bundle of joy."

Shirley spit the tea in her mouth all over Mother Johnson's front steps. She leapt from her seat and ran into the house.

EIGHTEEN

∞

When Shirley came back outside, Ma Dear and Mother Johnson both were standing. "What happened, baby?"

Shirley knelt and wiped the steps with the warm, soapy rag she'd gotten from the kitchen. She was afraid to raise her head. She could hear concern in Mother's voice. "What happened, Shirley? Is something wrong?"

She cupped the wet rag in her hands, sat back on her heels, and sighed. "You didn't happen to hear what the girl's name was, did you?"

"I'm not sure about her last name, but her first name is Windy, with an *i*, is what I heard."

Shirley dropped the rag, put her wet hands over her face, and moaned.

"What's wrong, baby?"

Shirley lowered her hands and told Mother Johnson and Ma Dear how she had met Windy. "I gave her a ride. I still can't believe I gave her a ride." She told them all the stories Windy had told her about her family. "Are you sure her grandmother doesn't know her?"

Ma Dear said Mildred could have passed the child on the street and not known her…except for her hair and eyes. Miss Lootie Belle said Mildred told Jack the almost white hair and bright blue eyes were the spit of her daddy.

Shirley told them how the girl had said she was her grandmother's favorite—and about the baby bed and the decorations. "She said her grandmother was putting up pink flowered wallpaper."

Ma Dear clucked her tongue. "If you ask me, like grandmother, like granddaughter."

"Ma Dear, this is no time for that," Mother chided her friend.

Shirley could hear her voice rising. "And you're sure about what they said about Windy's father?"

Ma Dear nodded. "They say he's crazy as a bed bug and ten times as mean—a chip on his shoulder big enough to fill up the Grand Canyon."

Shirley shook her head. "I brought her into town. I'm the one that dropped her off at the store." Shirley looked up at the sky. "God, what are You doing to me?"

Mother Johnson whistled. "The Lord works in mysterious ways."

Ma Dear began to glide slowly. "Well, hello, Mary Lou! I believe things are about to get interesting around here."

After a full dinner of fried chicken wings, red beans and rice, fried cabbage, and cornbread—along with a touch of peach cobbler—Shirley bowed on her knees with Mika and Lex to say their prayers.

"Mommy, can we sing the song you taught us?"

"Why? Are you feeling scared about something, Lex?"

"No, ma'am. I just like the song." So they sang it together. It was the song Shirley sang to herself when she was a child.

Rock me, baby Jesus
Hold me, baby Jesus
Keep me, baby Jesus
So I won't be afraid.

Even if the kids didn't need to hear the song, she sure needed it. It was no joke about God and His mysterious ways. *God, I need You to help me out here.*

That night when she lay in the bed, she thought over and over about Windy—especially about her eyes and her hair. It was as though they were speaking something to Shirley that she was trying to forget.

When she fell asleep, she dreamed of her mother, and of the last time she saw Sheri...

Shirley thought she heard Sheri. That Sheri was crying and that she held her hand. Shirley fell back into blackness, and then she thought that she saw her mother walking down the street—her mouth like an o and her robe half on, half off. Shirley thought she saw her mother walking past the great rock— the rock that towered over her, the rock like the rock at Monk's Mound, the rock like the rock with the Piasa Bird—and her mother was wearing only one house shoe. She thought she saw her mother's arms in the air, and that she saw her mother tearing at her hair. Shirley thought she saw her mother walking right past her.

She shook her head, huddled closer to the rock and went back to sleep. Then her dream turned to visions of Danny. "Don't be a hero," she whispered to him.

When Shirley awakened in the morning, her pillow was wet, and she guessed that the dampness was from her nocturnal tears.

It had been a year, and she had heard it all since Danny died. Other people knew it all.

"Time heals all wounds."

"You're a young woman; you'll marry again."

"He had to die so that you could be all that the Lord needs you to be."

What people didn't know was that she was through with love. It was too hard and it was too much work and there was no guarantee. There was life insurance, but no life *assurance*. There was no assurance that after you worked together, argued together, forgave together, despaired together, loved together, and hoped together, that both of you would still be standing—still alive together in the end.

So Shirley wasn't hearing any messages about love—not from friends, not from family, and not even from God. She didn't want to hear any promises about love, not through her ears and not from her heart.

There was no point in telling anyone, though, because they didn't want to hear she was done with it. It was her ear that mattered, though, and her ear and her heart were blocked to love.

If she ever got over this heartbreak, it would be the last.

She turned on her side and daydreamed about California until she rose.

NINETEEN

he next few days passed with more peach cobbler, more hot weather, more sweet ice tea,
more Mister Bubble, and more news of Jack the
grocer's worked-up nerves.

The clerk's mama told her aunt that Jack was swollen
worse than a twenty-one-day tick. He was having fits, they
said, about too many people in his house, too much strain on
his wallet, and too little time with any peace of mind. Ma Dear
said Jack was starting to look a little used, like some of the old,
worn-out produce he kept bundling together on a special little
table in the store. Too many unwanted people in your house
could do that.

"Having Mildred and that girl, Windy, in his house is
putting a strain on him. And you know he never married,
never had no kids, so maybe the thought of a baby is just
upsetting his cart."

"Oh, by the way—" Ma Dear smiled at Shirley like she'd
just had the last piece of peach pie—"I saw that boy in town.
That Tony—well, actually, he's a man now—but I told him
you're home." Ma Dear nodded. "I do believe he's going to

come by here. I just thought you ought to know." Ma Dear was never going to give up.

Shirley shook her head and said nothing. It was just better not to say what was on her mind. Better to not begin a conversation in which she asserted that she and Tony had just been friends. Better to not tell Ma Dear that a lifetime, a marriage, and two children had passed between her and Tony Taylor. Better not to answer, because Ma Dear would have a response for whatever she said. Better to leave it alone.

That night while she lay in bed, Shirley heard tapping at the side door. She heard Mother Johnson move in her creaking bed, heard her feet hit the floor, heard the side door open, and then heard voices in the kitchen.

Things changed, but they were still the same. People were still coming to sit and talk at Mother Johnson's table. Shirley slowed her breathing so she could hear.

"I don't even know how the child got to Tyler and why would she come to me, of all people? I barely know her." Shirley didn't recognize the voice. "Her people, especially her father, have never been any good. Not that she could have been much influenced by him—he was hardly ever around. But I can't see why Windy would come to me."

It must have been Mildred.

Mother Johnson's heavy voice was even and calm. "Maybe she was trying to save herself. Maybe the child was trying to pull herself out of the pit, and you were the only person she'd ever seen who got away."

"But I'm not like any of them. I can't help her. I don't know anything about her."

"Maybe not, Mildred. But maybe you do. People don't get to be who they are just out of nowhere. That child didn't get to this point by herself. Maybe you *can* help her."

"But I'm telling you, Mother Johnson, I don't *know* anything about her. She's a liar and a thief—pretending she's something she's not. Now she's pregnant without a husband. I don't know *anything* about that."

Mildred's voice was rising. "Her people are thieves and they're ignorant. Hardly any of the children know who their fathers are. It's just a big, writhing mass of sadness and anger. That's why I had to get away. After so many years, I had given them all I had and I had to get away." It sounded as though she might be crying. "And Windy never knew her father. He was the worst of the lot—a liar, a thief, mean as they come—he got in trouble for starting fires and had to leave town."

Mother was swinging into action. Shirley heard her getting the kettle ready for tea. "All I know, Mildred, is that families have patterns, and those patterns go on for generations and generations." Mother Johnson spoke as she worked. "Nobody sees the pattern in themselves because they don't want to see it. But seeing it is the only way to break the pattern and get it changed."

Mildred's voice sounded perplexed. "Mother Johnson, you're confusing me. I came over here to get away and to try to get some peace of mind, at least for a moment."

Shirley could hear Mother stirring in the cabinets. "It's okay, Mildred, honey. We'll have a little tea, a little talk between friends, and a little prayer for peace. Is that all right?"

Shirley strained to hear Mother Johnson praying. Her voice was barely loud enough to be heard. "Lord, we're asking for peace. We're asking for the peace that passes all understanding.

And, Lord, we're asking You to show us the way to a lasting peace." Mother's voice lowered, and Shirley could no longer distinguish the words. There was silence for a while, then Shirley could hear that Mother Johnson was back in motion.

"Mildred, we've got so much to do during our journey down here on this earth. There's so much to figure out. It's just a little time to God, but we need every second to try to figure out where we been, where we are, and where we going." There were sounds as though Mother was sitting now in her chair.

Shirley could just imagine Mother's hands comforting her friend.

"Nobody wants to hear that there's a wrinkle in the family quilt. The last thing we want to hear is that there's been a slipped stitch or a misplaced one. But until someone figures it out and owns up to it, the family quilt is always going to be out of line."

Shirley could hear cups being set on the table.

"Well, it's a lovely metaphor, Mother." Mildred's voice was mildly sarcastic—or mildly defensive. "I just don't know what any of this has to do with me."

"All right, let me explain. You know Jacob in the Bible."

"Of course, Jacob the liar."

"Yes, the liar, but then he turned out to be a great man, one of the fathers of the Jewish faith, of our faith."

There was the sound of a chair pushing back from the table. "Mother Johnson, it's late. Maybe I should just go home."

"Bear with me a minute, Mildred. You came all this way. You might as well hear me out."

Cups, saucers, and chairs were being moved about in the kitchen. Mother cleared her throat. "Wait, let me run and get my Bible." There was more movement, and finally, the chairs sounded as though they were being dragged closer to the table.

Shirley wasn't sure she wanted to hear any of this. She had been having too many conversations already that she didn't want to have. She had already heard too many things she didn't want to hear.

California, by contrast, was sounding better every day.

It seemed strange, after so many years, to be looking out the same window framed by what looked to be the same curtains. She was back in the same bed, smelling essentially the same smells in the house. It felt as though she was starting over—like moving back to *Go* in Monopoly without collecting two hundred dollars.

It felt good to be home, but she was afraid to trust it. She didn't want to be like those people who could never leave their hometown or live their own lives. Nor did she want to be like those souls who kept coming back, who kept starting over when things got hard so that they never finished, but always kept returning to and retreating from the same hard place.

Perhaps her time in Tyler was over. She had gotten to see the town, Ma Dear, and to spend time with Mother. The children had met Mother, hugged her, and kissed her. So now they also had memories of cobbler, fruit trees, and the prayer house.

Maybe it was time to go. Or at least it was time to go to sleep.

Mother Johnson's voice interrupted Shirley's escape. "So, like I was saying, here it is about Jacob. Right here in Genesis."

"I know the story, Mother Johnson. I go to church, Bible study, and Sunday school, too. You know that."

"Oh, honey, I know you do. I'm not trying to offend you, Mildred. I know you know the Word, but just humor an old woman."

"Mother Johnson, you're not any older—"

"Mildred, let's just go through it and see if you get anything out of it. Just humor me." Mother cleared her throat. "So, here's Jacob—and you're right, we call him liar and trickster. That's even what his mama named him—*Deceiver*. We always talk like the story began with him, but it didn't. Abraham, Jacob's grandfather, deceived the king of a strange land when he traveled there with his beautiful wife. He thought if the men there knew his true relationship with his wife, Sara, they would kill him and take her. He thought he had a good excuse to do it, but Abraham lied.

"When Abraham had a son, the same pattern showed up in *his* life. When Isaac traveled into the same strange land with his beautiful wife, he told the same lie about his relationship with his wife...so that he could protect himself."

"I already know that, Mother Johnson."

"But do you see the pattern? By the time it got to Jacob, he didn't even recognize the lying and the cheating. It was just the way they did business in his family, but he was the one that they called *Deceiver.*"

"Mother Johnson, I have always heard that it was his mother that taught him to trick and lie."

"I think that's right, too. She was a trickster like his father. And the truth is, it seems that whatever is broken in us, we seem to seek in out in other people. It may be a different flavor, but it's still ice cream."

The women were sipping tea. Cups were clicking on the table. "I see what you're saying, Mother Johnson, but I still don't see how it relates to me. I'm not Jacob."

"It may be, Mildred, that we are all like Jacob. We don't see our own broken places that are messing up our lives, or the missed stitches that are ruining our family quilts. It's easier to see the pattern in the family members before us, or those that come behind us. But it might be that we only recognize what's wrong when we get alone, when we wrestle with God's Spirit and with ourselves like Jacob did."

Mother Johnson cleared her throat. "The good news is, if we will get honest with ourselves, if we will struggle to see what is wrong, we can change it. We can repair our quilts. We can make changes in our families that will bless for generations to come."

"This was a good lesson, but I still don't get it."

"Spend some time wrestling and praying. Maybe your granddaughter came because she sees what you don't, that you *do* know the way to fix the quilt and to rescue her. She may not live the way you want her to live, and she may not believe what you want her to believe, but that doesn't make her your enemy."

Mildred's voice sounded agitated. Shirley could imagine her clutching her tight, starched collar. "But, Mother, you haven't seen her…her hair, her clothes. She lies and like I said, they're all thieves!"

"That don't make her somebody for you to hate. It makes her somebody you should try to love. That's why Jesus has us here, to love like He loved. To love until it hurts." Mother cleared her throat. "Don't make her your enemy. That baby needs your love. 'Cause she's not what you want her to be, don't hate her. You won't try to help somebody that you hate. I don't know about you, but I wasn't always so good either, Mildred."

Shirley could imagine Mildred shaking her head and pulling the tail end of her skirt close around her. "That's easy for you to say, Mother. I did things too, but not like her. She's a liar. You don't have to live with her. She's on her way to jail as far as I can see."

Mother's voice was calm. "That child is already in prison, Mildred. That's why the Lord sent her to you. She in prison in her mind and in her spirit—all she know is what she seen all her life. She hungry—all she knows is what she's heard and what she's been fed all her life. You talk about how she look, but she's wandering around lost, wearing all she know to wear right now. You got the key to unlock her prison; you just have to share what unlocked your prison. You can feed her the same word and love that has fed you and made you full. You can offer the same Holy Spirit clothes that cover you now. You got the key to unlock her prison, but first you got to unlock your heart and give that child some of the love you got locked up in there."

Shirley could sense a warm, sweet smile in Mother Johnson's voice. "God's love come alive when you give it away."

Shirley closed her eyes against the moonlight, and, closing out all that she heard, she fell asleep. As she slept, she dreamed of her mother, of Tony, and finally of her father.

"Wake up, Shirley. Wake up, baby." Then a shake—*"Wake up, Shirley."* Then a kiss—*"Come on, precious."* It was Daddy. *"Look at you all balled up like a roly-poly."*

Shirley flopped over on her side, then slowly opened her eyes. "Daddy?"

"It's all right, baby. Don't worry. Everything is going to be all right."

"You promise?"

His kiss on her forehead was warm and firm. "I promise."

Daddy smelled of Old Spice. "Come on now, sugar. Get up. Don't you want to fix your bike, so you can get back on and ride?"

"I don't think I want to ride, Daddy."

"Sure you do, Shirley." He pulled the covers back further. "Let me see that ankle." She held it out and he took it in his hand. "Look at that! It looks good as new. And your mama and your uncles told me how brave you were after the fall."

Shirley looked at her ankle and sighed.

"You know why you feel that way, baby?"

She laid her head back on one of the pillows. One of her braids moved as she shook her head from side to side.

Daddy smiled. "It's because the last memory you have of your bike is a bad one—the accident. You just have to make a new memory. We'll do it together."

"Can't ride worth nothing." Shirley could still hear her cousin's voice. "Girl, you bleeding! Look at your ankle." She sighed again.

"Come on, Shirley." Daddy pulled her onto his lap. "Listen to Daddy." He hugged her. "I want you to always remember this. When you fall down, you have to get back up. That's just how life is. If you just lay down, the bad memory wins. If you lay down, you'll just be scared and unhappy all the time. We fall down, but we have to get back up and try again. Then try again, if we have to. Okay?"

Inside she felt more like a no, but she said, "Yes, sir."

He held her in his arms. "Everything is going to be all right. I promise." He loosed her and stepped back.

TWENTY

S hirley loved the smell of bacon and scrambled eggs. The bitter and sweet aroma of brewing coffee added the perfect complementary bite. Her stomach growled.

"Why don't we let the children sleep a little late while you and I just spend some time together?" Mother Johnson set turquoise blue plates on the table. Beside them, she set brown ceramic mugs. "Grab the butter and jelly, will you, baby?" Mother heaped the plates with soft scrambled eggs and crisp strips of bacon. After grace, they tore into buttered toast hot from the oven.

Somehow, the food tasted better at Mother Johnson's table. Shirley closed her eyes against the pleasure of a bite.

"You get a good night's sleep, baby?"

Shirley opened her eyes and shrugged.

"What's the matter?"

"I'm not sure, Mother. I've been thinking—as much as I hate the thought—it might be time for us to go. It might be that I'm feeling restless because we've already been here long enough." Shirley faked a smile. "We don't want to wear out our welcome."

Mother took a sip of coffee. "You know that's impossible to do here. You're not welcome—you're home."

"We were on our way to California. We're never going to get there at this rate."

"Have you done everything you came here to do?"

Shirley just wanted to eat her breakfast. She didn't want to answer questions. Toast was about all that she could handle. "I don't know what I came here to do. Who knows, maybe it was to risk my children's lives by bringing that crazy girl here."

"Are you feeling guilty about that?"

"Yes!" It surprised Shirley how quickly she answered. "I don't think that I'll ever be able to face Miss Mildred, or Jack either, for that matter."

"Well, don't be guilty, honey. You did more good than you know. There's some things that needed to be straightened out and God just used you as the vehicle."

"You mean the chauffeur."

Mother laughed. "That, too."

"Well, I'm glad He's straightening out everyone else's life, because mine sure feels like a mess. Honestly, Mother, I don't know whether I'm going or coming."

"That's just how you're *feeling,* baby. If you could step back and look, you would see that you are doing a fine job. Your chirren are healthy and happy. You're being too hard on yourself. Have you been praying? Have you talked to the Lord about it?"

"Me and the Lord haven't been talking much lately. I'm having crazy dreams—dreaming about Danny, my mother, and my father. It seems like I've been dreaming about half the free world. Dreaming? Yes. But, no, I don't feel like me and God are communicating. I've been praying, but it doesn't seem like He's listening. At least He's not talking back to me."

Mother Johnson nodded. "The Lord's always talking. Maybe you got so much stuff blocking that you can't hear. Seems to me, you got some stuff in your life you might need to get out of the way. Then you might be able to hear. But it could be that God is saying something to you that you don't want to hear.

"Don't run, baby. You got plenty of time to go. Stand still and let's see what the Lord is going to do." Mother leaned forward in her seat. "You've been through a lot. You're still grieving. Grief is a place we all have to go, at one time or another. You just can't stay there. Grief is no place to build a home."

It was always easy for other people to tell you to stand, to work through the hard places. They weren't the ones hurting. She had hurt enough and she was ready to let it go. "But I was…we were on our way to California to start over. I was thinking I could go to nursing school—just so we could start over and put some stuff behind us."

"It could be, baby, that what's going on in your life now is less about starting over than it is about finishing the race that you've started to run." Mother poked at her eggs. "It's okay to take time to puzzle over it. Trust the Lord. He'll work it out."

The breeze was cool that evening and it invited them outside. Shirley sat on the steps and watched Lex throwing his Nerf football in the air. Mika alternately tied and untied her home-made Cabbage Patch doll's hair and, using colored pencils, sketched fashions on a tablet she had near her.

Shirley talked to and smiled at them, and prayed on the inside. *Lord, I feel so anxious and out of place. Here is this cool, beautiful evening, my kids are happy and healthy, but my mind is not on where I am, but on where I'm not.*

None of the stuff I planned, none of the stuff I thought would be, is. And You're watching all this and letting it happen for some reason. I don't get it and I'm tired of not getting it. I'm trying to figure out where I ought to be. So, if You're listening, God…if You still listen to me, I could use some help. God, I could just use a laugh.

"Hey, watcha doing, little girl?"

It was a man's deep voice and it startled Shirley from her thoughts. The man that spoke was standing near the gate—close enough to Lex to grab him.

TWENTY-ONE

The man at the gate had a bag in his hand—and a broad smile on his face.

"You haven't changed at all." He smiled and then he turned his head and lowered his eyes. Shirley's heart clutched. It was Tony Taylor.

He was just above medium height and medium build, which seemed pretty hefty compared to the skinny boy he had once been. She never would have recognized him, except for his shy presence. Shirley could not help but smile. "Hi, Tony." It was funny, but what she saw was a shadow of who he was superimposed over the person standing before her.

He smiled in return and then looked down at Lex. "Hey, little man. How about throwing me that ball?" Lex obliged and Tony caught it with his left hand. "Good throw, man. You look like quarterback material to me." He tossed the ball back to Lex who laughed and fumbled the catch. Tony smiled at Shirley again. "Definitely quarterback."

He opened the gate and stepped inside. "I can't believe it."

Shirley wasn't sure how to behave. It had been a long time. Should she stand, or would standing send him the wrong message? What would Mika and Lex think? How could she make it look like nothing? What would she have done if she was a long-lost girlfriend? It was too much to think and too little time to think it, so she sat still. She tried to look calm, but not too calm. Happy to see him, but not too happy. Shirley pulled at her hair and then moved over on the step so that Tony could sit down. "I never would have recognized you."

Tony looked at her in a way that was inviting, but that held within it a hint of vulnerability. "Age is not so kind to everybody. Some of us have to take our lumps."

She wasn't sure what the look meant or how to feel about it. She tucked her skirt around her legs. "You know that's not what I meant, Tony." This was not a conversation with the boy she knew.

He smiled at Mika. "So does this princess belong to you?" It was strange that his voice was deeper.

Mika smiled and nodded. Her two front teeth, larger than the rest, announced her age.

"Yep. These are my babies. This is Mika; she's eight." Shirley nodded at Mika and then at Lex. "And your quarterback is Lexington—Lex for short—and he's three."

It was so peculiar that Tony was now a man. Shirley kept herself from saying, "You're all grown up." There was a glimpse of her old friend in his profile, but not much more.

He smiled down at Mika. "You're beautiful, just like your mother." The little girl beamed at him. "And you, little man, I don't see anything short about you." Lex's chest expanded at Tony's words.

Shirley nodded at Tony. "Mika and Lex, this is Mr. Taylor. We went to school together when we were…what…like Mika's age?"

He looked at both the children. "I would like it better if you called me Tony."

"*Mister* Tony would be fine."

Tony smiled at Shirley. "Wow, I've moved into that category now. Time is moving." He rubbed his hand across his hair. "Ma Dear told me you were home…I mean she told me you were in town."

Shirley smoothed her hair again. "I'm sorry she pestered you. You know how Ma Dear is. She's stuck in a time warp— she thinks we're still getting ready for the high school prom."

Tony reached and briefly touched her hair. "No more Afro, huh?"

It felt strange for a man to touch her in any way—even innocently. Inwardly, she shied from his touch. Outwardly, she willed herself not to move. "Not for a long time."

Tony lifted the bag that was in his right hand into the air and crooked a finger from the other hand at Lex. "Come here so I can show you guys what I got." Lex scrambled up onto the porch. Tony opened the bag wide so that Mika and Lex could look inside.

"Oo-oo!" they said in unison.

"Reach in and get one."

They each pulled palm-sized cookies from the bag. "Wow!" Lex's eyes were almost as big as the cookie.

Shirley clapped her hands together. "Moon cookies from the blind man's store." She stomped her feet. "It's been *years* since I thought of them." She looked at Mika and Lex. "Aren't they good?"

The children nodded, but couldn't answer because their mouths were stuffed. Crumbs dotted their cheeks and chin. Tony pushed the bag toward Shirley. She grabbed a cookie and bit. She closed her eyes and the taste took her back to her first year at Mamie G. Griffin Elementary School and the bench and the recesses she spent with Tony when Tony was Tony.

"I planned to come as soon as Ma Dear told me you were here, but I didn't want to come without the moon cookies. The blind man's store is long gone. I had to hunt all over to find a distributor. I had to drive to the next county to pick them up." Tony grinned. "It was worth it just to see your face."

"Well, look at this. A porch full!" Mother Johnson stood in the doorway. Darkness had slid in unannounced, so her body was silhouetted by the light from inside the house. She nodded at Tony. "It's been a month of Sundays since I've seen you, baby."

"Good evening, Mother Johnson." Tony stood and nodded.

She smiled at him. "But it's sure good to see you, baby."

"Yes, ma'am."

"How are things going? How's the family?"

"Fine. Just fine."

"When was the last time you were in Frankston?"

"It's been a while, Mother Johnson. I really haven't been back there since my granddaddy passed. But, all in all, everything's fine."

Mother Johnson smiled at Mika and Lex. "And what is that in your mouths?"

Mika and Lex held up their moon cookies.

"My goodness, don't you want some milk with those things? Those are some cookies needing milk if ever I saw one."

Tony held the bag toward the door. "Have one?"

"Oh, no thank you, honey." Mother Johnson opened the screen door and then nodded at Tony. "You sit on down, now, and the two of you take your time getting reacquainted. Me and my two friends here are going to go in and get some milk. Then we're going to hit the hay." She pointed at Mika and Lex. "Come on, you two. Hurry before we let the mosquitoes in." Mika and Lex, cookies in hand, stood up. "Say good night to your mother."

"'Night, Mommy." They turned and kissed her, sweet crumby kisses that only mothers love.

"'Night, you guys. I'll be in soon." Shirley looked in Tony's direction, then back at Mika and Lex. "What about the moon cookies?" The children mumbled something around the pastry in their mouths that sounded like *thank you*. Shirley hugged them and kissed them again as they moved toward the door.

Mother Johnson held the door. "Come on now. Those mosquitoes are trying to beat you inside." The door closed behind them, and Shirley could hear Mother's voice trailing behind her. "No, we don't want any bugs in here—they say everything grows big in Texas and the mosquitoes ain't no exception."

Tony laughed and then, in the darkness, Shirley could feel him looking at her. "It sure is good to see you, Shirley. How long has it been?"

Her laughter sounded strange to her ears. "I don't think there's any reason to strain ourselves counting."

His voice lowered. "I'm sorry to hear about your husband."

"Yeah." She focused on the sounds of the night—the crickets, the frogs, dogs barking down the street.

"I hope I didn't do wrong to bring him up."

Shirley was glad that it was dark. "No, I just don't talk about it much."

"I can understand." He cleared his throat. "I've never been through it, but you know..."

"Yeah." She turned to face him. "So what about you? Our

local FBI agent—or MBI agent—tells me you're not married.
Any kids?"

"MBI?"

"Ma Dear's Bureau of Investigation."

Tony chuckled, and his voice blended into the night.
"You're right about that." He laughed some more. "MBI" He
shook his head. "Well, actually Ma Dear's right, I'm not married. And no kids. I came close once. To being married, I
mean. But…things didn't work out."

"I'm sorry."

"I'm not. If I can avoid a mistake, I figure I'm ahead."

She listened and tried to analyze his voice for sounds of
anger or bitterness. Shirley wasn't sure how to answer him, so
she let the background noises fill in the dead air.

Tony shook the bag. "Another moon cookie?"

"No, one is plenty." Shirley patted her stomach. "How did
we ever eat so many of those things when we were little?"

"Not we, baby—*you* were the one that had the jones, the
craving. You had to have those moon cookies."

"I don't remember you turning them down, Mr. Taylor."

Tony's voice sounded as though he were smirking. "How
could you remember when you were so busy feeding your own
face?"

Shirley slapped him on the arm and soon they were laughing about the cookies, the school playground, and their favorite
bench.

"It sure is good to see you, Shirley." His voice sounded
slightly self-conscious. "How many times have I said that
already? It is good, though. After you left, and I heard about
you getting married, I never thought I'd get to see you again."
He touched her cheek in the darkness. "You're still the same. I

knew you'd turn out to be a beautiful woman. I would have known you a mile away."

She turned her head and said nothing. She was being silly. He was just trying to be friendly. Still, she couldn't help feeling uncomfortable, feeling that she was doing something wrong.

Tony sounded embarrassed when he spoke again. "Here, keep these." He jiggled the bag of moon cookies. "You might need a fix tomorrow, and it looks like your kids have inherited the same addiction." He stood to leave and held out his hand. "Walk me to the gate." When she stood to her feet, he let go of her hand. "I don't mean to push, okay? I remember you taught me that when we were kids. I'm just happy to see you. But just friends. No pressure, okay?" The moon glow frosted his hair. "I would just like to be able to visit—not that I'm such hot company. I kind of stay to myself, so my conversational skills may be kind of rusty. But no pressure."

"Okay," Shirley said when the gate closed behind him. She held on to the cookie bag and waved with the other hand. Shirley stood at the gate until he disappeared from under the silver street lamp into the darkness of the night.

The taste and smell of moon cookies awakened her several times that night. When she slept, though, she dreamed of Tony.

He sat on the wooden bench right next to Shirley. Right next to her, almost on top of her. She scooted over, careful not to let the splinters from the old wooden bench stick the back of her legs. It was two bad girls couldn't wear pants to school. The other children were playing and there was lots of school-yard noise—kickball, hopscotch, jacks, war with little green plastic army men. Maybe if she stayed away from the fun, maybe the fun would call him and he would leave her alone. Shirley was stuck on the bench, and Tony was stuck next to her.

Maybe if you talk to him with a prayer in your heart and a little honey on your tongue... she could hear Mother Johnson's voice counseling her.

Shirley turned to look at Tony and frowned—he was just staring at her like she was from another planet. It was impossible. "What are you doing?"

Tony shrugged his shoulders.

"Why don't you leave me alone?" Tony shrugged again. Shirley's chest filled with air and a sound more like a whistle, less like a sigh, escaped her mouth. "Are you trying to be in love with me? Because if you are, I am way too young to be in love." She gave him her most stern, most grown-up look. "You are barking way up the wrong tree. That's all I've got to say." Tony shrugged. "Don't you talk?" He shrugged. "Are you going to keep sitting here?" He nodded.

Shirley shook her head and surrendered. "If you're going to sit here, you might as well talk." Tony said nothing. "I said, if you're going to sit here, you might as well talk." Tony said nothing. Shirley stood up. "All right, I'm going then. I'm going to—"

"Okay."

Shirley stared at the boy and froze. "Okay," he repeated, and Shirley sat down. Now what? She looked around her, then thought about her moon cookies. She bought them at least once a week from the blind man's store on the way to school.

She pulled out her bag. "You want a cookie?"

Tony shrugged. Shirley jumped off the bench, ready to stomp away.

"Okay. Yes."

There was something about his voice that surprised her, something that was far different than what she would have imagined.

Shirley woke from the dream, then rolled on her side to stare out the window, watching the moonlight, until she drifted back to sleep. There was still something about Tony's voice that was unexpected. Perhaps, as an unconscious act of loyalty, the last dream Shirley remembered was Danny. He was playing the guitar.

"Oh yeah, remind me to tell you something when I get back."

"Tell me now."

"No, wait until I get back. It's going to blow your mind. It's something you never would have expected in a million years…"

TWENTY-TWO

Shirley lifted the hair that kept falling down the back of her neck. It was so hot, and she was so sweaty, the hair plastered itself to her like some sort of wet webbing. It was miserable.

"So, how was it? I'm predicting a wedding." Ma Dear swayed back and forth on the porch and hummed the bridal march. "I know you'll be wearing white, but me and Mother will have to work on our fashions. Maybe we'll even have to go to Dallas to find something just right."

Shirley took a deep breath and wondered why she hadn't seen this coming. She laid the book she was trying to read on the step beside her. Thank goodness the kids were in the house. What was Ma Dear thinking? "Ma Dear, it's not like that." She tried not to sound impatient. It was early and it was too hot to be so early in the morning—not that time of day mattered. It was actually too hot to be any time of day. And the last thing she felt like discussing was marriage—either old or new. "I have more going on in my life right now than men, than trying to get married."

"Well, what else is there, honey?" Ma Dear stood up and did a little spin.

"Ma Dear, that may be how women used to think." Shirley's temples were pounding, and she felt as though there were a band tightening around her head. "But we have more choices now. Who I am is not determined by the man I have on my arm. I don't need—I'm okay like I am!"

Ma Dear stopped short. "Oh, baby. You know Ma Dear is just teasing. I just want to see you happy, and you know I know if anyone knows—and I got a string of ex-husbands to prove it—marriage sure won't make you any happier than you are. You know that. What's the matter, baby?"

Mother Johnson stepped out onto the porch. "The kids are out back making mud pies." She was fanning and smiling. "Mika says she's in charge of production and Lex is the head of sales." She cracked up. "Those two are a mess."

She looked from Shirley to Ma Dear and back again. "What is going on out here between you two? Whatever it is, it's thick enough that I can cut it with a knife."

"It's just hot, Mother. Ma Dear and I are fine." Shirley wiped her forehead with the back of her arm. The paper towel she had been using had died several wipes ago. "It's just hot."

"Is that so?" Mother sat in her glider. "How about you, Ma Dear?"

Ma Dear mumbled something unintelligible. Then she put on a smile. "Everything's fine. Just like Shirley said, it's just hot."

"What's that song that boy sings—'If You Don't Know Me by Now,' I believe it is. Well, if you don't know me by now. Now either you birds can start singing, or I'll just keep picking at the feathers until I find out what's underneath."

Ma Dear sang first. "I was just teasing Shirley about Tony Taylor, that's all. I shouldn't have been doing it." Ma Dear looked innocent and contrite. The older woman played dumb, but she knew the fastest way to avoid one of Mother's grillings was to just come clean—the first one to shine was the winner.

Shirley rolled her eyes and muttered under her breath.

"What was that?" Mother fixed her with a look. "What did you say?"

"Nothing, Mother." She was grown. There was no way, unlike Ma Dear, that she was going to cave in to Mother Johnson—no matter how much she loved her. "Everything's just fine." Shirley winced. It was one sentence too much. That's how giveaways were. It was one step too much, one word too much, one look too much that told the sly investigator—in this case, Mother Johnson—that someone was trying not to give up the goods. Shirley could have kicked herself. She knew Mother Johnson scoured each television episode of *Ironsides* looking for new interrogation techniques, looking for new tip-offs that would tell her that someone had not come clean. She looked at Mother Johnson and knew that it was already too late.

"All right, Shirley. What's going on out here?"

"Just like Ma Dear said, she asked me how things went when Tony visited." She smiled at Ma Dear. If she was going down, Ma Dear was going with her. "And she just asked me if we should start planning the wedding."

Ma Dear flopped down in her glider and looked at Mother, eyes wide, lip protruding. "Mother, I said no such thing. The word *planning* never crossed my lips. This girl and Tony haven't been talking long enough to be planning a wedding. I believe they're just friends."

Shirley turned on the steps so that she could get a really

good look at Mother, and especially at Ma Dear. "Well, she didn't say *planning*, exactly. But she asked about what color dresses the two of you should wear. She said maybe the two of you would have to go to Dallas to find something suitable."

Ma Dear narrowed her eyes at Shirley. "Mother, you've known me for years." She batted her eyes at Mother. "You are not going to take the word of a child over an adult, are you?"

Mother Johnson looked at the two of them. "You know what? I think you two were right in the first place. It's hot—it's too hot." She fanned herself. "First the two of you are looking mad and ready to fight. Now you're acting more like children than children. I'm finished." She blew air up toward her forehead. "It's too hot to get myself involved in foolishness that's just going to work me up and make me more hot."

Mother fanned her head. Ma Dear fanned her chest. Shirley kept fighting with the hair at the back of her neck.

Two girls walked by with their hair braided in cornrows. "That sure does look cool," Ma Dear said. "I wonder, am I too old for something like that?"

Mother Johnson cackled. "Ma Dear, you live your life doing things folks think you are too old for—it's never stopped you in the past."

"Mother, are you saying something not so nice about me? Because if you are, I can go sit on my own porch and sweat...*alone*. If I'm bothering the two of you—and I am feeling a little unwelcome about now—just let me know."

"You know what, Ma Dear? There ain't nobody I would rather spend a hot day with. I don't know why, exactly. But that's how I feel. Besides, if you go home, you can sit, but you won't have any sweet ice tea."

Ma Dear smiled at her old friend. "Thank you, Mother." She looked at Shirley fighting with her hair. "Maybe you should try it."

Shirley wiped her forehead, again. "Ma Dear, I told you that marriage is the last thing on my mind! I'm not lonely and I can't count on a man to take care of me. We've managed to make it fine for a year. I have to take care of the kids and myself. That's why we're headed to California. I've been married. I'm just not ready—not for Tony, not for anyone!"

Mother Johnson and Ma Dear glided slowly in tandem, almost as though they were on the swing that still hung on the back porch. "Mmm-hmm," Mother said.

Ma Dear blinked innocently. *"I* was talking about getting your hair braided, baby. What are *you* talking about?"

Shirley picked up her book and pretended to read.

Mother Johnson scooted forward and touched her shoulder. "Maybe it would be fun getting your hair braided up. Sometimes something small like that can change your whole attitude."

"My attitude is fine, Mother!"

Mother Johnson resumed her gliding pace. "I see."

Shirley slapped at the hair on the back of her neck and tossed her book aside. "Okay. I give in. You'll have to tell me where to go."

Mother Johnson nodded. "We'll watch the kids."

"Just two more rows to go," the braider said. "You doing all right?"

"Mm-hmm." Shirley was glad she had taken the girl's

advice and taken some Tylenol before she began braiding. It had been hours—what with the girl taking telephone calls, stopping to eat, and stopping to change her baby. Olivia was friendly, though, and the price was right. And, if Shirley could make a determination based on how tightly her scalp was pulled—the braids should last for a few weeks.

"You trying to make your hair grow longer?" Braiding would make her hair grow, Olivia told Shirley. Some people said braiding would break the hair, but not if you had someone that knew what they were doing, the girl said. "I got growing hands. Everybody whose hair I do, they hair grow."

The girl took a big gulp from a pink transparent plastic tumbler filled with red Kool-Aid. "You're gonna feel a whole lot cooler with your hair braided, that's for sure." The baby had the same red Kool-Aid in his bottle. Olivia nodded her head in time with the music coming from the radio that sat on her table, then spoke above the volume of the television playing in the background. "I only wear my hair in cornrows in the summer. It's too hot for all that hanging down hair."

The girl used the green wide-toothed comb in her hand to make a part. She motioned toward the jar of yellow hair oil that Shirley held in her hand. "Could you hold that up a little higher?" The girl used her finger to dip a small amount from the jar. The smell was both oily and fragrant. The girl deftly rubbed the oil down the length of the part she had made and then began braiding, again. "One more row, after this one. I'll pin it up and you'll be ready to go."

Just as she was finishing the row and about to braid the last one, the baby hollered. Olivia tapped Shirley on the shoulder. "It won't be long now. But if I don't feed him, we'll never get through."

Shirley stood in line at the take-out window of the Dairy Queen. There was no point in trying to take ice cream to the kids. By the time she got it home, there would be nothing iced about it. She talked herself out of feeling guilty. She wasn't leaving them; she was just having some ice cream, just a brief moment to herself. The hairdo and the ice cream weren't much out of the family seed money—it was a small investment in her sanity. Like the stewardesses said, put your own oxygen mask on first. Shirley touched her hair, it really was worth it; it was much cooler.

"No cone, just a cup, please," Shirley told the woman behind the counter when she placed her order.

She settled on a shade-covered bench and pulled the book she had been reading from her purse. Shirley was beginning to form a theory about novelists, or maybe just about the people who read their writing.

She dipped her white plastic spoon into the ice cream, then sucked the cold, smooth sweetness from the spoon.

Some novels, like the one she was reading, were heavy on description and light on dialogue. Maybe those writers, Shirley speculated, were more fascinated by observation—they enjoyed solitary analysis of the world. Then there were the dialogue-heavy writers—like the one she had just finished. Maybe for those writers what was important in their lives was the next conversation, the next human interaction. Shirley took two more bites. It could be that the former writers were introverts given to reflection, while the latter were extroverts who only came alive when they were conversing with others. It might be a good subject for a research paper, Shirley mused.

She could feel her shoulders relaxing. The muscles in her neck—even in her face—felt looser. Mother Johnson and Ma Dear were right; she'd needed to get away. Shirley ate more ice cream and then found her place in the book.

"Your hair looks really pretty."

Shirley looked up, smiled, and squinted her eyes against the sun. It was nice to get compliments. All she could see, with her hand up to her eyes, was the outline of a girl against the sun.

"I wondered if I was going to see you again," Windy said.

TWENTY-THREE

Windy shifted her weight to one leg. "I wanted to thank you again for giving me a ride to town. My grandmother wanted to find you to give you a reward or something. She is just so excited—and you should see the baby's room!"

Shirley adjusted her position on the bench so that she could see Windy's face without being blinded by the sun.

"You would not believe it." Windy had a broad, silly grin on her face. "I keep saying, 'Granny, you are doing too much!' But she just says that this is her great-grandchild and I am her favorite granddaughter so she can fuss over the two of us as much as she pleases." Windy waved one hand in the air. "You are not going to believe this, but she is planning a big—no a *huge*—baby shower right now, even as we speak." Windy smiled and shook her head.

"No, I don't believe it."

"Me, neither. But I guess that's how love is. I told her, 'Granny, I don't know how people will feel about coming to a shower since I'm not married or anything.' Well, my grandma told me to keep my head up high. 'Let the one who is without sin cast the first stone,' is what she said. Can you beat that?"

"No, I can't."

"And guess what else?"

"What?"

"My daddy's been calling and calling, begging me to come home. 'Baby, come on home. I can change. I can make a place for you and the little one, for my grandchild. Come on home to your daddy who loves you, baby.' It just tears at my heart, you know? I know my daddy means well, but what is he going to do and say when the people in his church start putting pressure on him and start saying things behind his back. I don't know…I love him, too. But I have more than myself to think about now. I have to do what's best for me and for the baby. Besides, my grandma's already done so much, she would be heartbroken if I just up and left."

Was the girl crazy? Was she just a liar, or were there a few rungs loose on her ladder? Shirley could feel her neck beginning to tense again, and there was sweat on her neck and brow. Whatever Windy's problem was, the day was too hot for foolishness. "Windy, I already know about everything."

Windy kept smiling. "Isn't that funny about small towns? Everybody knows everything. I mean Tyler isn't small, but compared to other cities… Isn't that something, you know all about the shower and everything." She raised her shoulders and hands in disbelief.

"What I mean, Windy, is I know about your grandmother."

"Isn't she sweet? It's a miracle all she's done for me and the baby. I can't get over the wallpaper. But she keeps telling me that nothing's too good for her favorite granddaughter."

"Windy, will you cut it out?" Shirley didn't mean to yell. She lowered her voice after a few people's heads turned. "Will you stop all the favorite granddaughter stuff? You used me to bring you to Tyler with this hopped-up crazy story. Only your grandmother doesn't even know who you are. I know there wasn't any bus ticket, there is no baby shower, and there for sure isn't any pink flowered wallpaper."

Windy's face turned pink and her chin began to tremble. "I don't know what you mean."

"I mean I've been hearing all kinds of crazy stuff about you, your grandmother, and Jack. I mean, how could you *do* that?"

She looked to her right and then to her left as though she were looking for a way of escape. "Well, you must have been hearing about someone else. They must have me confused with someone else. My granny said—"

"Windy, it's too hot, okay? I know all about it and it's pathetic. Your grandmother was at my home the other night, so don't try it. I know about the store; I know about everything. What is up with you?"

Windy dropped her head. "Sorry." Her voice was a whisper. "I'm sorry."

"Sorry? Do you have any idea how this makes me feel? I don't know how I'm ever going to face your grandmother." Shirley shook her head and talked more to herself than to Windy. "I can't believe that I was stupid enough to bring you—to give you a ride in the car with my kids. Who knows what you really did to end up at the police station."

The girl wiped her face with the back of her hand. "I did the same thing you did, nothing. Okay, I lied about my grandmother, but that doesn't mean I lied about everything else."

"Windy, you lied about your father. Is your father a preacher?" The girl was mute. "So, like I said. What didn't you lie about?"

"You don't understand."

"You're right. I don't understand." Shirley snatched her purse off the bench and stuffed the book inside. "I don't need to understand. You've had your fun with me and my family. I don't know what your family's going to do with you, but I'm done." Shirley stood, tossed her ice cream cup in a waste can near the bench. "Don't worry about the hamburger money, I'll just consider it a lesson worth learning. But do me a favor; the next time you see me, act like you don't know me." She walked quickly to her car.

Mother Johnson kneeled in the prayer house. The children sat on the back porch, the creak of the old swing amused them and reassured Mother Johnson that they were nearby and safe.

"Lord, it's hot out here. I know You know that, if anybody does. And it ain't Wednesday. 'Course You know that, too. But nothing wrong with a little conversation between old friends. And I hope You don't mind, Lord, but I'm going to ease off these old knees and sit down on one of these pillows. 'Course, after I sit down, I'm gone have to ask You to help me get back up.

"I'm not beating the pans today, Lord, or shaking the tambourine. I got two new little friends over there and I'm trying to keep this prayer quiet between me and You. I'm not coming to You because anything's going terrible wrong. Actually, Lord, I'm coming because I see You trying to put some stuff to a wonderful right. It's just, Lord, that sometimes when we've been struggling so long, when we've been in the darkness so long, it's hard to get adjusted—it's hard to recognize the light. We get satisfied with dark, and even dim light looks good. But don't let us get content, Lord. Help us to shine.

"It's pretty clear to me that You're working and that You've got a plan. Seems like, though, the people You working for don't see it. I know how tricky this changing part can be. You know, when we're not feeling bad so much anymore, we're just not all the way there. Lord, I'm just asking You and the heavenly host to keep working. Lord, I'm asking You to work with them so that they don't give up. I'm praying for the folks in my life who have hung on, who have made it through the darkness. All I ask today, Lord, is that You let them pass into the marvelous light."

"Your hair is so pretty. You look like a queen."

Lex was covered with bubbles—he had even put a scoop of them on his head for a crown. He didn't beg for baths, but with bubbles, Lex was pretty easily persuaded to hit the water. A son that didn't mind bathing—that was enough to make most mothers drop to their knees with gratitude.

Mika sat nearby on a towel rubbing lotion on her legs. She was probably using enough lotion to cover at least two kids her size, but Mika wasn't about to miss a spot. Whatever Mika did, she took seriously.

Shirley couldn't help but smile at them. They were such sweet kids. She was so blessed.

Lex picked up a glob of bubbles and blew them so that they floated into the air. "Mommy, what is California like?" Why did she feel a sucker punch coming? "Is it fun?"

"Yes, baby, it's fun. Sure it is." Shirley was using a soapy washcloth to wash his arms. Lex called them his wings.

Mika was still applying lotion. She pushed up the arms of the cool cotton nightgown she wore so that she could give more attention to her elbows. "Are we going to like California as much as we do here? We like it here."

Shirley felt a knot in her stomach. Maybe it wasn't a knot, maybe she was just feeling closed in—feeling that the children, Mother Johnson, Ma Dear, the money in the tan envelope, and life in general were conspiring to keep her in Tyler.

Mika was really working to massage the lotion into her knees. "Yep, we like it, Mommy. Mother Johnson is funny, and there's a big backyard. Are we going to have a house and big backyard in California?"

What was she supposed to say to that? Adult questions were supposed to be complex, but it was the simple questions that children asked that were difficult to answer. Well, it really wasn't difficult to answer.

She could tell the truth.

No, we're not going to have a house and, chances are, we won't have a yard. It probably won't be a lot of fun because I'll be working long hours trying to afford the crummy little apartment we will live in. I'll be scuffling along to keep the lights on and to keep food on the table, so we won't be able to afford luxuries like Mister Bubble, but we'll be fine. We'll make do.

What was difficult about her children's questions was the guilt and uncertainty that came with answering truthfully, particularly when her parental responsibility was to answer in a way that left Mika and Lex feeling happy, assured, and carefree. What were parents supposed to do when lies kept children happy, while the truth would make them anxious, or make them worry? "We're going to be great," she told them and made her voice sound cheerful. "We're going to be so happy. Wait and see." She tickled Lex, and the three of them laughed.

When the children were both bathed and dressed for bed, she tucked them in like a good mother and headed for bed.

TWENTY-FOUR

*E*arly the next morning, when the sun was just rising, Shirley thought she heard the gliders on the porch. She sat up, leaning on one elbow. It wasn't Ma Dear's voice she heard. Shirley concentrated—it was Mildred. Shirley lay back down. She had enough of her own to deal with. Shirley put the pillow over her head and tried not to hear.

Mildred's soft, silver hair was pulled into a prim bun. "I don't believe in all that healing and hollering. The way she carries herself—it's not dignified."

Mother Johnson liked the early morning. It seemed cleaner and clearer than any other time of day. "No, sometimes it may not be, but I think God loves and uses the undignified just as well as he uses the dignified. Praise His name for that, because otherwise He wouldn't be using me."

"But all that ridiculousness about being a healer. I don't believe in that. Even my pastor doesn't believe in that."

Mother let her patience show in her smile. "Maybe so, but

141

Ma Dear believes the Word of God tells her she can heal. That's what she reads. And I don't know it all. What do I serve by tearing her down? Trying to make her just like me? Maybe she is supposed to be a healer, but what if I spend all my time trying to tear her down and make her believe she's wrong? What happens when someone needs healing, and she's not there or she doesn't believe enough in herself to try? Not to mention that *I* didn't do what *I* was supposed to do 'cause I was too busy telling her how she should think."

Mildred sniffed. "I just don't believe that all of that yelling out loud is necessary. All of that hollering is offensive. God can hear me if I make no sound at all. The Bible warns us not to make a show of prayer in front of other men."

"To tell the truth, it's not Ma Dear that's hollering, Mildred. I'm the one that hollers. I know the Bible speaks against praying to show off. Do you really think that's what I'm doing? Do you really judge my heart that way?"

"Well, I wasn't talking about you, Mother. I was speaking about Ma Dear… I'm not trying to judge *you*. We were talking about Ma Dear. But, if you really want to know, I do question people who have to make so much noise in what's supposed to be service to the Lord."

"We could argue back and forth all day, Mildred, and I could quote the Bible; then you could quote some. But maybe that's the problem. Maybe we spend too much time judging when we're not ready to judge."

"What do you mean, Mother?"

Mother Johnson stared out the window. "Maybe we've got it all wrong—I mean about praying—especially about the school prayer thing. Maybe we *lost* the right for our children to have prayer in school. I mean, I don't think some puny man—

or woman, for that matter—has the power to take away prayer. Maybe we lost the privilege because we didn't honor the prayer."

Mildred frowned and shook her head. "What do you mean, Mother? I don't understand. I reverence prayer."

"Maybe God allowed us to lose the right to pray because we took it for granted. Because when we prayed, He could tell by our voices, by our words, that we didn't know how sweet it is to be able to pray. Maybe we were judging too much, arguing too much, and loving too little."

Mildred folded her arms across her chest. "Mother Johnson, I'm sure I really don't know what you mean. And I'm not sure what any of this has to do with Ma Dear."

"I don't know for sure, Mildred. It could be that what we're doing right now—separating ourselves and questioning each other's ways, instead of working together and trying to get along—grieves God.

"Maybe He allowed our school prayer to be taken away because our thoughts weren't on thanking Him or talking to Him when we prayed. Teachers were thinking about lesson plans and paychecks; kids were thinking about recess and home time; and Baptist principles were thinking they weren't going to be letting any Catholics lead prayers in their schools, as if the prayers belonged to them. Maybe Presbyterians were thinking that they weren't going to let any Pentecostals be leading prayers in *their* schools."

Mildred lowered her arm and then her head. "You know, Mother, I never thought about it that way."

Mother Johnson stirred the liquid in her teacup. "It just makes me queasy on the inside when I think about it. But maybe that's how it was. Maybe folks in the North were saying no one with a Southern accent was going to lead prayer in their schools, and vice versa. Maybe black folks wouldn't listen to white folks, and white folks felt the same, and let's not even *talk* about them letting other folks talk to God for them. Maybe our prayers just started to stink, and God had to turn His head away."

Mildred trembled. "Oh, Lord, have mercy on us! Mother, it makes me just want to fall on my knees."

"It's a frightening thought. And I ain't no preacher, but maybe we lost the honor of being heard because we lost our humility. Maybe we had to lose the prayer to appreciate it."

"You mean like missing the water when the well runs dry?"

Mother frowned. "That's just what I'm afraid may have happened. Maybe we didn't appreciate the prayer—the living water—until it dried up. I've been thinking, then, that instead of fighting and protesting, we need to be telling the Lord we're sorry, asking Him to heal what has gone wrong, and humbly asking Him to give us back our prayer."

Mildred wrung her hands. "Mother, I don't even want to think that we were the cause… I understand what you're saying, but I still don't feel comfortable with…with yelling…and praying out loud. I'm sorry, Mother. I don't mean to offend you. It's what I've learned and how I feel. It makes me uncomfortable."

Mother Johnson got up from the table and added more water to the kettle. It didn't seem like it should be so hard to get along. Sometimes it felt like it would be easier to give up, to just stay to herself. It was a lot easier following the Lord when she didn't have to deal with people!

While Mildred sat quietly at the table, Mother Johnson wiped the countertop. When she couldn't avoid finishing the conversation any longer, she returned to her seat. She knew the truth. Part of loving God was doing the hard work of loving other people, different people.

Mother touched Mildred's hands with her own. "I respect your right to feel as you do. I just don't think that should keep us from praying together, rocking together, or sipping a little sweet ice tea together. Maybe it means you don't want to pray with me when I go to the prayer house…'cause I'm bound to holler there…I can't help myself. But sometimes you can still come by, can't you? Differences shouldn't stop us all from being friends. 'Sides, Mildred, I still need your solemn prayers. I'm a hollerer, that's true. But, some days, Mildred, God looks and sounds just like you. Sometimes, I can hear His voice through you.

"We've got to start appreciating each other instead of tearing each other down." She shook her head. "And think about the way we fight…the way it must look to people that don't know the Lord. We must not look like any family they would want to be adopted into."

Mother Johnson looked over at her good friend's chair. "Oh, Ma Dear has her rough edges. But I don't look for what's wrong with her. I just hold on tight to the good I see in her. In my mind, I can see her praying for me. Calling me back from death's door. When everyone else had given up, she was the one who came and prayed and believed God would heal me. Why would I hate her for that? I'm alive! Hallelujah! I'm alive!"

Mother patted Mildred's hands. "I don't have to understand it—everything's not required to fit in with what I think or know about God. But Ma Dear believes God can do through us right now, today, what He did through the disciples a long time ago. Who am I to argue with that?"

Mother Johnson nodded at her new friend. "I don't know it

all, Mildred. I'm trying to find God. Every day I'm seeking Him and trying to know His ways. Maybe you can teach me something with your quiet, solemn ways. Maybe *you* can learn something from *me*—or even from Ma Dear."

Mildred looked up and down the street. "People already talk enough that I'm friends with a black woman."

"Well." Mother felt tired at that. She was supposed to love others, but how much was too much? How much patience was she supposed to have? What in Mildred's mind made it so easy for her to think and say what she had just said? Mother sighed. "It seems like you got some choices to make, like you've got some thinking you have to do for yourself. I don't know everything, but I do know that we're not going to get to Revelation from here."

Mildred frowned, clearly perplexed. "What do you mean by that?"

"You know where it says something about a number that no man can number?"

"You mean about every nation and every tongue?"

"Yes, that's what I mean. How do you think we're going to get to that point from here? When we're scared to just be seen with each other? Let alone to pray." Mother nodded sadly. "You know, Mildred, I want to be friends. But not if being friends means I have to be less than all of who I am, less of all that God has made me to be. God loves me just like He loves every other person He made. If I have to deny what and who He has been in my life—that's too high a price to pay.

"I believe that we can hear from God…that when we pray, if we listen with our heart and mind and spirit, the Lord will speak back to us. That scares some people. They don't want to know God like that. But that's what I believe because of what I've read, what I've studied, and what I've experienced. He's been speaking into my life just about every day I can remember."

Mildred folded her hands in her lap. "Well, I don't hold with any supernatural God. That's just a bunch of religious hogwash. That's what keeps people from believing in us as Christians. They think we're all just full of superstition."

"Maybe so, but I just figure our whole relationship with God is supernatural. God—just God by Himself—is pretty supernatural. He parted the Red Sea. God's Son, the Word, gave up His position in heaven. And you know that's got to be supernatural, 'cause how many preachers you know that would be willing to give up their position just on account of my good? You know that would make some folks howl." Mother scratched her head. "It would make *me* howl for that matter.

"But we believe the Son of God gave up His position, came to earth, and then died in our place to atone for our sins. Then we believe that because He shed His holy blood, we have everlasting life. I don't know, Mildred. It sounds pretty supernatural to me. Just seems like I don't have the right to tell God—" Mother stood up and shook her finger—"'Now, that's enough with that supernatural stuff. Cut that out, God.'"

Mildred smiled and then covered her mouth with her hand. "You make it so funny. I don't know…" She sighed and beckoned for Mother Johnson to sit back down. "Maybe Ma Dear is just a little too much like my husband. He was always so noisy, so busy laughing at everything. 'Course, he was so busy laughing he never had time to work—not much. We lived in squalor. Cootie Town they called it. I just needed to get away from all that. Here no one knows I was a cootie. There's no drugs or drinking. I get to be a new creature."

"That's what we all want."

"Don't let's let any of this separate us. I want to be among that group with you, you know? Among that number that no man can number. I want to learn and to understand."

"This is all a dress rehearsal."

"Yes, Mother Johnson. And I wanted to tell you that I had been thinking about our conversation the other night. You know, about my granddaughter Windy. Maybe I've been trying to do the same thing, in my own way. To run away from who I was, or who people thought I was, so that I could become someone better. I thought that you might be right, she might be trying to do the same thing."

Mildred lowered her voice. "I got pregnant young, too. Only we got married right away, and no one asked us any questions, so…there I was living in that horrible place and the children were so angry about how they were treated…about being poor, and being treated like they were worse than trash. People called them names. *Cooties* is what they called my children, like they were vermin or bugs. Even the teachers laughed. My son Kenneth was so angry, he was just mean. After Windy was born, he left. We'd hear of him here or there, mostly in some kind of trouble. That's when her mother took her off to Oklahoma."

Mildred folded her hands and sighed. "Maybe I should have stayed, Mother Johnson, but I couldn't breathe anymore. When my husband died, I left. I had to get out. Now…here she is." Mildred shook her head.

Shirley dreamed that she heard someone talking about Cootie Town. She heard a woman's voice. Shirley was eight and the voice belonged to Mrs. Canada.

"You're going to have your own reading group—The Greenbirds. You're going to be their teacher."

Barbara was twelve, Misty was nine, and Ken was eleven.

Barbara was hard. She was tall and thick, had dirty-blond matted hair, wore lipstick, smelled of cigarette smoke, and it was rumored that she had been known to run away with grown men from time to time.

Misty was skinny and she always looked scared. She looked the least like the other Cooties. She wore clean clothes and ribbons in her hair. It appeared that her mother might have been trying to help Misty avoid the community stigma. To some extent, she was successful. During P.E., the other white girls would hold Misty's hands for games of Red Rover. During recess, however, she was shunned, for while the children would play with Shirley and other Negro children, they refused Misty's company. After all, ribbons or not, Misty was Barbara and Ken's cousin and she lived in Cootie Town.

Ken's fingers were stained brown from tobacco, which must have stunted his growth because he was short for eleven years. His hair was almost white, with a permanent coating of what looked to be soot. While Barbara was known for fighting, then smiling down at her victims if she had to, Ken was known for being plain mean. Anger crawled up his back, over the top of his head, and settled on his mouth and in his eyes—icy blue eyes. He wore a perpetual snarl. He was not interested in reading or in school games, only in the canned meat sandwich, which he pulled unwrapped from his pocket on the Greenbirds' first morning in the cloakroom.

Barbara looked amused by Shirley, by the little colored kid in front of her trying to teach them to read. Misty looked confused. Ken was silent, but surly. It was clear he hated being in the cloakroom. He never looked anyone in the eye—anyone except Shirley—when they were assembled as the Greenbirds. What Shirley saw in Ken's eyes said that he knew his position. He knew the rules and was willing to abide by them. He was a Cootie and he was willing to be shunned, to be angry, to be invisible. But he seethed at the breaching of the social contract. Teachers might humiliate him, but he was not to be humiliated by a little colored girl. He was better than that. He was too good to be banished to the cloakroom with someone like Shirley.

"What can you teach me?" Ken snarled from the cloakroom corner where he sat. "You ain't nothing but a—a—little old girl!"

It was pretty clear that he didn't use Vitalis—his hair was dusty, white-blond, and dry, not slicked back and parted like the men on TV. His hair was uncombed and looked more like animal fur.

He looked away from Shirley and clamped his arms tightly across his chest.

She glared at Ken. It was hard, too hard. They couldn't remember the sounds or the smallest words, and Ken didn't even try. At least Barbara and Misty pretended to be interested or looked amused at her efforts to teach them to read—unlike Ken. Shirley wanted to punch him.

But if she could just hold out…just a few more minutes.

Brrring! Brrring! The bell!

Shirley sat up, sweating. She looked around the room, needing to see something familiar. She was a grown woman with two children and a life very far from the third grade and East St. Louis.

Shirley was awake, but she could still see Ken's image in the dream. The icy blue eyes, the hair…

Suddenly, Shirley understood. It was what Windy's eyes had been trying to tell her, what had seemed so familiar.

Ken was Windy's father.

TWENTY-FIVE

*T*ony Taylor jabbed the box cutter into the seam that was apparent through the packing tape. A thin line appeared where the blade had been. He followed by cutting the side panels free. Then he used his hands to tear the box open. He pulled the bottles of cleaning solution from the box two at a time. The box was located beneath the shelves, so as he reached in, he moved the bottles to the storage shelves above.

It was morning and it was quiet. He liked it that way. He had breakfast in the morning, if he wanted. He watched the news, if he wanted. He showered first thing, if he wanted. He dressed, if he wanted. Some days, when his work didn't require him to go out, he worked all day in what he slept in, if he wanted. He exercised, if he wanted. He cooked or made a sandwich or got fast food, if he wanted.

He was calling the shots, and there was safety in that. There was no discussion and no risk that someone would—or could—disagree. There was no risk that there would be a fight. Even more than that, there was no risk that he would feel something he didn't want to feel.

He didn't have a lot of money, but it was enough to keep and take care of him and let him do what he liked to do. Tony wasn't responsible for anyone, he didn't hurt anyone, and he liked it that way. It had taken him a long time to find this peace, to find a system that worked. It was trial and error for him. Some people just seemed to know how to do it, how to live. But Tony didn't. It had been years of a series of missteps until finally he had discerned a pattern that worked, that kept him from getting gouged, punched, kicked, or burned.

That was what he had in life. It was safe. He had figured out a system and that made him feel safe.

Which was why he was thinking long and hard about this Shirley thing. What exactly was the point of it? Tony threw the box he had finished unpacking to the side and grabbed another. The box cutter slid easily into place. It was even stupid to be thinking this much about it.

In fact, it was dangerous. He knew the signs. The last thing he should ever do was get involved in something that made him feel anxious, that made him feel he might have to raise his voice or defend his position. Shirley was not a diversion kind of girl—no, woman. And he was already feeling it. That feeling that made him crazy…the feeling where he kept replaying in his head what he had said, and then spent way too much time worrying about what she might have said or thought.

Like the other night. *No pressure.* What was that? And the whole moon cookie thing—hunting for the things and driving all over to get them. That was just not…not smart. What was worse was telling her about it. He shook his head. This was not good. Besides, she had kids and that added a whole new dimension. He was going to shut it down before it got started.

He shouldn't have gone to see her in the first place. What

was that? They hadn't seen each other in years. All that stuff he had felt when he was boy, that he had held on to as a teenager—all that was behind him. It was stupid to be carrying all that around. No, it was dangerous to even think about it. Shirley had been married. He needed to keep his life in order and it was easy to see she was not in order.

She had that I-can-take-care-of-myself thing on the outside, but he could feel the upset just drifting around her. Shirley was not his responsibility, but it was easy to get sucked in to that kind of thing. And that—getting sucked in—did not make for a safe and peaceful life.

Shirley—no matter what it looked like or what she looked like—was not the person she used to be. But no matter who she was, she was not his business.

Tony wasn't even sure how he had ended up sitting on Mother Johnson's front porch steps with her.

He remembered thinking about Shirley every day since Ma Dear stopped him to tell him she was home. Okay, so it was natural to think of someone that you had been friends with for years. No big deal, right? Except that he kept thinking of her. But it was just natural curiosity, the same feelings he would have had for anyone else he hadn't seen in a long time. They had never really even been involved, so it was overreacting to panic. It was okay to be friends with an old friend.

So he had let himself think about her. That's how he got to the moon cookies. He kept thinking about her eating the cookies, and it was funny how he could remember even seeing crumbs on her chin—crumbs he didn't tell her about because she would have brushed them away.

He'd debated over the cookies, about getting them and whether it would send the wrong sign, whether it would signal something that he didn't intend. But it was stupid to put so much importance on cookies. If she were his cousin or a guy friend and it was about some ribs and sauce that they liked, he would have gotten it and not thought about it. So he was making too big a deal of it. Which is how he ended up actually finding the cookies and buying them, because he didn't want her to think that getting the cookies was such a big deal.

But if the cookies, and getting them, wasn't such a big deal, why did he even mention it to her?

This was the unsettling feeling he hated. Here he was, a grown man, worried about what she thought about cookies, and she probably had thrown the bag away and not even given him a thought.

What he needed to do, though, was not worry about her, but to think his way through this so that he could make a rational, unemotional decision. So once he had the cookies, then the debate was whether he should actually go see her or not. It was probably safer not to see her, not to call or do anything. But what did it matter—since it didn't matter? She was an old friend, and he would have gone to see any old friend. So he decided to go.

He had thought about going to see her during the day, but he had to keep his priorities straight. Work was first, and he wouldn't have taken off from work to go see an old guy friend. So he decided it was more natural to go see her after he finished working. But after he finished working, he was sweating and dirty. He changed into slacks and a shirt, but he wouldn't have worn them to go see a man, so he changed the slacks to jeans and the shirt to a pullover.

He had told himself on the way there that he would see an old friend and all the high drama would be over. Things would go back to normal. They would have a few laughs, promise to see each other again soon, and then he would be able to stop thinking about it. Only when he saw her, he hadn't expected to feel the way he did when he was a boy.

First of all, the timing was bad. He had meant to arrive in the evening, but it was night. Night always signaled courting, and that was *not* the message he was trying to send. Then he had started out playing with the kids, which is what men did when they were trying to get in and get over. That wasn't why he did it, they were just nice kids. But he knew better.

What didn't help, either, was that her laugh was still the same, and she still had the same look in her eyes—like she wasn't sure that she should trust anything he was saying. She still talked and moved confidently, but her eyes still gave her away. And the look had the same effect it had when he was a kid; he wanted her to know that he wasn't one of the ones that she couldn't trust. She still looked away from him when she talked. When he saw her, he knew it had been a long time, just like he had figured—but he had held her hand, like he hadn't figured. And he had pretty much promised her that they were going to be friends, so if he didn't keep his promise, it would deepen that look—that wounded look that was in her eyes.

Tony threw another empty box to the side. *No pressure, okay?* He shook his head and looked around his storage room. He could feel knots forming in his stomach.

The boiled egg Shirley was eating felt like hard clumps when she swallowed. There was too much on her mind. Too much thought about Ken and Windy, too much thought about how she was going to take care of Mika and Lex. Too much thought about her family, about Danny, about what Tony meant when he said no pressure—and too much thought about why that should even matter to her.

Mother Johnson sat across from her pretending to be solely focused on her own eggs and toast. Shirley, after years with her, knew better. Mother was reading every signal, every nuance.

Shirley shifted in her chair. "So, Mother, I was wondering. I never asked you how it came to be that you got me from the hospital or whatever that place was. Why was it you that came and got me?"

Mother paused, a slice of bitten toast en route to her mouth, and looked over the top of her glasses. "Is that what's on your mind this morning?"

Shirley sidestepped Mother's pointed inquisition. "No, really, I've always wondered why you came."

"I never thought about it. It was something that needed to be done, and I did it. I was a stranger to you, but you wasn't no stranger to me. Me and your mama and uncles stayed in pretty regular contact. Your mother wrote me for years and sent me pictures. They were always saying that they were coming to visit me when they came to visit Demosthenes. We didn't see each other much, but time and distance ain't got nothing to do with real love. When your daddy passed, and I got word from your uncles about your mama, you know I was praying for you."

Shirley nodded.

"Well, when you ended up in that institution and your uncles couldn't get to you, they were able to get word to me. 'Course, they got word to other people, too. But I'm the one that could come, so I came. Wasn't nothing to do but get you and bring you here." Mother sat the toast down and took a sip of coffee. "There was relatives closer, but it doesn't matter who's closer, what matters is who steps in. The good Lord always knows what He's doing. Nobody comes into your life by mistake. You needed somebody. I didn't know I needed somebody, but the Lord did." Mother smiled and went back to eating her breakfast. She looked up. "That all that's on your mind?"

Shirley nodded, then she shook her head. "I heard you this morning…talking to Mildred."

"Oh, baby, I'm sorry we disturbed you."

"No, it's not that, Mother. It's that…since I first saw Windy, I felt like I had seen her before, like I know her. I didn't know until the other day on the porch that she and her grandmother were from East St. Louis. But, I don't think it clicked until this morning."

Mother Johnson wiped crumbs away from her mouth with a paper towel. "Oh, baby, I thought you knew that. It's a small world, ain't it?"

"Mother, I know Windy's father."

Mother Johnson seemed unconcerned. "Do you now?"

"Well, not now, but I knew him when I was a girl. I spent a lot of time with him." She looked down at her plate and then back at Mother. "I'm probably making a big deal out of nothing."

Mother laid her knife and fork across her empty plate. "No, I think it probably feels important to you because it is something important between you and that girl. Mildred said the child barely knew her father, I'm sure it would mean a lot to her to know that you knew her daddy and that you could tell her about him."

"I'm not so sure that she would want to hear what I know."

"Maybe what you know would put her heart at ease. You never know. You think it's an accident you meeting that girl, her being on her way to Tyler, and her grandmother being my friend? Just think if Mildred and me hadn't had that conversation this morning, if you hadn't been awake." Mother shook her head. "Ain't no accidents."

Shirley pushed her half-eaten boiled egg around on her plate. "I'm not sure that I want to talk to her, Mother. I'm not sure that I want—or that I'm supposed—to have any more to do with Windy than I already have. She lies—even her own grandmother thinks she's trouble."

"Well, nobody can make that decision but you. You know in your heart what's best." Mother continued drinking her coffee.

"Mother Johnson, I've got enough to deal with right now. I've got two kids and I'm a widow—I'm not saying it for anyone to feel sorry for me. It's just what my life is. I'm trying to get to California so that we can get a fresh start." Shirley sat up straight in her chair. "Actually, I'm excited about starting over… It just doesn't feel like a good time to be getting involved in other people's lives. It just makes things more complicated."

"More complicated? Or are you just trying to say that Windy doesn't fit into your plan? That, from where you're sitting now, it looks a little too messy for your taste."

Shirley blinked. "Mother, I'm handling a lot now. I can't handle any more people. Me, Mika, and Lex is all that I can manage."

"Says who? It's never a good time to welcome people into our lives. Things never settle down in any of our lives long enough for it to be a good time. We're always on our way to or back from somewhere. We're on our way from our old life or on our way to our new life. We're leaving one relationship or entering into a new one. It's never a good time, according to us, which is why God usually doesn't ask us what we think about it."

Mother's words were difficult, but her expression was pleasant.

Shirley lowered her head. "Never mind, Mother. I'm sorry that I brought it up."

"I wanted us to have these times alone in the morning so that we could talk. So don't be sorry." Mother smiled tenderly. "But, baby, you keep saying *people*. Windy's just one person. You got somebody else on your mind? Somebody else that makes Windy add up to *people*?"

"Mother, I'm just trying to stay focused on what I'm doing. That's all."

"Maybe your staying focused on your plan is not part of God's plan."

For once, Shirley wished Mother wouldn't say any more.

TWENTY-SIX

*I*t was cooler at dusk than it had been for a while. Shirley, Mika, and Lex ran after fireflies in the front yard. Mika held the jar lid and Lex cheered while Shirley ran back and forth across the yard after the insects. "I used to be able to catch these really easy." Shirley tried not to sound like she was out of breath as she smiled at Mother Johnson, who moved slowly back and forth in her glider.

"Me, too!" Mother laughed. "You used to think it was worth all that running, though."

Shirley slapped her hand over the jar. "It still is." There was a firefly inside. "Quick, Mika, give me the lid." The insect buzzed inside the jar. Mika looked almost as amazed as Lex. Shirley saw another firefly near a bush and began stalking it.

"I thought hunting season was over."

Shirley stopped just as she was about to cup her hands together to capture the second firefly. Tony stood at the gate, smiling. "Hello, Mother Johnson."

Mother smiled and waved. "Come on up."

Shirley kept her eyes zeroed on the one that got away as she spoke to Tony. "That firefly is thanking you for his freedom right now."

"Glad to do what I can."

Mika and Lex ran to the gate to show him their treasure. "Look, Mr. Tony." He showed the proper amount of admiration, then put his keys in his pocket and joined in the hunt. In short order, the collection had grown so that Mika and Lex sat staring at the jar, fascinated.

Mother stood. "Well, come on, you little ones. We've got baths to get, stories to read, and you have to get your rest so you'll be ready to hunt again tomorrow."

"Mother, you don't have to do that. The children can stay up a little longer."

Mother Johnson waved her hand at Shirley. "It's no bother, honey. Me and the chirren are gone have us a good time." Shirley hugged and kissed the kids and watched as her comfort trailed into the house behind Mother.

Shirley glanced at Tony, trying to convince herself she wasn't nervous. "How've you been?"

"So-so." He folded his arms across his chest.

"What brings you by?" She tried to sound light, then wondered why it was so hard.

"I just thought I would stop by to see an old friend. And I was thinking today about that shoebox. The one we saved the money in." Tony laughed like he was on stage.

"It's still here. The kids found it and they've been keeping stuff in it."

He nodded, looked at the sky, and then back at Shirley. "So did you find her? You tried so hard to get to her. I can't remember her name, but I was thinking how determined you were for a little kid."

Shirley smiled and shrugged. "Her name was Sheri. And, no, I never found her...I mean I never really looked for her after I got grown and got a family… It was kid stuff, you know."

"It didn't seem like kid stuff."

She smiled, but not too broadly. "It was, though, just a little girl being homesick. Kid stuff."

"Like moon cookies."

"Yeah, like moon cookies."

They sat down on the steps. "So since you're not hunting Sheri anymore, what are you doing now? Are you planning to stay—?"

"No, I'm not staying here." Shirley answered before he could finish talking. "I'm sorry. I just came here to visit Mother and so the kids could see her rather than just hearing me talk about her all the time. And *I* wanted to see her, you know?"

"Makes sense."

"I mean, I've already stayed longer than I planned. But soon we're going to California."

"Okay, California. What part? So you have other relatives or friends in California?"

"Well, I'm not exactly sure where. We're just going to pick a place on the map, I guess." She sounded like an airhead. Or like a teenager dreaming about being anyplace exciting, anyplace other than her room.

"You just need to get away."

Shirley sighed.

"I can understand that. Sometimes I'd like to get away. Actually, I did. I haven't been back in Tyler very long."

Shirley turned so that she could see him better as he talked.

"I moved up and down the East Coast, mostly. I don't know, just looking for something different. I tried a little bit of everything. For a while, I lived in the Midwest and I drove trucks."

"I can't imagine you driving trucks."

"Well, me neither. But it paid well, it had good benefits, and I could drive and think." A smile lit on his lips, then was gone as quickly as it came. "It also gave me an excuse to be away from home." Tony swatted at a mosquito. "I probably would have been driving still, except there was a strike. I hung in there for a while. But pretty soon, it was hard to tell who was right and who was wrong—I sure couldn't tell the good guys from the bad guys. It was all smoke and mirrors. It wasn't enough to commit to for life. I need to know who's wearing the white hat."

Tony stretched. "I looked around at the rest of my life and I didn't have any reason to stay there, so I made my way back here. I don't know if I'm here for good, but business is going okay. I'm comfortable working for myself."

"I guess I never saw you as an entrepreneur. Not that I know what one looks like anyway."

"It wasn't in my plans, but I realized I couldn't work for anybody. I still have too much stuff bothering me."

Shirley found herself relaxing. It was a conversation between old friends; it felt like one. "What do you mean?"

"That stuff that happened to you when we were kids…them dragging you out of the movie theater. I still think about you lying in that bed after what happened. It broke me up that I couldn't do anything about it. But what was I going to do? I was a boy. I would walk by the movies and think about setting it on fire, about burning it down.

"That theater has been shut down for years, but when I go past what's left of it, I still remember how they…how the white people threw you out of there. Out onto the street."

"Oh, Tony." Shirley reached out to touch Tony's shoulder, then pulled her hand back.

Tony stared straight ahead at the street. "It probably bothers me even more now, than it did then. When I look back on it…they were adults and you were a little kid. I don't see how people could do that to a child and then sleep at night. Of course, it doesn't help that I still have memories of how people treated my grandfather in Frankston, about how they disrespected him and talked to him. I still have a picture in my mind of this young white man plugging one of my grandfather's watermelons and calling him boy. My grandfather was in his sixties!"

He lifted one of his hands and wiped his face. "Maybe I should get over it. Some things have changed. White folks aren't calling me nigger out loud, anymore. Nobody's kicking me out of movie theaters. But I still have a hard time working for people and pretending like those attitudes just went away overnight, that suddenly there's no more prejudice. I can't pretend—when I see those same attitudes, those same expressions—that I'm not recognizing the same old racist mess."

Tony balanced his elbows on his knees. "It was bad for a while. Real bad. I was mad at God. I didn't want anybody coming to me talking to me about the white man's God."

"You were Black Muslim?"

"No, I couldn't get with that either. Like a lot of guys, I got caught up in the European images of Jesus, and serving the oppressor. It all looked good for a while. But when I started reading the Bible, it was clear to me that there were black Jews and black converts to Christianity before any Europeans ever came to Africa.

"And I couldn't walk away from what my family taught me…you know, 'train up a child.' I believe in God, and that Jesus is real, but some of the stuff that was done or allowed in His name makes me wonder about who He is, or at least about who the people are that are serving Him. How could God let all that stuff happen in His name?

"I was there when all the stuff was happening in the sixties and seventies, Shirley. We all were when all the stuff was going down. I know that God is. I pray, but…like I said, I still got a lot on my mind. And I feel about church like I did about the people calling the shots with the strike—I can't get close enough to the players to figure out who's real. Every day there's someone else that I thought was real that turns out to be a phony."

Tony shook his head. "No doubt about it, I got a chip on my shoulder. I'm not proud of it, but I'm not pretending it's not there. And I figure the best way to deal with it is to stay to myself until I work it out. That way I can control when, how, for whom I work—and who and how I worship."

Shirley let herself touch his arm. "It's hard to forget everything that happened, Tony. Really, I don't even know if we should. I mean, since I've been home the town looks different—more buildings, more roads, more businesses, more houses—but I've seen some of the same people. Now they smile like nothing ever happened. Like I should have wiped it out of my memory. I don't know how I feel about that. I don't know how I should feel. But what I do know is that I need God. When Danny died, there was no way I could have made it, except for God."

"I hear you." Tony shrugged. "I want to forget. I want to walk past grown men and not remember what they thought and said in the past. I want to believe that their hearts have changed and that when they employ me or work with me, they don't see me through the eyes and teachings from when they were kids. But if I'm still following what I learned as a child, why should I believe that they're not doing the same thing?"

Tony rubbed one hand up and down on the back of his neck. "I want to believe that they're different and I want to believe completely in God, but I'm just not willing to stake everything that I am on it. What if it turns out to be like *The Wizard of Oz?* I guess I'm afraid to hope."

"I don't know about men, either, but I know God's real, Tony. He has to be. Everything hasn't been perfect in my life. I mean, I didn't expect that I'd be a widow in my twenties or that I'd be raising two kids by myself. My whole world has been turned upside down. I couldn't have made it through if I didn't have hope. I never thought I'd be reading the Bible or going to church every Sunday without anybody telling me to do it." She smiled at him. "But the only reason I had for staying sane when my husband died was that God came and sat with me. I know it sounds crazy, but when I was going through it, I could feel Him so strong, feel Him holding me. When everything fell apart—when the kids and I had our backs up against the wall—I turned back to what I knew, to what I trusted." She looked up toward the dark sky. "When I needed Him and leaned on Him, He proved Himself. He was there."

"I believe you." Tony stretched his arms overhead and then back to his sides. "I'm working it out." He turned toward Shirley. "So what other dark secrets haven't you told me?"

She laughed and told Tony what she'd been doing, where they'd lived, and how she'd gotten to Tyler.

"You were in a jail cell?"

She nodded and told him the rest of the story. "So that's

that. Now, like I said, we're on our way to California."

They talked until he looked at his watch. "I better go." He stood. "This was good, Shirley. I mean, it felt like old times. Better than old times."

After he left, Shirley went in the house and found Mother Johnson standing at the counter, stirring sugar into a pitcher of tea. "Mother, you didn't have to bring the kids inside. They were okay."

"I know, baby. Sometimes it's just good for grown folks to have private conversation."

"If people are going to date me or be my friends, they need to know that I have children and that's part of being in my life." Shirley's face felt warm. She spoke rapidly. "Tony and I…we're not dating, Mother. We're just friends. So it doesn't matter. The kids can be there when we're together."

Mother stopped stirring and tilted her head to the side. She opened her mouth to speak, then closed it. She turned back to the tea she was stirring and nodded. "You're going to make it." She dipped up a spoonful of the tea and held it for Shirley to taste. "See? Sweet just like you like it. Mother knows what you like." She nodded again. "You're going to make it."

TWENTY-SEVEN

*O*kay, everybody up!" Mother Johnson had on a nice blue-flowered dress. "We're getting out of here. We're going to have us some fun and get us some sunshine. I'm about sick of us being holed up in the house." She was throwing open curtains, raising blinds, and clapping her hands. "Mika! Lex! Come on, let's get a move on. Come on sleepy heads."

Shirley turned over on her side when she heard Mother coming in the room. She put her arm over her face just in time to block the bolt of sunlight that shot across the bed. "Mother?" It was more of a whine than a question.

"We are going to get up and get moving. I've been making a picnic lunch. We're going to go to Woldert Park so you and the kids can swim. It will do us some good—it will do *me* some good, anyway." Mother stopped fussing in the room. "I didn't even think, baby, to see if you had other plans. You got other plans?"

Shirley's eyes were still closed. "No, ma'am."

"All right then, let's get this show on the road." Shirley heard Mother leave the room, then start running bathwater for the children. "We're not going to use a whole lot of this bubble bath, because you all will be having to bathe again when we get back from the park." Shirley could hear Mother moving. "Okay, now we'll have to get your suits and towels together. And we'll have to get your little outfits together. It's going to be a great day!" She started humming "He's an on Time God."

By the time they turned onto Glass Street, the park was already full of people who were dressed and strolling, sitting, or dancing near cars. Shirley was glad that Mother Johnson had pushed her to wear something nice.

"You don't want to just wear your everyday jeans, baby. People are going to see you. We're going into town."

Shirley had forgotten that, how in small Southern towns, going to town—even if town was just a few feet away—was an occasion to dress up and fix up.

"Your hair looks nice," Mother Johnson had told her. "Just put a little something on your cheeks. If you look thrown away, you'll feel thrown away."

Mother Johnson was right; she did feel better.

The pool was at the top of the hill. "Are you sure that you can make it, Mother?"

"Shirley, don't make me have to take a switch to you." Clearly, Mother was feeling feisty today. "I'm old, but my grave ain't turned over yet. And if you don't get to stepping, I'm going to leave you behind."

Mika and Lex ran ahead; they couldn't wait. They wore their swimming suits up under their summer outfits. "So it won't take us so long to be ready to get in the pool," Mika said. They carried their beach towels—Mika's was pink, orange, and yellow; Lex's was blue and green with red stripes—and plastic blow-up pool toys. Lex had a pair of goggles strapped around his head.

"Last one in is a rotten egg," he yelled to Mika.

They played in the shallow end of the pool—water wings helped keep Lexington afloat. The water was ice cold, but it felt good. The chlorine smell reminded Shirley of the pool in East St. Louis, and in her mouth she tasted the hot popped corn she had always eaten there.

The pool was crowded; there were knees, elbows, and feet everywhere. Mika and Lex jumped in and out, splashing and screaming. It had been a long time since Shirley had laughed so hard or so long. They waved at Mother Johnson sitting on a bench in the shade, just outside of the pool. Lex climbed out of the pool and walk-wiggled to kiss Mother through the chain-link fence that surrounded the pool area.

The lifeguards called for all the children to leave the pool. All the children, including Lex and Mika, groaned about what they wouldn't have to do when they got grown. They went and sat on their towels close enough to the fence that they could talk to Mother Johnson. Shirley took the free time to swim laps. Her arms cut in and out of the water, and she enjoyed the power she felt as her legs kicked and propelled her forward. The water kissed her face, and she closed her eyes. Swimming always made her feel insulated and alone with God. *Thank you, God.* She flipped her body so that she backstroked, then she did two laps on her side. She thanked God for Mother Johnson.

When the whistle blew, she swam back to the shallow end and waited for Mika and Lex to join her. The skin on their fingers and toes was wrinkled, and Lex's teeth were chattering despite the hot sun that reflected off the water. "Are you guys ready to get out?" Why even ask? She knew the answer.

"Not yet!"

They swam a while longer. "Okay, we need to go and eat so we can get snow cones." Bribes still worked.

While they were dressing—Lex kept asking when he was going to be old enough to go to the men's dressing room by himself—Mother Johnson made her way down the hill and found a picnic table for them near the car, a fountain, and the playground. By the time they were dressed, Mother had already unpacked most of the food. There was cold fried chicken, potato salad, and pickles. She had packed a chocolate cake, and there were chips, and sliced white bread. "You chirren get the paper plates and cups and the plastic forks."

Shirley brought the Styrofoam cooler, filled with cans of soda and ice, to the table.

Mother had covered the table with an oilcloth table cover. They sat on the wooden benches eating, talking, and laughing, while music from cars played in the background. Sly and the Family Stone sang "Hot Fun in the Summertime," followed by Patti La Belle singing "I Got a New Attitude."

"This is what we needed." Mother Johnson lifted her face. "A little fresh air and a change of scenery. Shucks, I got a new attitude myself!"

When the children were finished, Shirley took them for snow cones. The attendant at the stand stuffed large chunks of ice into the metal machine and ground them to tiny pieces, which he stuffed into blue-and-white striped paper cones. "What flavor you gonna have?" Mika chose cherry. The sweet, sticky red syrup pumped from a large glass bottle covered the curve of the ice, but settled to the bottom so that the base of the mound was dark red, but the crown was pale pink. Lex chose banana. "All right, little fella." The man expertly turned the cone around so that it was covered with syrup.

There was no talking, just sucking noises, as the three of them walked back to join Mother Johnson. Mother shook her head when Lex and Mika offered her a bite. "That cold ice just makes my teeth hurt." She held up her paper cup. "Thank you, but this cool water is just fine for Mother." She kissed both of the children. "You all are sweet to offer."

Shirley packed what was left of their food, stretched, then sat down. She laid her head on Mother Johnson's shoulder.

"Fun will wear you out, won't it?" Mother kissed her forehead.

Shirley nodded. When Mika and Lex finished their snow cones, they rinsed their hands in a spout that stuck out from the side of a nearby water fountain and then ran to play on the swings and sliding board.

"They could go all day, if we let them." Mother Johnson wrapped an arm around Shirley. "How you feeling, baby?"

Shirley answered by snuggling her head into the crook of Mother Johnson's neck. "Better. Tired."

Mother sipped at her water. "It's hard work putting off what you know you have to do. And it's even harder to fight against what God wants you to do."

Shirley thought to pull away from Mother Johnson, but she was too tired to lift her head. "Mother, if you knew how tired I was, you would know that I'm not fighting anybody, especially not God. I don't know what He wants me to do. If I knew it, I would do it. I'm tired of fighting, I'm tired of trying to figure it out—I'm just tired."

"Baby, just like I knew you were coming home, I know you

got some things in your life that you're not dealing with. You got it stuffed away in boxes in your closet and you got things piled on top of it all so that you don't have to look at it or think about it, but it's still there."

Shirley sighed. She didn't want to hear any of this. "Mother, it's a beautiful day. It's been a good day. Do we have to do this now?"

"There ain't no perfect day to deal with the stuff that's waiting for you. A good day is never going to come, you just have to make up your mind to deal with things and get it out of the way. It's just old stuff cluttering up your life. And the thing is, whenever you try to move forward, those boxes you got hidden just keep being more and more of a problem."

Shirley wanted to argue, but she was too weary. "Mother, I don't even understand. I don't know what it is that you think I'm hiding. Are you talking about the death of my husband, about my grieving? Because if you are, then I think I'm doing fine. It is natural and normal to grieve. I mean I have some bad days, but all in all..."

"It's more than that. You got some stuff hid away that was given to you. You didn't sign up for it or buy it, you just inherited it. But you still got to deal with it."

Shirley closed her eyes. "Mother, I really don't—"

"You've been covering all these things up for years. And I know you ain't been to see me 'cause lots of these things that hurt you, you left them here buried in my house. Least that's what you tell yourself. But, baby, those old bones are following you around and keeping you from the joy that the Lord has for you. You may have to cry while you doing it, but you got to clean out your closet.

"Your daddy been gone a long time. When he died, it must

have seemed like all the threads holding your life must have come apart. All kinds of confusion going on around you. I know you don't want to deal with all the sadness and the pain of that time, but hiding the memory of him away don't help either. You may be keeping the sadness away, but you keeping the joy away, too. 'Cause there's joy in who he was and how much he loved you. He was a smart man, and in his memory is lessons of life and love that would love you and hold you now, just like he did when you was a little girl."

Shirley pulled away and buried her face in her hands. She was tired of fighting her way through it all. "Mother, I just can't think about all of this now. I've got the children to take care of and I have to figure out where we're going…how we're going to get there. I just don't have the time or the strength for any of this."

Why wasn't where she was good enough? She and the children had made a lot of progress since Danny died. They were out of the dark place—why wasn't that enough? Shirley looked at Mother Johnson. "Why can't I just sit still, Mother?" Shirley shook her head. "I just don't think I can do any more."

Mother's eyes were full of reassurance and sympathy. "I know you feeling like you can't make it, but, baby, that's the best time. When we're weak, that's when God shows up strong. You're not fighting through this by yourself. There is more for you than those that be against you. Shirley, you remember what I'm telling you. You're never alone."

TWENTY-EIGHT

Shirley wiped sleep from her eyes. The house was quiet. It was even too early for Mother Johnson to be stirring. There was just the faintest touch of yellow light appearing at the edge of the fading night blue sky. Shirley turned to look back at her pillow. She didn't know what woke her. What she should be doing was sleeping, catching every wink she could. It was too late, though. The early light of day had her. She swung her legs out of bed.

You're never alone. She knew Mother Johnson meant well. People always meant well. It was easy for them to say that, to try to calm her with platitudes. *You're never alone.* Funny, but when she had to pay the bills, no one else was around that she could see. When the kids were sick or worried, and she had to comfort them, there didn't seem to be anyone else around. When she had to make decisions, there definitely was no one around that she could see except her.

It's just too much. The muscles in the back of her neck and her shoulders were so tight. Shirley rotated her neck to try to loosen them. Maybe what she needed was to get out of the room, to steal out onto the porch while things were still quiet, while she could still get away with stepping outside in her robe. A tender dawn breeze might soothe her.

Shirley tiptoed through the house, which was quiet except for the ticking of a clock, and eased the front door open. She stepped outside and closed her eyes. *You're never alone, baby.* If only that were true.

She opened her eyes to see, or maybe to feel, the same presence that she'd felt with her in the jail cell in Tuscaloosa. She could hear herself breathing. Everything was so quiet. It was difficult to comprehend what she saw. There were no wings, no halos, just the suggestion of an illuminated form. What held her in place was the feeling, mostly. It made no sense. She should be running, but instead she felt tension and fear draining from her.

She could hear Mother Johnson's voice comforting her. *There are more for us than those that be against us.* Then, like in the cell, she could feel the presence reassuring her.

"Don't be afraid. You are not alone."

Shirley breathed deeply and then closed her eyes.

"God hears you. You have a great journey ahead of you, but you are not alone."

When she opened her eyes, the sweet peace was still with her, but the illuminated presence seemed to be gone. Shirley touched her hands to her face, maybe to reassure herself that at least she was real.

She was not going to talk about it. This was not a sitcom, it was real life. There was no way she would have been able to explain it to anyone…she couldn't even explain it to herself. Shirley busied herself setting the table for the lunch that she and Mother Johnson were about to share. The kids were having a makeshift picnic out back, so it was just the two of them.

Mother Johnson always seemed to know everything—or to be able to fish the truth out of people. This, Shirley determined, she wasn't about to tell. Angels on the front porch? Not even Mother was going to go for that one. There was no way she was going to tell her.

"What's on your mind, baby?"

Shirley looked up to see Mother Johnson staring at her. Her laugh sounded fake, even to her. "Oh, nothing, Mother. You know." Shirley folded a frayed yellow napkin and laid it on the table.

"You sure?"

Mother hadn't moved. Shirley rolled her shoulders. She was not a little kid. She didn't have to tell Mother Johnson everything. She was not about to tell her—

"You look like you saw a ghost."

Mother was fishing, but Shirley was not about to let herself get hooked.

"Whatever it is, you know we're in each other's lives to help each other."

There was no way she could tell Mother about what she saw this morning.

"You know there's nothing you can't tell me, baby." Mother Johnson tilted her head. "Nothing."

Before she knew it, Shirley swallowed the bait. She was sitting at the table spilling all of what she never intended to tell to Mother.

Mother Johnson nodded her head. "Sounds like a heavenly visit to me."

"Mother, things like this just don't happen. I'm just under

too much pressure, too much stress." Shirley picked at the frayed ends of the napkin she still held in her hands. "It made me feel better, but it was probably just like the Sheri thing...just my mind trying to help me cope."

Mother Johnson's smile was full of love and her eyes sparkled with wisdom. "That may be so. But if God sent angels to David, to Elijah, to Mary, to Peter, and to Paul, why would you think He wouldn't send one to speak with you?" She laid a warm hand on top of Shirley's. "I believe that God is still at work today, revealing Himself to us just like in the days of old. Most of us are just afraid to admit it. Afraid that people will call us crazy." She squeezed Shirley's hand. "But isn't it something that the visit gave you just a little strength, just a little courage to go on." Mother nodded again. "I feel like you got something ahead of you, and God wants you to know that He is with you."

Shirley was startled. She hadn't told Mother what the presence had said. How could she have known...? "That's exactly what the angel said! I mean what the man said...what my mind said!"

"God wants the best for you. Maybe He sent a word a long time ago. Maybe your angel is just now getting to you to deliver the word, just like Daniel. Maybe your angel's been fighting his way to you all this time...like that story we talked about in the prayer house." Mother Johnson stared so deeply into her eyes that Shirley felt she was touching her soul. "God's trying to get you to the best. Don't be satisfied where you are, don't miss the best that He has for you."

Mother rose from the table and walked to the stove to fill the kettle. When it was full, she walked back to the table and stood behind Shirley's chair. "You know what, baby?" Mother

Johnson's hands rubbed her back. "You got a lot ahead of you, but you got a lot blocking your progress. When I think about it, it's almost like you got a baby you're about to deliver. In my mind, I see your stomach just big and fat and about to bust for having that baby. But you got these other things clogging you up and blocking the baby's path. This other stuff is old and dead, but you got to get it out of the way—it's got to be delivered for the new baby to get through. You may not feel like you got time or strength, but you got to do it anyhow. And you can do it, because you know you're never alone. You know that. Never alone."

Mother rubbed the back of Shirley's neck, and she laid her head back on Mother's arm. Why couldn't they just stop here? Why wasn't this enough? Why did Mother, why did it seem *everyone* wanted to push her forward? Shirley couldn't breathe.

"You have to finish the journey that you started."

"Mother, I don't know what you mean."

"Have you been to see your mother in all this time? Since your daddy died? Since your mother's breakdown?"

Shirley squeezed her eyes shut. She could hear the frustration in her own voice. "Mother Johnson, what's the point? What good is it going to do to dig up the past? She doesn't even know me. She wouldn't know me. What am I supposed to do? Why can't I just move on?"

"All of us are delivered into this world by our mothers. They are the angels that announce who we are in this world. Unless we find a way to make peace with who we are together—maybe not change it, but just make peace with it— we never get to be the people God intends for us to be. It don't matter whether we like it or not, it's just how it is."

Shirley turned her body so her face was buried in Mother

Johnson's bosom. "But when I think about it—when I think about going back, I feel like I'm going to drown, like I'm never going to get out." She was stammering. It was hard to force the words from her mouth. "It's not that I don't love her. I'm just trying to save my own life. I'm trying to hold on to my own sanity. I'm trying to keep my head above water."

"I will never forget that day you was going to the prom with Tony and that special delivery letter come to the house. I was hoping it was from your mama." Shirley could hear Mother's voice rumbling in her chest. "But it was from your uncles. Just more hard news for you, telling you they was in jail. Caught up in some mess that might mean they'll be in jail for the rest of they lives…just because they was freedom fighters…trying to make sure that we could walk around free. Now they in jail."

Mother began to pat Shirley on the back. Her voice sounded as though she was wrestling with anger, with frustration. "You know them men, your uncles. Good men! You know they ain't murdered nobody, and one day it's gone be proved. But, honey, what I remember most about that day was them telling you in that letter that they loved you. I remember the look on your face. It had been a while since I had seen something crack through, but your uncles got to you."

Shirley could hear calm ebbing into Mother Johnson's voice. "Then I remember what they told you. That you got to go home. That if *they* never saw you again, you had to get to your mama and try to make it right." Mother Johnson stroked her hair, and Shirley could feel the calm trying to spread to her. "I know it's got to be hard, baby. But you can't save your life and not try to save hers. When the Lord saves us, we got the responsibility to at least try to go back and save those that He has put in our lives—no matter how scary it is. It ain't no promise that they are going to accept the peace you try to bring them. They got the choice, but we still have to try.

"It's not easy, baby. We got to be willing to give up our own life sometimes." Mother lifted her face. Shirley knew that Mother wanted to look into her eyes, but she would not open them.

"You prayed for me, baby. Nobody thought it would do any good. They thought I was gone and dead. But God specializes in bringing things back from the dead, and He used you to do it. He just needs one soul down here that is willing to try." Shirley could feel one of Mother's hands cupping her face. "Maybe your mama won't get up, maybe it's too late, or maybe she won't come back to life, but don't let it be because you didn't pray or because you didn't try."

Tears squeezed from the corners of Shirley's eyes. She didn't want to go back to Illinois. There didn't seem to be anything to go back to but painful memories—or even more hurt.

Mother's voice was soothing, but determined. "You got a journey before you, Shirley. And I believe you come here for strength, just like Elijah when he went to stay with the poor widow. That widow shared with Elijah just the little bit that she had to strengthen him and encourage him. You are a child of promise, Shirley. The Lord knew you before you were formed in your mama's womb." Shirley wrapped fists in Mother Johnson's apron.

"And just like the Lord sent a divine messenger to Elijah, I believe He sent one to you, Shirley, to encourage you and to let you know that it's time to finish your journey. Sometimes life has hurt us so bad, we figure we'll just hide out. We'll be satisfied with where we are or satisfied with less. We just so happy to be out of the valley. We give up thinking about ever getting to the mountaintop. We just so happy to be out of complete darkness, we settle for the shadows. But the Lord never meant for you to stay in the shadows. It's okay to travel through grief and sadness, but we not supposed to move in and stay."

Mother pressed a kiss to Shirley's forehead. "When you was just a little girl, the Lord sent you to me to prop you up. Now you back for just a little strength for your journey, just a little rest. You got to finish the work ahead of you—you got to get things cleaned up so you can do and be all that the Lord intended for you before this world was ever formed. It's some joy coming to you, baby. Your angel just delivered the word. It's a mountaintop waiting for you. You won't find joy hiding in the shadows."

Shirley put her arms around Mother Johnson and wept.

TWENTY-NINE

*T*ony lifted Lex into the air and slung him over his shoulder. "You sure you know how to bowl, man? You sure if I have you on my team that we're going to beat the girls?"

Lex, upside down, snorted and chortled. In the past couple of weeks, he and Tony had become a potent team dedicated to symbolically demolishing the threat to male domination. That threat was represented—at least in Tyler, Texas—by Shirley and Mika. So far, the dynamic and manly duo was being soundly thrashed. The enemies had met on the fields of putt-putt golf and water volleyball. Now they were facing off at Green Acres Bowling in South Tyler, not far from the GE plant.

There was a war going on, but for Shirley it was good to play, to have a moment away from the things that troubled her. During their outings, she didn't worry about angels or journeys. "Baby, rest and joy are part of the journey, too," Mother Johnson told her. Shirley surrendered herself to the mission at hand—teaching the men who really kept the world tilted on its axis!

"We can't let them beat us again, man. We won't be able to show our faces around here. The brothers of the world are counting on us."

Shirley and Mika just laughed. There was no reason to comment. Those who can't, talk. Those who can, do.

Tony worked hard to win, but Mika and Lex spent more time playing pinball games and eating fries. With only half teams, Shirley and Tony eventually called the contest a draw. They drank lemonade to salute their friendship and sat on a bench where they could watch the kids play.

The lemonade was a little too sour for Shirley's taste. She looked up to see Tony smiling at her frown. *"That's* a face I would expect to see in *Essence* magazine."

"Right, Tony." She smiled at him and then looked back at the kids. It had been a while since she had felt so peaceful, since there had felt like nothing was missing. She thought about telling him, but decided it wasn't a *friend-type* thing to say. "The kids have been having a good time." That seemed like a reasonable compromise.

He nodded, but didn't say anything. He wasn't helping.

"Tony, I've been thinking about that night, you know when you came by Mother Johnson's. It's funny, but that meant so much to me."

"It's no big deal. Why wouldn't I come by to see a friend?"

What did *that* mean? "Oh, I know. Right. But what I meant was that when you said that, about still thinking about what happened to me at the movies all those years ago. I don't know…it touched me." Was she saying too much or sounding stupid?

"You mean you're glad that I'm still messed up about it," he teased.

"What I mean is, not that I'm happy that you're angry, but

it's nice to know that you've been thinking about me all these years. And that it was on your mind...you know, even as a kid, to protect me."

He nodded at her. "We're friends. Nothing will ever change that."

She felt like he had pushed her face. Her cheeks felt like they were burning. *Why, what difference does this make? I'm not trying to date him. We're friends...just having a friendly conversation.* "Yes, we're friends."

"Special friends," he said, and squeezed one of her hands. Shirley was confused and used Mika and Lex's pinball game as a way to extract herself from the conversation.

Dating language was too hard to understand. No one taught it in school, or if they had, she must have been absent that day. Friends, *special friends*—what did that mean?

She loved men, but *relationships* always unnerved her. Especially that weird, unmapped area between friends-special friends-boyfriend-lover-husband. Shirley was good at the extremes, but the middle confused her.

Mika and Lex were standing together at the Ms. Pac-Man machine, and she joined them. Their love and friendship were safe, they were uncomplicated—they spoke the same language, and the dynamics were pretty much constant.

Shirley watched the Ms. Pac-Man character running across the board, running from monsters and trying to gobble fruit that gave her power as she ran.

"Turn and get them, now, Mika!" Lex yelled when Mika's character was full and energized. But Mika, in her excitement, fumbled the controls and, just when she was about to pursue the monsters, her character lost its power and was pursued again instead.

Shirley shook her head. Why pay to play a game that she could live in real life instead?

Mother was gliding when Tony dropped them off at the gate. "The kids are tired," Shirley had told him, when she saw he was about to park.

"You have a good night, Tony." Mother waved as he drove away. Mika, holding onto Shirley's hand, stumbled up the steps. Lex slept with his arm around her neck. Mother started to rise. "You need some help, baby?"

Shirley shook her head and whispered. "No, Mother, don't you move. You've done enough. Let me get them in bed and then I'll come back out. I think I'm going to try my hand at gliding…bowling's not my thing."

When she came back outside, pieces of the moon could be seen through the branches of the trees. Mother was humming "He's Sweet I Know." She paused. "You take it easy gliding now. It can be pretty tricky for first timers."

Shirley sat in Mildred's glider and began to keep rhythm with Mother Johnson. "It's not so hard. It must be in the blood."

They rocked and watched the moon. "Mother, how long is long enough before a woman starts to date or talk, you know, again…after, you know."

"Oh, I don't know. I don't know that it's written in any book or anything." Mother slowed her rocking. "Some reason you asking? You and Tony…"

"No, Mother, I just wondered, that's all. Tony and I are just…special friends."

"Well, I guess I just figure it depends on the person—I

guess the person is ready when she's able to talk."

"What do you mean by talk?"

"Well, you know death is hard on all of us. But it's even harder when there are things between a couple that never get aired out...just like between family members. Once you get those things aired out, well then it seems like the pathway is clear."

"Danny..." She was drifting, and it was difficult to speak. "Danny, don't be a hero, okay?"

He continued to play, and laughed within the mood of his accompaniment. "What else can I be, baby? I've pretty much messed up everything else I've tried to be...I'm not going to get any medals for fatherhood or being a husband." He chuckled again. "Maybe I can get this one thing right." The guitar strings squeaked softly as he pressed and fingered them.

"Mother?"

"Yes, baby?"

"I don't talk much about Danny. You know—I loved him and... Sometimes I think it's because I'm trying to protect him and protect his memory. But sometimes I think I'm trying to protect myself. I don't want to hurt about it anymore, and I guess...oh, I don't know, Mother. Why does life have to be so complicated?" She was glad that the darkness hid most of her face.

"You don't owe too much to anybody, and you don't have to talk about anything you don't want to share. But keeping it bottled up is not the way to keep it from hurting. What I learned from life was that when I tried to keep stuff that hurt me from getting out, it kept me churned up on the inside."

Shirley rocked a while longer. "Danny was a good man. He made me laugh and he loved the kids. When I needed him, when I cried, he was there." Shirley could see him. She could smell him. "We were just like everybody else, I guess. We had some hard times. And I could never understand it—I thought about it over and over until I realized I was just never going to figure it out. I just could never figure out why Danny died just as we, just when we…when he finally trusted me. Just when he started to pray, then he's gone." Shirley looked away from the moon and into the dark bushes.

Shirley could hear sympathy in Mother's voice. "It's a hard thing, ain't it? I know, in my soul, that we don't understand death. We all feel like if we could have had one more day, or one more time to say good-bye, then we would be fine. The truth is, it's never a good day to lose someone you love."

Shirley forced herself to say things she had kept hidden away. "Sometimes he drank too much." She was minimizing, but she knew that Mother would know. "And he wasn't always faithful. But I stayed. I loved him. I kept thinking, *Someday.*" Shirley's voice quieted. "When someday came, he wasn't with me. I wonder, sometimes, what it was about. Why I stayed, and if it was worth it."

"You said that he had just started praying when the Lord took him?"

"Well, he believed in God—kind of, but…"

"But you said things changed before he died?"

"Danny was praying and talking to the chaplain."

"You know, baby, when I hear you talk, I can hear in your voice that you loved Danny. Your children loved him."

"Yes, ma'am."

"Just the time that we have with someone, even if it's just a minute, that's a gift from God. It is. If they bring any good into our lives, that's a gift from God." Shirley nodded and Mother

Johnson continued. "And, if he learned to know God through knowing you, ain't that a blessing, too?"

"Yes, ma'am. It is."

"I wouldn't ask you this if I didn't know you, if you didn't know that I loved you. If you had to make a choice right now…if you could choose between losing him, but knowing that Danny found his way to God, or having him alive but lost to God, which would you choose?"

Shirley looked at Mother Johnson. "I don't think I should have to choose, Mother. Other people live and never have to choose."

Mother laid her hand on Shirley's hand. "Baby, God had to make the choice for us. He let His only Son die so that we could find our way home to Him. You know that was a hard choice, but that's what God did. That's love. We have to trust God, that He knows what's best. And the same gift that God gave to the Lord Jesus Christ, He also gave to Danny. If Danny was willing to believe and to accept Jesus as Lord, God promised to make Danny one of His sons and to resurrect him just like He resurrected Jesus.

"You may not answer me now, but I know which choice you would have made. The Lord knew which choice you would make. The only choice that says love." Mother lifted her hand and then folded it back across her lap. "If you knew that the love you gave Danny would save him, even though it would cause you this pain, you would have loved him anyway. The Lord knew you would say yes. He knew that you were the one to send into Danny's life."

Mother Johnson began to hum. It was an old spiritual— "We'll Understand It Better By and By." When she began to speak again, her voice was full of strength as well as tears. "I'm an old woman. Sometimes on this life journey we lose things that are precious to us. I've lost some things that brought me to my knees. But I can tell you; I never lost anything that the Lord didn't somehow open to me something better, something that made me better. I know the widow's cry because I've cried it myself. I also know that the Lord will come and sit with you, because He sat with me. Some days, the only way I could make it was to read His Word. I read it and prayed it so much, I can quote it by heart." Mother spoke, and Shirley could hear the mood of the hymn still ringing in her voice. She recognized the Scripture that Mother Johnson quoted.

"'Do not fear, for you will not be ashamed;

Nor be disgraced, for you will not be put to shame;

For you will forget the shame of your youth,

And will not remember the reproach of your widowhood anymore.'"

Mother Johnson moved back and forth in her glider. "I held on to that word. I knew the Lord was speaking to me, right to me. He told me to trust Him that He was real and to put my hope in Him. Sometimes I hurt so bad—" it sounded as though Mother was crying— "it was like I had a big old wound in my side that everyone could see. The Lord told me not to be ashamed of my tears, that my heartbreak wasn't going to last forever. That someday my pain would just be a memory."

The Scriptures tumbled from Mother's lips again.

"'For your Maker is your husband,

The LORD of hosts is His name;

And your Redeemer is the Holy One of Israel;

He is called the God of the whole earth.'"

Mother Johnson leaned forward in her rocker. "It was lonely—I felt unsafe and uncovered. I was alone with my daughters. There was just me it seemed, but the Lord put His arm around me and told me that He was there. I had so much leftover love; I didn't know what to do with it. The Lord said to give it to Him. He was my husband and my protector. Because I trusted in Him, He wasn't going to leave me, the God of the whole universe was going to stand with me."

"'For the LORD has called you
Like a woman forsaken and grieved in spirit,
Like a youthful wife when you were refused,'
Says your God."

"Those words told me that God knew how deep my pain went. That my husband's death didn't just make me feel lonely; it made me feel rejected and unloved. I wasn't a rejected woman, God was asking for my hand."

"'For a mere moment I have forsaken you,
But with great mercies I will gather you.
With a little wrath I hid My face from you for a moment;
But with everlasting kindness I will have mercy on you,'
Says the LORD, your Redeemer."

Mother breathed deeply. "I know these Scriptures because I had to bury them in my heart. They were what kept me going. Baby, I have lived a long time. I've had a whole lot of regular, human people do me wrong. I can count the number of apologies on my one hand. People would rather fight you and kill you than admit that they hurt you. They not willing to humble themselves.

"But here was God of the whole universe. I'm telling you, girl—even now it gets me right in my stomach. Here was God Almighty telling me He knew He had hurt me. God don't have to apologize to nobody, but God puts His heart in the hand of every widow. He said to me, I know I hurt you, Mavis Johnson.

I'm God all by Myself, but I want you to know that your God know the pain of a widow and the pain of a woman without children, and I promise to make it up to you. And it ain't a promise for one day, the Good Lord says it's for everlasting."

Mother Johnson touched the hem of her apron to her face as though she was dabbing away tears. "The Lord made me a promise, and He ain't failed me yet. No sir. He ain't failed me yet."

Shirley kneeled next to her bed and, with her Bible turned to Isaiah 54, she began to read quietly to herself and to God. "'Sing, O barren, thou that didst not bear; break forth into singing, and cry aloud, thou that didst not travail with child: for more are the children of the desolate than the children of the married wife, saith the LORD.'" She skipped to the fourth verse. "'Fear not; for thou shalt not be ashamed: neither be thou confounded; for thou shalt not be put to shame: for thou shalt forget the shame of thy youth, and shalt not remember the reproach of thy widowhood any more. For thy Maker is thine husband; the LORD of hosts is his name; and thy Redeemer the Holy One of Israel; The God of the whole earth shall he be called.'"

She set her Bible on the nightstand. "God, I'm trying to believe You. God, help my unbelief. It hurts, God. I don't know how I'm supposed to sing in the middle of all this. If You hear me, if You're still listening to me—it still hurts. I'm trying to find joy, but I'm not even sure I know what it looks like anymore. I'm afraid to hope for joy in my life again.

"And I'm afraid, God. I don't even know, yet, what it means that You'll be my husband.

"God, I don't know if I want another husband—even You. Why should I want to love again? How do I know that if I love somebody, if I open my heart, how do I know that he won't die, too?"

The Scripture she had just read came to her mind, as though someone was speaking to her heart. *"Fear not; for thou shalt not be ashamed: neither be thou confounded; for thou shalt not be put to shame: for thou shalt forget the shame of thy youth, and shalt not remember the reproach of thy widowhood any more. For thy Maker is thine husband; the* LORD *of hosts is his name; and thy Redeemer the Holy One of Israel; The God of the whole earth shall he be called."*

Shirley crawled into bed and sang the song she had been singing since she was a child. It was the song she had made up to protect her when she was afraid.

Rock me, baby Jesus,
Hold me, baby Jesus,
Love me, baby Jesus,
So I won't be afraid.

THIRTY

❧

Mother Johnson and Ma Dear were in their usual places. The children, within earshot, played a game on the side porch. When Shirley stepped out the front door, Ma Dear looked smug.

Shirley looked at Mother and did her best to ignore the other older woman. "So, Mother, you're sure you don't mind my leaving?"

"Shirley, you go have a good time, baby. I'm the one that's getting the best of this bargain. You go on now, and don't leave that boy waiting."

"Boy?" Ma Dear looked like the cat. Shirley, dressed in a canary yellow jersey and baseball cap, was appropriately attired. "Did you say *boy*, Mother?" Ma Dear's eyebrows moved up and down.

Mother Johnson shook her head as if to say *it's just no use* and didn't answer.

Ma Dear was not to be denied any information, especially information about a man. "Are my loved ones holding back on me? I remember hearing a lot of stuff—*Oh, Ma Dear* this, and *Oh, Ma Dear* that. Well, let me see now."

Shirley shifted her weight from foot to foot. Here it came.

"Let me see if I can figure out who this mystery *boy*—this mystery *date* might be."

Shirley rolled her eyes and began to inch her way down the steps. If she moved too quickly, Ma Dear was sure to pounce.

"Nobody's giving up any information, so I guess that the MBI was right after all! You going to meet Tony Taylor, ain't you?" Ma Dear's smile was smug. *I told you so* was written all over her face.

Shirley shrugged and put on her sunglasses. "We're just friends, Ma Dear. We've been friends just about all our lives. We're not going anyplace special. We're going to Burger King. Does that sound like a romantic date to you? We're friends, just special friends."

"Special friends!" Ma Dear lifted an eyebrow. "You know a lot of things have changed in the eighties. People are dressing like they been thrown away on purpose. Movie stars is presidents. Women are wearing shoulder pads bigger than a football player's. Hair is standing up in the air and looking crazy, and ain't no telling what color it's gone be from day to day. But some things don't never change. There was code language when we was girls." She nodded at Mother Johnson and waved a plump hand. "And it's still code language now. You can fool some of the people all the time. You can fool all the people some of the time. But you ain't woke up early enough in the morning yet to fool Ma Dear. I know a wedding is coming. I'm feeling it in my bones. Every time I pass a flower shop, I get a little hitch in my side!"

Mother Johnson laughed. "Ma Dear, if you get any louder you gone wake the dead!"

"Well, if they get up, they better be dressing for a wedding!

I knew it! You can't fool Ma Dear!"

Shirley continued edging toward her car.

Ma Dear furrowed her brow and pointed at Shirley. "You can try to slide on off if you want to, Missy, but you know Ma Dear is right. Somebody's gone get married!"

Shirley got in her car, started the engine, and began to roll away. She waved at Mother and Ma Dear. Mother laughed. Ma Dear stood up and kept talking. "You and that boy ain't fooling nobody. You hear me? And going to Burger King, that don't mean nothing. It just show that you at the 'I like you but I'm trying not to be too obvious 'cause I'm not sure you like me' stage. We did the same old thang years ago. Ma Dear wasn't born yesterday. I'm gone call the preacher!"

Shirley stared at her image in the front window of the Burger King. Tony had called. He wanted to see her. *Marriage?* If Ma Dear was waiting on her to marry, she was going to be waiting a long time.

"I like that cap." Tony slid into the booth seat across from her. "Am I late?"

Shirley shrugged. "Like I would know? When have you ever seen me wear a watch?"

Tony looked at the menu board. "Anything look good?"

"Very funny." Shirley studied Tony's profile. Burger King was a funny choice, a funny place to meet. "Did you have a taste for a Whopper or something?"

Tony looked flustered. "Yeah." He shrugged. "Burger King, Wendy's, McDonald's, whatever." Tony regained his composure and looked back at the menu board, then at Shirley. "You want to go someplace else?"

Shirley shook her head. "I came because you called me, right?"

Tony jumped to his feet. "Come on, let's eat." He ordered enough food for two men. "You want a pie? A shake?" He carried the tray back to the table, unpacked the food, and waded in. Tony ate two Whoppers with cheese, his fries, her fries, and finished his large drink.

"So, Tony, what's—?"

"Wait just a minute." He almost sprinted to the counter for a drink.

"Tony, what is the matter with you?" she asked as he slid back into the booth.

"I thought we needed to talk."

Shirley's stomach clutched. She wasn't sure she wanted to have this conversation. She wasn't sure she *didn't* want to have this conversation.

"The other night at the bowling alley. Well…"

"You know what, Tony, this is ridiculous. What are you trying to say? What are we trying to say? What am *I* trying to say, for that matter?"

"When we got to Mother Johnson's house, I just kind of got the feeling… Look, Shirley, we've been friends for a long time. Well, a long time minus some years, but I guess they count."

Shirley pumped her straw up and down in her drink. "Tony, you told me already, remember? We're special friends." She smiled brightly.

Tony sat his drink to the side. "You're not going to make this easy, are you?"

"Make what easy? We already know how to be friends."

"Look, Shirley, the last thing I need—or the last thing I thought I wanted was to get involved with somebody."

We're special friends. She could hear the words even now. "Are you involved with somebody?"

"Come on, Shirley, okay? I'm sorry. You scared me. I got scared, all right?"

She wanted to keep going. *Scared of what? Why?* But he was her friend, and she could see that he was struggling. She knew the feeling. So, instead, she took a step too. "Look, Tony, I don't know what we're doing, either. I feel something; I don't know what it is. I mean, I know, but I don't know. And I don't know if we…I don't know anything." Shirley looked around the room. She would never see Burger King the same.

Tony pressed a napkin to his brow. "I've got a business, and like I told you the first day, I keep to myself, pretty much. We're just friends. That's what I've been trying to tell myself since you got here. But if we're friends, why am I scared? Why do I feel like running?"

Burger King. They were talking about their lives in the middle of Burger King. "Tony, I'm not trying to do anything to you. I'm not trying to trap you."

"I know. But I know how women are."

Shirley felt her last good nerve work. One eye began to twitch. "You know what, Tony? Maybe you're having this con-versation with the wrong *special friend.* Because the truth is, you don't know me or how I am. You knew me as a girl, but you don't know me well enough to lump me in with all the other females that you've encountered."

Tony leaned back in his seat and smiled. "You've said spe-cial friend about twenty times since we got here. Can we start over? I can see I'm not doing to well here."

Shirley wasn't ready to smile. Yet. "Look, Tony, whatever we're talking about is hard enough without us bringing other people into it and acting like we know each other because we've been disappointed or hurt by other people. Whatever somebody did to you, it wasn't me. And if you think you're the only person who ever got hurt or used, then you're kidding yourself. You just don't know." Shirley looked out the front window. *I told You I hate this relationship stuff, God. I told You I didn't want to do this.*

"Fair enough. Can we start over?"

Shirley looked at him. "Where do you want to start from?"

Tony's smile was less than self-assured. "Well, I would start from the first night, but the moon cookies are too hard to get. Can we start from the bowling alley?"

She smiled. "Okay. But instead of the bowling alley, can we go sit in the park? This booth is wearing me out."

They pulled their cars into the parking lot side by side, then went to sit on a bench.

Tony let out a deep sigh. "I've been trying to figure this out since you got here."

"Maybe we're both trying to do too much figuring."

"Yeah, but it's practical that we have questions. That we figure out where each one of us stands."

He was talking like a man, thinking like a man. Why did they always have to do that? "Why does that matter, Tony? Why can't we just take it like it comes? Why can't we just see where it all takes us? Because maybe we're going somewhere, or maybe we'll just stay friends. It doesn't have to be that complicated."

He frowned.

"What, Tony? What does that look mean?"

"It means…it means that…look, Shirley, I don't want to get hurt, okay? I don't want to get all involved with you and the kids, and then you look up one day and say 'I'm off to California,' or 'I'm going to see Sheri.'" He clamped his mouth shut and folded his arms. He turned his head toward her. "What I want to know is what you want from me?"

God, I told You I hate this stuff! "How do I know, Tony? Do I want to stay in Tyler for the rest of my life? Right now, I don't think so. But that could change. And I don't know where that Sheri thing came from. How do I know where I'm going to be ten years from now?"

He sat forward, put his elbows on his knees, and his face in his hands. "This is why I'm scared, Shirley. I know you don't want to hear it, but I've been through this before. It feels like déjà vu. I've been through this before with other women, and I've seen it before with you. You're looking for something; I can see it in your eyes. It's the same look you had when you were saving that money. I don't want to get caught in your wake again."

Shirley shook her head. *Is this how it's supposed to feel? What is good about this?*

"I can see myself loving your kids. I can see us having something real. But I need you to make peace with whatever it is that I still see in your eyes."

Shirley drove from the park wondering why she had ever agreed to meet Tony. It was better…it would have been better to leave it as it was. And even worse, everyone knew. Ma Dear and Mother were watching. It was all going to blow up in her face. She was going to look like a fool.

Fear not; for thou shalt not be ashamed.

God, I don't know how to do this. I don't know how to have a relationship and trust it to You. I don't even know if we're having a relationship.

Fear not; for thou shalt not be ashamed.

"Okay." She took a deep breath, then pulled into the parking lot of Jack's grocery store.

Peck, peck, peck.

The sound startled Ma Dear and Mother Johnson, previously deep in conversation. They both looked toward the front gate. Mildred rapped at the front gate with the ring on her finger.

Ma Dear frowned openly at the woman. "Oh, shoot!" Her whisper was loud enough to be heard. "Here's the end to a perfectly good afternoon."

Mother Johnson patted Ma Dear's hand. "Behave, Ma Dear."

"Humph!"

Mother waved, smiled, and raised her voice in Mildred's direction. "Hey, there, Mildred. Come on up. Your chair's here, free and waiting on you. We were just hoping you would come by."

Ma Dear rolled her eyes and snorted just loud enough for Mother Johnson to hear. "We? I know it wasn't too long ago I was just saying the opposite. Look at her with that starched collar. It's as stiff as she is. "

Mother ignored Ma Dear and waved Mildred toward the empty seat. "Come on up."

Mildred shrugged and stayed lodged outside the gate. She nodded her head in Mother's direction. "I hate to bother you, but could you come down so I can talk to you alone for a minute?" She eyed Ma Dear.

Ma Dear pursed her lips. "Oh boy, here we go. Another episode for the Phil Donahue show—Tired Old Women Who Just Won't Go Away!"

Mother Johnson kept smiling in Mildred's direction while she whispered to Ma Dear. "You behave, you hear me, girl. You are about to lose your seat—not to mention that the sweet ice tea supply is drying up real quick." Mother waved her hand and started to rise. "Hold on, Mildred, I'm coming."

When Mother Johnson got to the gate she could see that Mildred's eyes were red-rimmed and her cheeks were splotchy. Mother leaned close. "What's wrong, Mildred?"

"Oh, Mother Johnson, I didn't want to come here, but I didn't know who else to talk to. I'm about at the end of my rope." A tear fell from the corner of her eye and she swept it away with her hand, as though she didn't want anyone to see. "I came here to get away from all of this. It's Windy." Mildred pulled a small white handkerchief from her pocket and dabbed at her eyes. She looked up at Ma Dear and then back at Mother Johnson. "I shouldn't have come."

Mother Johnson nodded. "You came to just the right place. Whatever is going on, what you need is prayer. And me and my friend sitting up there, we are some prayer warriors. Oh, honey, you are at the right place."

Mildred's voice quavered. "I just think it might be too late, Mother Johnson."

Mother Johnson pushed the gate open. "Now, you come on in here, Mildred." She linked arms with her and turned Mildred toward the steps. Mildred looked up at Ma Dear and wouldn't budge. Mother tugged at her arm. "I know you and

Ma Dear here have been having a good time having this little feud, but if what's going on is as serious as I think it is, you can't afford to be picking and choosing who you want to have in the battle. Come on here, girl, and let's get this worked out."

Mildred wept quietly and followed Mother Johnson up the steps.

THIRTY-ONE

a Dear crossed her legs and puffed up like a spoiled, angry cat when Mother approached the steps with Mildred. She huffed and looked away from the two women, but Mother could tell that Mildred's tears were more than Ma Dear had expected.

"Mildred, you know my good friend, Ma Dear. The two of us been friends for years." Mildred looked toward the roof over the porch. "Ma Dear, you know Mildred." Ma Dear looked toward the side of the house.

Mika and Lex came around the front of the house chasing a red, white, and blue plastic ball.

"I know," Mother said, "the two of you don't sit horses. I don't know why, since neither one of you knows the other one. But we got work to do here—the *Lord's* work. And it seems to me you two grown women should be able to get along at least as well as those two children." Mother unlinked her arm from Mildred's. "But if it ain't important to you, I got things I can be doing inside the house."

Mildred moaned and let out a loud wail. Mika and Lex

stopped running and stared. "What's wrong, Mother?" Mika asked.

Ma Dear stood up, smiled, and waved her hand. "Ain't nothing going on, just some old ladies being silly."

Mildred started fanning with the handkerchief and collapsed into the chair. Mika and Lex were frozen. They looked from Mother Johnson to Ma Dear. Ma Dear waved them around the side. "You all get your ball now, and keep on playing. Nothing going on up here that you need to worry about. Miss Mildred just got a little hot under the collar. You all go on and play." Ma Dear wiped her brow when the children were gone. "Lord, have mercy!" She slumped into her glider.

Mother was all business. "All right, now. What is going on?"

Mildred looked at Mother, then at Ma Dear. Finally, she looked back at Mother Johnson and started to cry. "It's my granddaughter, Windy, and Jack. The two of them started off on the wrong foot when she got here. Something happened at the store, and…well…things have been strained between the two of them. Well, Jack said she can't stay at his house eating up his food and taking up room in his house and not contribute. So she got a little part-time job down at the store. I mean, it wasn't the best solution, but it was close and it was convenient."

Mildred blew her nose with her handkerchief. "I thought to myself, well it could be worse, you know. I thought to myself, 'If Windy could just stay out of Jack's way, it could at least work out until she has the baby.'"

Mildred looked earnestly at Mother Johnson. "Windy and I have been having some good conversations lately—she even came to church with me last Sunday. Then yesterday at work…" Mildred covered her face. "Everything exploded. Jack got to yelling at her about something—I still don't know what. But before you know it, he said she was chucking cans of green beans at him. One of them caught him in the shoulder, and one bounced up and hit him on his bad knee."

Mildred sat up and looked at Mother Johnson and Ma Dear. "I tried to talk to her and reason with her, to get her to apologize. She wasn't even the girl that I have come to know. She was like a wild woman, and she started yelling that she wasn't going to let any man push her around. No matter who he was."

Mildred reached out for Mother Johnson's hand. "Well, that was the last straw for Jack. He said he wants her out of his house and out of his store. I tried to talk to him, to remind him that she was pregnant and needs our help." Mildred began to sob. "He told me she had three days to go and he told me that it might be good for some other people to be looking for a place of their own, too." Mildred cried so hard that she couldn't catch her breath. "What am I going to do, Mother? What are *we* going to do?"

Ma Dear appeared to be speechless. She looked at Mother, at Mildred, then back at Mother. "Well, do tell," she said finally.

Mother Johnson scratched her head. "I think this is a little more than I can figure out." She dropped her head.

Ma Dear was incredulous. "What do you mean, Mother? Of course, the only thing to do is pray. We got to pray. It's Jesus Time!"

"You think so?" Mother Johnson thanked God in her heart—there was nothing parted that God couldn't mend. She wouldn't lift her head because she didn't want the two women to see her smile. "You think so?"

Ma Dear was indignant. "I *know* so. This woman needs

help, Mother. This ain't no time for doubt. I'm surprised at you! What she needs, what her family needs, is a united prayer—an unexpected prayer." Ma Dear grabbed Mildred's hand. "I know how it is. Sometimes you just can't pray for yourself. But don't you worry, you come to the right place.

"You and me, we've had our differences, but that won't stop us from doing God's work. In fact, it's just gone fool the old devil. See, he's not counting on you and me praying together, so he won't be on the lookout to stop this prayer. By the time he and his henchmen get together, this prayer will already be through and the answer will be on the way." She looked at Mother. "Come on, Mother, grab that girl's hand. We got to pray It's Jesus time!."

"Amen," Mother Johnson said. "Amen. Is there anything too hard for God?" Mother Johnson shook her head.

Ma Dear shook hers and smiled. "Not a thing in the world, Mother. There's not a thing in the world too hard for God." Mildred looked back and forth between the two women, and Ma Dear patted her on the knee. "Don't you worry a bit. Me and Mother, here, been praying together for years. Ain't that right, Mother?"

"That's right, Ma Dear."

Mildred shrugged her shoulders. "The situation just looks impossible."

Ma Dear laid her hand firmly on Mildred's shoulder. "God specializes in doing the impossible—that means He specializes bringing dead things back to life—dead situations, dead relationships. Whatever you need, God's got it. Sometimes things get hard, and it's tough to pray for yourself. But don't worry, sister, like I said, you've come to the right place." She looked at Mother Johnson. "Come on, sister, let's get to work."

Mother smiled and nodded. They were back in business. "Lord, I declare I know that You are up to something. Everywhere we look, it looks like there is no way. This child's granddaughter ain't much more than a baby herself, and here she is with a baby and no husband. Now it looks like she's got no home—and even like Mildred here might be without a home. But, Lord, we know that You are working it out. Look what You already done, Lord. Here we are, the three of us praying together. Who would have thought such a thing could happen...even just an hour ago, who would have believed it?"

Ma Dear waved her hand in the air. "Amen to that! I know I wouldn't have, Lord!"

"So we need You to show up, Lord. Your Word says that You are looking to and fro throughout the earth looking to show Yourself strong on the behalf of someone that loves You. Well, Lord, here are three women that love You. Now, show up, Lord! Put your eyes on us!"

"God, please help us," Mildred said.

In a short while, each of the three women had her head bowed. They prayed together, cried together, and even sang together.

Mika and Lex tossed the ball back and forth in the backyard.

"What's wrong with that lady?" Lex frowned.

Mika shrugged. "I don't know."

"She was crying."

"I know." Mika looked at the prayer house. "When Mommy gets back, we'll tell her about the lady and we can pray for her."

"Why can't we pray now?" Lex bounced the ball, caught it, and then held it in his arms.

Mika and Lex walked to the prayer house. They never went inside alone. "Drop the ball, Lexington. We're going in." The door creaked when she opened it. They stepped inside and knelt on the pillows just like they had done the first day. "Here." Mika handed Lex a pot and a spoon.

"No, I want that." He pointed at the tambourine.

"All right." Mika handed it to him and kept the pot for herself. "Okay, we're going to do it. But be quiet. We don't want them to hear us, we don't need to make too much noise." She looked at her little brother. "Say what I say." Mika drummed her pot softly.

"Okay." Lex closed his eyes and lightly shook the tambourine.

"Dear God, help the lady."

"Dear God, help the lady."

"We don't know what's wrong with her, but help her, okay?"

"We don't know what's wrong with her, okay?"

"Thank you. Amen."

"Thank you. Amen."

Mika opened her eyes. "Oh, I forgot! Keep your eyes closed, Lex."

"They're closed already, Mika!"

"Lex! This is serious!"

"Okay!"

"Thank You, God, in Jesus' name."

"In Jesus' name. Oh, and don't forget about the puppy. Amen."

Mika and Lex opened their eyes. Mika shrugged. "I guess that's it."

Lex nodded in response. "Last one to the ball is a rotten egg!" Both children ran for the door. "Our prayers are on the way to heaven! Just like Mother Johnson said. Remember?" He grinned at his sister. "She said when we pray, we don't see our words go to God's ears, but we don't have to. But that's how it is."

Mika nodded. "We don't see Him give our answers to angels, either."

"And sometimes those angels have to fight hard to get past the prince of the air and his dark angels. Just like in Daniel. There's a war going on. We can't see it, but that don't mean that it ain't going on."

"And our answer is on the way," Mika nodded. "Just like Mother told us." The two children pretended to sword fight. They exchanged imaginary blows.

"I'm the angel fighting!" Lex stepped up his onslaught.

"Let's both be angels—we can fight together and get the answer to earth faster!" Mika stood at her brother's side and they pretended to wield weapons and shields at their unseen adversaries.

Mother Johnson's encouragement was the background music for their fight.

"Before you get a puppy, your mama has to get a place, find the puppy, and get everything ready. Your mama has to fight through some circumstances to be able to keep her promise; it's hard, but it's what she promised she would do. Some of it you can't see; you're a child and she don't want you to see, but that don't mean it ain't going on."

"You mean I'm going to get the puppy?"

"That's what it means, baby. At just the right time, you're going

to get that puppy. The same thing for Daniel—God promised and He's going to make sure that it gets there at just the appointed time. We can't see evil fighting to keep our promise away from us, but that's what's happening. We're children and we don't need to see everything, we just need to keep believing God. That's why we have to be like Daniel, we have to believe and pray. Even better, we got to fast and pray, and sometimes—sad to say—we got to cry. The good news, when the devil is fighting, God got even more reinforcements He can send in to get the job done. We can't see it, but when we pray, God is listening. Just like your mama, or even better than your mama, it may take some time, but God is going to keep His promise."

"We're winning, Mika!" The two children fought shoulder-to-shoulder and back-to-back.

"Yeah, Lex! Somebody's praying!"

"At the end of all that crying, praying, fasting, and angel fighting, Daniel got his promise—he got his word. Your mama is right, don't ever give up. Your answer is just a prayer, a fast, or maybe even a tear away."

Mika acted out the defeat of their last enemy. "Lex, it's over, the battle's over—we won!" The children held their pretend weapons in the air and began to dance in victory. Lexington hooted. "My puppy's on the way!"

They yelled together, "Never give up!"

Shirley looked at the store sign. *Jack's Groceries.* She needed stockings for church on Sunday, but she wasn't even sure why she came to Jack's store. He was the last person she wanted to see. Well, maybe not last. She didn't feel like seeing Tony now. She didn't want to see Mildred, either.

Of course, she wanted to see Windy even less than she wanted to see either of the other two.

"I need you to make peace with whatever it is that I still see in your eyes."

What was it that Tony saw in her eyes? What was it that Mother Johnson saw?

"Baby, just like I knew you were coming home, I know you got some things in your life that you're not dealing with…"

Shirley stopped just before she stepped on the sensor for the automated door. "Okay, God. You show me what You're showing them. You lead me and I'll follow, okay? It's too hard to fight. I don't see it, but if You lead me, I'll follow." Shirley stepped on the pad and stepped inside the store.

THIRTY-TWO

Shirley walked up the produce aisle. The refrigerator cases and shelves were more modern than she remembered. There were bananas, apples, and peaches galore. She picked up a bunch of red grapes and smelled them. Shirley could taste the sweetness just from the fragrance.

Okay, God. Shirley picked through the produce. *None of this is working out like I planned. I said California, but here I am in Texas. I said a fresh start and put the past behind me, but everywhere I go the past keeps following me. I give up. If You are answering prayer, then God speak to me. Give me a sign. If You want me to go home, I mean to really go home, give me a sign. If the kids and I are supposed to pick up and go to California, just give me a sign.*

Give me a sign! She laughed to herself—she was beginning to sound like one of those movies they made about unscrupulous televangelists—the televangelist always had to be unscrupulous. Then again, she was sounding like one of those big-budget Cecil B. DeMille movies. *Right here in Jack's Groceries, Lord, give me a sign.*

Shirley wandered up and down the aisles looking for stockings. She found them on the next to the last row. She searched through the colors. Tan, off-white, nude—there was no coffee. There were never any coffee-colored stockings—at least not in the smaller stores, not in the stores that weren't on the right side of town.

There was a sound from the last aisle, almost like a kitten mewing. Shirley ignored it and kept moving the stocking packages, hoping that somewhere hidden in the back was the pair for which she searched.

She laughed to herself again. A sign in Jack's Groceries. That would be the day. Maybe there would be a bolt of lighting, or maybe Charlton Heston would throw down his staff and part the boxes of cereal.

Shirley heard the pitiful crying sound again. It was none of her business, so she went on with her fantasy. She imagined mile-high walls of cereal, creating a kind of tunnel, and people in togas following a lone figure toward a celestial light at the end. Or, better still, maybe Edward G. Robinson could throw a big party in the housewares and cleaning aids aisle.

What is *that sound?* Shirley's curiosity got the better of her. She walked to the end of the row and peeked up the last aisle. Windy sat on the floor, surrounded by small packing boxes. Shirley backed up, hoping to avoid a conversation before it began. She turned to make her way back up the stocking aisle.

"Shirley, is that you?"

Windy had seen her.

They sat outside on a wooden bench painted forest green. Nothing about the meeting felt peaceful. Windy was making the same mewing sound, in between whining and complaining, that Shirley had heard her making in the store.

"I told him nobody was going to push me around—especially no man. I don't need nobody. Me and the baby can take care of ourselves." Windy wiped her nose on the sleeve of her smock. "I knew I couldn't count on him. I knew I couldn't trust him."

Shirley dug in her purse for tissue. When she handed it to Windy, Shirley noticed that today the girl's nails were a bright metallic green.

"Well, I don't need his help. Nobody never gave me nothing! Nobody never went out of their way for me!" Windy cried harder. "Well, I'll show them. They don't want me here, I'll go home."

Oh no, God. Shirley looked up in the sky.

"I'll go back home, just like I come. But I'll tell you one thing—" Windy's cheeks were beet red and her face was wet— "when my baby comes, she won't never be treated like this. She won't have to count on people that don't want her around. That don't want to be bothered. She'll have somebody she can count on—I'm never gonna leave her. Never!"

Shirley dug in her purse for more tissue. All she could find were napkins from the Dairy Queen. She handed three of them to Windy—no need in giving them to the girl all at one time. Windy looked like she had a lot of crying to do. "So, what are you going to do now?"

Windy began to mumble and moan into her napkins.

"What did you say?"

"I said I don't have no choice. I got to go back home." She shook her head. "Three days to get out. How can he be so hard-hearted and ornery? Three days? How am I gonna get enough money to get home in three days? I been givin' all my money to him for rent." Windy began to rock as she wept.

God, please…I know I asked for a sign…

"So, I been prayin'." Windy wiped at her nose. "I been going to church with my grandmother. She knows so much about the Lord. And she really is a godly woman." Windy told Shirley how her Granny Mildred had been caring for her and spending time with her. "I know I made all that stuff up before—" Windy looked Shirley in the eye—"but this is for real." Windy wiped her tears. "I been asking the Lord to give me a sign."

Shirley looked up toward heaven, frowned, and then looked back at Windy. "So, is your grandmother going to help you? Why can't your grandmother help you?"

Windy began to wail again. Shirley dug for more napkins.

"How is she gonna help me? Granny ain't got much money herself, and Jack is threatening her, too." Windy pressed the dry napkins to her eyes.

"So what are you going to do?"

Windy balled her hands into fists and hit them on her knees three times to emphasize her words. "I don't know!" She blew her nose. "My mother died more than two years ago." Windy's eyes looked faraway, as though she was seeing beyond the parking lot in front of her. "If my daddy knew I was in trouble, I bet he would help me. But—" she looked apologetically at Shirley—"I guess you know I ain't never seen him either." Windy cried so hard that she wheezed. "I guess I won't *never* see him; I won't never know nothing about him!"

Shirley put an arm around Windy's shoulder and sighed. It was her fault, she guessed. She had asked God for a sign. "Stop crying, Windy. I know some things I think you ought to know."

THIRTY-THREE

I can't believe the three of you were together praying."
Shirley stared at Mother Johnson, then loaded clothes into the washing machine. She needed to wash, and besides, it was a good way of keeping her mind off of Tony.

"That was almost like my Ten Commandments sign in Jack's Groceries." Shirley gave Mother Johnson details of her meeting with Windy at the store. "Between Windy at the store and Paris Peace Talks right here on your front porch in Tyler, I guess I'm going home." Shirley switched the temperature dial to warm, and then she measured powdered detergent in a cup and poured it under the jetting water. "I figured I better get things together for me and the kids."

Mother sat at the table sipping tea. "Well, it might be better for the two of you—you and Windy, I mean—to go and leave the children here. That'll be less pressure and responsibility on you."

Shirley thought about it. Really, it was a good idea. The children would stay with Mother and she could do what she needed to without worrying about them. They decided the children would stay. "You're right, Mother. I hate it though. I hate leaving them. I'm going to miss them. I'm never away from them."

"Are you making peace with it, with going home?"

"Sometimes I think so. Except sometimes I have this bad feeling. Really, I've always had a bad feeling that if I went home…well, something bad would happen." Shirley tried to look upbeat. "It's just being silly. I'm not a little girl anymore." She smiled and tried to look calm as she grabbed a load of laundry from the dryer. "Anyway, after I told Windy what I knew about her father, I promised her I would take her. I don't know why…anyway, it's done."

While Mother studied her Bible, Shirley carried the dried clothes in a basket into her bedroom. It had been years since she'd thought about Ken, Barbara, and Misty; about the Cooties and about the Greenbirds. Now that Shirley was grown, it seemed even more strange that her third grade teacher at Morrison Elementary School, Mrs. Canada, had assigned her to teach the Cooties to read. The Cooties, her students, had all been older than she was.

Shirley could still see them sitting together in the dark cloakroom. Could still see Ken—mean, nasty Ken—making no bones about letting Shirley know that he was displeased a black child had been appointed his teacher.

That was long ago, though, and Shirley was sure that things had changed in East St. Louis.

Mother Johnson flipped through the pages of her Bible, but her thoughts were on Shirley—young Shirley and how troubled she'd been when Mother first saw her. Mother hadn't known, when she went to fetch the girl, what kind of state she would be in, or even if the people at the hospital would let her have Shirley. What she was certain of was that she had to try. There was no one else to fight for the child.

It was a long bus ride from Tyler to Illinois. Mother Johnson had read and prayed all the way there. She had to be ready to face the doctors.

And face them she had.

"So, are you trying to tell me I can't take the child?" One of her eyebrows raised.

"No, you're her closest blood relative." The doctor made his fingers into a tent. *"It's just that we're concerned about her being off the medication."*

Mother forced a smile. "Well, I'm concerned about her being on it."

"That's understandable. You're not a physician and have little knowledge of such things."

"You know what, Doctor? You might be right about me. But I do know the greatest Physician that ever live, and I'm pretty sure that He will take the case."

The doctor smirked. "That's just what she doesn't need. She's already been through a severe trauma, and she's having difficulty determining exactly what reality is. The last thing she needs is to be exposed to superstition."

"How long has she been here, Doctor?"

"Nine months."

"Has she gotten any better? Have you been able to lower the amount of medicine you're giving her?"

"It's not that simple, Mrs. Johnson. These medicines are very complex, and while we've had to adjust them several times, Shirley hasn't made sufficient progress to justify lowering the medication. We have to be patient."

Mother Johnson leaned forward. "Well, I tell you what, Doctor. You just pack up my baby's things and bring her on. We've got a bus to catch. And if we leave right now, we'll get to the Trailways station just in time."

Mother Johnson was sure that she had looked way more confident, facing the doctor, than she'd felt. I can do all things through Christ, which strengthens me. *She had said the Scripture over and over again to herself. Sometimes you had to fake it until you felt it.*

What was certain was that the child needed somebody. Young Shirley needed someone to put her arms around her—someone to tell her that she was going to make it. That the trouble that she was facing wasn't permanent. Shirley had been through enough heartache for three grown women. If ever there was a tender lamb that needed a shepherd, Shirley was the one.

Mother could still see Shirley, no bigger than Mika was now, sitting next to her on the bus ride home. She had patted Shirley's leg.

"Don't you worry about a thing. You go on to sleep. You'll be waking up soon enough." *Shirley nodded and her head fell on Mother Johnson's arm.*

"I don't know everything, baby. But I do know that you have been through a lot. It will probably be some time before you feel like talking—before you're ready to tell the tale. That's all right. Everything's probably looking dark to you, looking like night, like you can't make heads or tails of where you are.

"What I can tell you is God never sends us anyplace by mistake. One time I walked through a dark place. There were shadows everywhere, and in every shadow it looked like there was a boogeyman. But God was in the shadows, too. I couldn't see Him, but every once in a while He would reach out and touch me…let me know He was there."

She squeezed Shirley and kissed her on the cheek. "I walked out of the bad place. And now I'm free indeed. I walked out of the shadows. Baby, count on it—you're coming out, too. And you just remember I told you so."

Mother Johnson closed her eyes. "Lord, I thank You for what You've done in this child's life, in this woman's life. She's still got a ways to go—that darkness she was in is far behind her, but Lord, You lead her into joy. Be with her, Lord, as she goes. Be with her, Lord. Keep her from dangers seen and unseen. And encourage her, Lord, as she passes into the light."

THIRTY-FOUR

There was still time to back out. What was packed could be unpacked. What was planned could be unplanned. Shirley looked briefly in the rearview mirror at Mika—wearing pastel pink lace fingerless gloves, hair bow, and anklets—and Lex—wearing red and black pants covered with zippers and matching red shoes with Velcro closures—playing in the backseat. Was it really worth leaving her kids? Maybe it was better to leave *everything* the way it was.

They were on their way to the library, then on to meet Tony. She turned the radio down and turned her eyes back to the road ahead of her.

It was silly to trust a man. It was dangerous. She had already been through it once. Why take a chance with Tony?

Danny had almost killed her and there wasn't anyone she could tell. She wasn't the victim of a wounding that was detectable. It was invisible, except to others who had been similarly wounded.

There was a time, when they were stationed in Alabama, when Danny had had an affair. The other woman rode around with her Danny, with the man Shirley loved, on the back of her motorcycle. She wasn't beautiful; she wasn't rich or intelligent. In fact, Virginia, the other woman, was worn looking and poorly shaped. She talked too loudly and smelled of cigarette smoke. Virginia didn't love Danny—she just used him like toilet paper to wipe away something in her life that she didn't like. Her husband had died, she didn't want to feel the pain, so Danny wiped it away for her.

Danny was good at it—wiping away pain. Shirley knew that about him. He was intelligent, he was handsome, he was a passionate lover, and he was not satisfied unless he was healing someone's pain. So he rode away on the back of Virginia's motorcycle.

Sometimes when she remembered, Shirley wondered why she didn't run after him. Why couldn't she show him enough of her own pain to keep him satisfied? Why was it that she was too afraid to let him see that she needed him—that she ached but just let her love ride away. Danny was gone and when he came back—smelling of martinis or beer—she always found some way to take him back.

It wasn't just Virginia, though. Over and over, she had seen Danny with rejects—broken people with issues. My God, she remembered thinking, what was he doing around them? Why would he want to be around them, when he could be around her? Or around the children? Danny loved her—Shirley knew he did. She was easy to love.

Now that he was gone, though, she realized the rejects were all her. She was them. What drew him to them, was her. He loved her, but she couldn't let him close enough to her to heal her, so he found her needs, her weaknesses, her pain, and her flaws in other people. He sought out her need for attention in other women. He found her fears in their eyes and comforted them. She couldn't let Danny close enough to heal her.

Shirley wondered, as she drove, if he might have left to cause her pain, to give her some pain that he could heal. But when Danny came home, she still was unable to show him her pain. Shirley just smiled, prayed, and moved on. She had kept smiling and working and forgiving and praying and washing and cleaning, but she couldn't give Danny what he needed to stay. She couldn't let him close enough to her to heal her.

She shook her head. All of this was silliness. She loved Danny—like the fool she was—but he was a womanizer. That was the real truth. There was no point in getting philosophical or poetic about it—he was a jerk. Just like all the books said, she suffered from low self-esteem. He couldn't be trusted. He was like all men. Shirley's jaws tightened. Her mother's voice whispered memories to her and made cold rings around her shoulders.

Mama gave a look that gave Shirley chills. "I'll tell you one thing I know for sure." She looked at Shirley. "You can't trust no man. Don't ever count on one, because you will be disappointed every time!" Mama put her hands on her hips. "You remember what I say now. Don't ever trust a nigger!" She looked back at Shirley's uncles. "And you two are just the same." Mama wiped her mouth and stomped off from the table.

This whole thing—this whole stupid idea about dating Tony was just that. It was stupid. It was stupid and it was asking for trouble and heartache. Better to think on other things.

There was still time to back out of everything. Like how she figured she was going to help Windy—what exactly was the point? The girl was in a bind. Of course, she was also in a bind—the bind leading the bind—she knew it should be *bound*, but bound wasn't funny, and Shirley was going to take any laugh she could get at the moment.

What exactly was she going to accomplish taking Windy to East St. Louis? How was it going to help Windy to recite a lot of stuff to her about her dad? Basically, he was mean and nasty and he couldn't read. That was sure to help the girl. What was the point of seeing her own mother for that matter?

The bar was dark, even in the daytime. In the early afternoon, the smell of mold and must was a little more noticeable. There were few patrons, just a few regulars. The seat on which Tony sat made a grinding noise when he moved. The rusted, red leather bar stool next to it was identical, except that the seat part of it wobbled from side to side. Tony had chosen the lesser of two evils.

He tapped the bottom of his glass on the worn wooden bar. Why had he even called her? Things were better off before. The last thing he needed in his life were arguments, yelling, and angry, disappointed women. Tony took a drink and pursed his lips.

He was probably about to lose a good friend—if he hadn't lost her already.

"What you doing in here, young blood?" The old preaching drunk, Lucille's husband, slid onto the bar stool next to Tony. "I don't remember seeing you here during the day. This is my regular hideout—" holding his glass in his hand, he gestured around the room—"but, like I said, I ain't seen you here at this time before."

Tony shrugged. "Just thought I would stop by."

The old man laughed. "Woman trouble, huh?"

"I know better. I know better." Tony shook his head.

The old man laid his hand on Tony's shoulder. "I know I complain a lot, but life is not so sweet without a little taste of love. And the only way to have it is to take a chance."

Tony looked at the old man and then back at his drink. "Being alone ain't so bad. It's predictable."

"Yeah, some people like it that way." The old man studied Tony. "You don't look like that kind of somebody." Tony frowned and stared into his glass. "I just think I hear a little bit of bitter in your voice."

Tony laughed. "That makes me about the same as every other man that steps up in here."

"You think the crowd in here's that bad?"

The stool groaned when Tony turned to face the old man. "Really, pops, I don't know about the other men. And I don't know if *I'm* really bitter. Just wiser."

"Um-hmm. Somebody used you and hurt you bad, didn't they?"

"I had to learn, just like everybody else."

The old man's seat wobbled and he grabbed the bar to hold on. "This chair's a wild mouse ride if ever I saw one." He took a sip from his glass. "I don't know about your situation, but it seems to me I see mens over and over again going for the same kind of woman. And I ain't talking about looks—I mean women with the same ways. Then we act surprised when we keep getting treated the same way. Why you think that is?"

Tony shrugged and looked away. He came into the bar to be alone.

"Sometimes, I think it's cause we keep picking what we

know." The preaching drunk rested his elbows on the bar. "You know, like the only car I know about is Fords. So, when I go looking for cars, all the possibilities I see is Fords. Don't even occur to me to try something else." The old man rapped a knuckle on the bar and nodded to the bartender for a refill. "Of course, if I keep picking Fords, all the cars I get are gone drive and act like Fords. I think that might be what we keep doing with women."

Tony turned his head and hoped the old man would know he wasn't interested.

"Of course, sometimes we luck up and just happen up on something new and special." The old man was oblivious to, or ignoring, Tony's feedback. "Only thing is, we keep looking and thinking we seeing that old woman on the new woman. Why you think we do that?"

"Maybe Freud would know?" Sarcasm might send the old man away.

The old man wiggled his head. "I guess if I could answer that question, I could write a book and get enough information to buy this old bar." He looked around the room. "If I bought it, I would fix it up. That's for sure. First thing, though…" he wiggled on his seat. "I'd get rid of these old stools." He took a drink and winked at the bartender. "Just like I like it." Then he looked back at Tony. "If you find a good woman, give her a chance."

Tony opened his mouth to tell the old drunk to mind his own business, to tell him that he didn't know anything about his life and what he had been through, about how he had been hurt. Tony opened his mouth and then closed it. Better to just leave it alone. If he responded, he would just be encouraging the old man. Tony sloshed the ice around in his drink.

"That's ginger ale you're drinking, ain't it?"

Tony sat back on his stool, pulled his lips tight, and nodded. He knew what was coming next.

"Why you come to a bar to get ginger ale? You can get it at the store for fifty cents or so. Why you want to pay for ginger ale here?"

What was the use? The old man wasn't going away. "I like bars. I don't drink anymore, but I like…I just like to come here."

The old man nodded. "A creature of habit, huh? You like doing what you been doing all along." The old man adjusted his sitting position. "Was you a big drinker?"

"For a while. It got to be too much and I quit."

"You think you was drinking like a painkiller? I see lots of fellas doing that—trying to dull the pain. Trying to make themselves be able to live with working at a job, doing something, or living with somebody they don't really like. If they can get a little something to take the edge off they can get by. So they come in and have a few and say it's fun. What you think?"

Tony shrugged. "I like the people, mostly. And it's quiet in here, kind of like a cave." It was funny. The old man was irritating him because he didn't want to talk. But most times he liked the conversation, even the old man's.

They sat in silence and listened to Lou Rawls singing, "You'll Never Find a Love Like Mine."

"'Course, the other thing I see is that lots of men spend time with the wrong woman—sometimes, no woman—but mostly the wrong woman. There's probably lots of different reasons, but mostly I think it's just like drinking—to take away the ache. Somebody that dulls the pain. Trouble is, she can't never give you the real pleasure and help God intended. She seem safe, like she'll do to just take the heat off—and since you don't care, she can't hurt you. But a woman you don't love can still bring you to your knees…and when the right one come along the wrong one already got squatter's rights. Lots of mens is married to women they don't love. Painkillers can kill you."

The old man took a big gulp and swallowed. "You look like a nice young man." Tony nodded and smiled briefly. He waited for the old man to ask him for a drink. "You go to church?"

The question surprised Tony and it took him a while to answer. "I'm not big on church."

"You don't believe in God?"

"It's not God, it's church that I don't like."

"You been to a lot of churches?" The old man hunched forward over the bar. "Hope I ain't asking too many questions." It was a little late to be asking now.

"Not many. It didn't take much for me to get the picture."

"That's too bad." The preaching drunk waved a hand in the air. "Too bad. 'Cause churches are pretty much like bars." Tony cocked his head. "You can't judge one bar by another. You got to search around until you find the one you like, you know, the one where you feel comfortable and where you likes the people. Funny, people won't give up on finding a bar, but they'll sure give up on finding a church."

"You still go to church? You just don't seem…"

"Well, no, not much anymore." The old man looked down into his glass. "I ain't much welcome no more. But I remember…" He looked up from his glass and then patted Tony on his back. "Don't give up, young blood. I believe any day now, things are gone turn around."

THIRTY-FIVE

⁂

"There's Mr. Tony's car!"

Lex was smiling at Mika, pointing and straining against the seat belt. Shirley spotted Tony sitting on the bench where they had met last time.

"Just wait a minute, Lex, until Mommy stops the car."

Her car bumped over the gravel; then she pulled into a parking space. "Mika, you and Lex stay on the playground near the car so we can keep an eye on you all." While she locked the doors and got the water cooler from the car, the children ran ahead. They hugged Tony—he and Lex exchanged high fives and exchanged imaginary punches—then they ran to the swings.

The bench was in a great spot. There were two grills nearby, a water fountain, and the playground. The grass was green, and the large trees near the bench were giving off ample shade. It was lovely, and what made it even nicer was that there were hardly any people in the park. The setting and the privacy would have been perfect if they were really dating. But...

Shirley realized it was taking her a long time to walk the

fifty feet or so to the bench where Tony sat. Things felt so complicated. Nothing had really happened. It just felt like it. She
dragged herself to the bench, sat down, and tried not to look
like she felt—like she was dreading their meeting. "Hi."

"Hi." Tony didn't look any happier.

"The kids are always really happy to see you." She made
herself smile. "They like you."

"I like them, too. You know that." He looked at her and
then looked away.

She would be brave. She would start first. She would take
both of them off the hook. "You know, Tony, you are a great
friend. You are. I appreciate you."

Tony gave her a tight-lipped smile. "Here it comes, the old
I-appreciate-you speech. I thought there might be something a
little more original."

"Tony, don't make this hard for me and don't put it all on
me. You don't look like you're so happy, either. Maybe it's best
if we're just friends."

He nodded. "That's what I thought. Well, better sooner
than later."

"Look, Tony—" Shirley tried not to raise her voice or give
Mika and Lex any indication that anything was going on—
"both of us are uncomfortable. Not just me. I know how to be
your friend; we figured that out a long time ago. But I'm a
widow and I still don't have *that* all figured out—I don't know
what to do. And the kids…that's another thing. I don't know
how long is long enough. And…" She stared into his eyes. "I
promised myself, after Danny died, that I was going to have a
relationship like God says. But I don't know what that
means—that I try to do things in the right order, to get the
spiritual and emotional stuff right first. It just seems like all this

ought to be easier. It ought to be more natural."

She looked away from him. "I don't know what happened. One minute we were smiling and the next minute I'm neurotic. I don't get it."

"I should have followed my mind. I shouldn't have brought it up."

"Maybe we're thinking about it too much, Tony. Or maybe we're just meant to be friends. Friends is a good thing."

Tony looked as though he were smiling to try to make it easier on her. "Yeah, friends is a good thing."

The air was hot, but not scorching. There were parts of the landscape that were like green carpet, while others were like chunks of green thrown against red clay. Mika and Lex were sliding, running from the bottom of the board to the metal stairs so that they could climb up for their next turn. As they sat waiting to slide, they rocked from cheek to cheek. Shirley remembered that feeling, the metal slide being a literal hot seat.

Tony leaned back and laid his elbows over the back of the bench. "Look, Shirley. I'm not trying to marry you tomorrow."

"Is that what we're talking about here? Marriage? I told you my husband—"

Tony held up a hand for Shirley to stop talking. "Look, I'm a serious person. I'm not a player. I tried it and I got played a lot more than I ever played." He shook his head. "No, I was broke down. I was so messed up and hurt, trying to run women and pretend—when all the while they were seeing through me and running me—I ended up broke, a joke, and disgusted. Man, I was doing everything…I started drinking.

"One night, I was in this bar drunk, bothering some people—that's how bad it had gotten. They didn't know me— just two couples. But there I was standing there trying to badger them into buying me a drink. Telling them there wasn't any difference between them and me. Really, I don't know what I was saying. Probably, I was just mad because they were couples.

"One of the dudes finally had had enough of me, jumped up and knocked my stupid drunk self down. I ended up halfway under a table, laying in other people's trash and looking up at other people's mess."

Tony looked away, then turned back to her. "It took that to get me to listen to myself. I wasn't a drunk; I was trying to force myself into a life I wasn't supposed to live. I was drinking to take away the pain. I knew it. I knew it all along, but it took lying there on the ground looking like a drunk to admit that was what I was turning myself into. And I wasn't even a nice drunk—" Tony rubbed his hand over the hair on his head—"I can't believe I'm talking this much. But I don't wear casual well. I can't do '*it don't matter to me*,' or '*we're just friends*,' or '*we'll see where it heads*' relationships. I had to fall under a table to realize that. I was a serious boy; now I'm a serious man. So if this is something temporary you're doing just until you move on to find your rainbow, let me know. I'm a giver, and I have to be careful that I don't give out."

"I'm not trying to use you, Tony. I'm not trying to hurt you." Shirley pushed her braids back behind their ears. "I don't know. I don't know how it happens for other people. I don't know how people make the transition from friends to…whatever. Maybe if we just didn't think about it so much. Maybe if I didn't have so many different issues in my life. Or maybe something just happens to sweep people away to get them past thinking and to get them caught up in the moment."

Tony looked at her. "Like what?"

"Like a shipwreck and they're stranded on a desert island, or a plane crash—"

"And they are stranded on a desert island." Tony nodded.

"You know, it's just something to let the couple know that they really want to be together. That it's worth overcoming whatever is in between them."

Tony leaned back against the bench. "I get the drift. Well, I guess it's not going to happen for us. The chances are slim to none of us getting stranded on a deserted island in Tyler. But…"

Shirley and Tony looked at the children swinging. Mika and Lex were both standing in the swings, pumping back and forth. He nodded his head in their direction. "You leave tomorrow, right? I'll drop by to see them while you're away." She nodded at him.

Eight to ten cars pulled rapidly into the parking lot and into spaces surrounding their cars. People began to unload from the cars. There were men, women, and children. Tony and Shirley stopped talking and watched the activity.

One man wearing a Jheri Curl jerked a large metal cooler from the trunk of his car, as what appeared to be his wife and children piled from the car. He carried the cooler over near the grill, set it down, and stripped his white summer shirt off down to a sleeveless T-shirt. "Cameron," he yelled to his son. "Get the charcoal and the lighter fluid and come on. We got to work fast." The man stacked the charcoal in kind of a pyramid and lit it.

While he worked, another family tumbled out of an old blue station wagon. The driver lowered the car's back gate and slid an old-fashioned ice cream freezer out of the back. He set it on the ground. His wife, wearing a pink sundress, sat on the car gate. Her legs dangled over the edge. She bent forward and began to crank.

The driver of a third car set a large boom box with speakers on the roof and cranked up the volume. Al Green told everyone in the park "Let's Stay Together."

Several women came from another car, talking loudly and excitedly. Three of them left the pack and walked toward the bathrooms at the top of the hill. The others began to argue over where they were going to place two metal arches that they carried between them. "It will look prettier on that hill," one woman said.

"Yeah, and then next thing you know, Baby Sis, we'll be tripping and rolling down that same hill. It's better to put it where it's flat."

The women argued for a few more minutes, then settled on the flat land.

Once the arches were in place, the women began to drape tulle over them and to wrap ribbon and silk flowers attached to wire around the arches. The flowers were gathered in clusters of muted pink, purple, and peach—even more vibrant against the cloudless blue sky. The ribbons were the same colors and the tulle was cream.

Shirley noticed that Mika and Lex had slowed the frequency of their swinging. They, like Tony and Shirley, were focused on the activity of the group.

The woman in the pink sundress had a dreamy expression on her face. Seemingly oblivious to the rest of the people, she cranked the ice cream to the beat of the music.

"I think we in business now!" The man in the sleeveless T-shirt said to no one in particular. He opened the cooler and began to lay slabs of ribs on the grill. Next he laid out chickens that were cut in half. The girth of his stomach hanging over the belt of his pants said he knew at least a little something about what he was doing. "If don't nothing else happen, we gonna be eating good up in here." No one seemed to doubt the man's word.

He used a large, two-pronged fork to arrange the meat on the grill. Then he yelled in the direction of the other cars. "Big Mama, you got the sauce, right?"

A short, plump, gray-haired woman poked her head out of one of the cars and stood up. "Oh, baby, you know I got the sauce. If you see Big Mama, you see sauce."

As they talked, four more cars pulled into the parking lot and five men wearing suits, at least one of whom appeared to be a preacher, got out of their cars and strolled to meet the others. The preacher wore a traditional black suit coat, but the four other men wore loose, brightly colored jackets—grape, electric blue, emerald green, and neon yellow—that were boxy and big-shouldered. The jackets were paired with white shirts with turned up collars and thin intentionally loosened ties. None of the four appeared to be wearing socks.

Other men, women, and children followed the five. Big Mama waved at the man cooking the meat. "All right now. Things are coming together." She looked at the five recently arrived men and smiled. "All right now. I was starting to get a little worried."

One of the women that had been working on the arches clapped her hands. "This is going to be so beautiful!" A baby sucking on a bottle walked along with her, holding on to her leg. The smell of the grilling ribs and chicken provided an aromatic and palatable backdrop for the setting.

"Who got the paper cups?" A woman in a green dress

yelled. "I got the paper plates, napkins, and the knives, forks, and spoons. Who's got the paper cups?" She put her hands on her hips. "Ain't nobody got the paper cups?" She shook the plastic cutlery in the air. "I knew it. I knew somebody was going to forget something and mess everything up. I knew it!" She shook her hands frantically over her head. "I knew it!"

"Ernestine, if you don't quiet down. And stop making a big to-do about nothing." Big Mama was giving Ernestine the evil eye. "This is not *your* day. This is the Baby Sis's day. I would thank you kindly to keep it down to a dull roar." Ernestine, in the green dress, froze midwave. "Thank you." Big Mama nodded. "And by the way, I got plenty of paper cups."

Tony looked at Shirley, then leaned forward as though he were trying to figure it out. Mika and Lex joined them on the bench. "Don't stare you guys," Shirley whispered as the four of them stared. Shirley thought she recognized the bottle baby. The girl who braided her hair—it was her baby. Shirley looked amongst the people standing in the group for Olivia, but didn't see her.

"All right," Big Mama hollered. "Put the music on; it's time." The man cooking the ribs put his shirt back on, unbuttoned, and the group gathered together near the arches. The three women, who had gone toward the bathrooms, emerged. One wore a peach-colored gown, while another wore purple. The other woman, who Shirley now recognized as the hair braider, Olivia, wore a cream-colored gown with a matching veil.

It was a wedding. The three women walked down the hill, leaning back so they wouldn't pitch forward in their high heels—swaying to the rhythm of Whitney Houston singing "The Greatest Love of All." The woman in the pink sundress kept cranking, and the woman who had helped decorate the arches clapped her hands and breathed, "Beautiful!"

The three women in gowns were joined at the altar by three of the suited men, plus the preacher. A teenaged girl left the group watching the couples and ran to a car. She came back with a plastic grocery bag. She went to the women in gowns and handed each of them a bouquet. "I almost forgot," she said.

Shirley could see the preacher's mouth and hands moving, but she was too far away to hear him speak. While he talked, the bottle baby joined the three couples, wrapping himself around his mother's legs. The woman in the pink sundress kept cranking, and the man in the white sleeveless T-shirt kept looking toward his grill.

Ma Dear needs to be here, Shirley thought.

Suddenly the preacher began to flap his arms. Shirley strained to hear.

"By the power invested in me by the great state of Texas, I now pronounce you man and wife!"

The bride jumped up and down, and the baby held on for dear life. The groom leaned forward and put his arms around his bride, careful not to crush the baby, and kissed her passionately.

The bride, after she had hugged her other guests, waved to Shirley. She pointed to her head. "Your hair is still holding up good!"

In a short time, Mika and Lex had joined the children from the wedding party and were laughing and eating homemade ice cream. The couple—the entire group—looked happy.

The sun had softened, and the air had cooled slightly. Shirley turned to look at Tony. His profile—somewhere in it she could still see the boy he had been. She slid her hand on the bench so that it was touching his. He turned to look at Shirley, then lifted his hand to cover hers.

"It would be nice to be in love." She sighed. "But I just don't know."

THIRTY-SIX

hen he stepped from the afternoon light into the dark of the bar, Tony jerked the bottom of his T-shirt out of his pants. If he could have chucked off his heavy work boots he would have done that too. He looked down at them. They were scuffed, gashed, and stained with dirt and oil. If he took them off, he would pretty quickly be the only person in the bar. No doubt about it.

He looked around to see who was there and noticed the old man, the preaching drunk, at the bar. For some reason Tony didn't understand, he was happy to see him. As he walked toward him, Tony realized he had never asked the old man his name.

"Leviticus," the old man told him when he sat down beside him. "Leviticus Lamentations Jones. That's a mouthful, ain't it?" The old man laughed. "I guess that's why most folks just don't bother." The old man closed one eye and looked Tony up and down. "You seem to be in a more better mood than the last time I seen you."

"Maybe." Tony tried not to smile.

"A new girl?" Leviticus Jones tilted his head. "The last time

I had that expression on my face, I had just met Lucille." He took a drink. "God bless her soul." The old man took a drink and then sat back to get a good look at Tony. "So what kind of lady is she?"

"Nice." That was a good answer.

"The way you smiling, she seem like somebody you really like."

"Yeah. We've know each other since we were kids—I liked her then, but…"

"Oh, your meet," the old man said.

"My what?"

"Your meet—you know, your mate. The one that's intended for you. Your fit." Leviticus shook his head. "It's hard for a man to make it to his meet. The path is strewn with all kinds of pretty distractions, but the man that makes it to his meet is a happy and complete man.

"We are the sons of Abraham. We been given a gift. Our seed is strong, just like Abraham's, and it produces a big crop for generations to come. If we plant in good ground, we gone get a good, rich harvest. 'Course, the flip side of our blessing is a curse. If we plant among weeds we get big—" Leviticus frowned and spread his arms out wide—"nasty, ugly weeds. Lots of them for generations to come." He laid his hand back on Tony's shoulder. "You done the right thing, young blood. The Bible say it ain't good for a man to be alone. You need a good woman." Leviticus tapped Tony on the shoulder. "She saved?"

Tony nodded.

"All right now. Nothing like a church girl." Leviticus laughed out loud.

"Maybe. Maybe not. You know what I'm talking about?"

"'Deed I do." The old man nodded. "We always got a war going on inside of us about that." He smiled at Tony. "A church girl. You know you got to get yourself right then, don't you? She say anything to you about that?"

Tony shook his head. "We haven't talked about it."

"Most times women don't like to talk about it, but it's one of the most importantest things they is."

Tony stared at his drink. "I don't see what difference it makes. Half the men I know in church are saying one thing and doing another—raunchy men. Half of the other half, you can't tell if they're men…or if they are…they're just watered down or what. I don't want to be like that. I don't want church if that's what it does to you. I don't want church if I have to give up my manhood…and 'cause that's not the same thing as not knowing God."

Leviticus took a drink and then wiggled around on his stool like he was settling in for a long sermon. "Ever since God first blew life into us, we been struggling with our nature as mens. God made us to be men, you hear me? *Men.*" He slapped his hand on the counter. "Not some tame, limp thing, but *men.*"

Now this was a sermon Tony didn't mind hearing. "Yeah! That's what I'm saying! I don't want nothing that's going to make me into a weak man."

"I know that's right, young blood. But at the same time, we got to make that nature so that it obeys the voice of God. If we don't listen to God, every man does what he thinks in his own heart is right to do. And that sounds like a good thing to us men, every man doing what he thinks is right. That is, until you run across a man who thinks it's right to murder, make men slaves, use children, and the like. Then it dawns on us we need some kind of order and the only order I been able to figure out that makes sense for all men is God." Leviticus shook his gray head. "We got to, as men, listen to the voice of God. A man with no God is a raging beast. Like a team of wild horses out of control. You need God to harness and direct a man's power. On the other hand, a tamed man with no power and no strength ain't much good to nobody."

Leviticus held his fists in front of him, moving one up and the other down. "It's a life and death balancing act, and most mens can't figure it out. So, most of us just stay away from God. But that ain't the answer. If we stay away, we lost. By not choosing, we choosing death. But we not just choosing death for ourselves, we choosing death for our families and for generations to come. Staying away ain't the answer."

Tony took a big swig of ginger ale and then hunched his shoulders. "What does not going to church have to do with it? I pray to God. I believe in God."

"When we stay away, we keeping ourselves from the very source of our power. When we stay away, we leave the women to have to do it all—they got to be warriors because we're absent from our posts. And then we leave another generation of young boys with no guides—nobody to show them how to be mens. When we stay away, we miss hearing from God. We miss learning to know His voice, 'cause we got to hear and study His Word to begin to recognize His voice."

Leviticus frowned and shook his head. "No, staying away ain't the answer. Losing our manhood ain't the answer. Somehow, we got to somehow figure it out." Leviticus kept moving his fists up and down again, trying to make his hands balance. "We keep saying, 'God show us a man who got the answer. Show us a man that can show us how.' But I'm thinking it ain't no one can tell us how to do the balancing act but God, that's why we got to draw near to Him. If we can get the Lord to whisper to us how to be godly men, we can raise up a whole generation of men behind us."

Tony asked the bartender for a refill. "I hear you talking, Leviticus. But I've been doing all right on my own so far."

"Have you?" There was silence between them.

Leviticus drained his glass. "What you got now is a saved woman. How you gone love her like God want you to love her, how you gone take care of her like He want you to take care of her, if you don't even know what He trying to say to you? Man's ways is not God's ways. We think we doing right and come to find out in God's eyes we doing wrong.

"We need the love of a good woman. It's not good for a man to be alone; the Word says so. But a man out of control will kill a good woman. Why you gone hurt her when you got the remedy to keep from hurting her right at hand?"

Tony shook his head. "I don't know. There are a lot of things…"

Leviticus lay one of his hands on Tony's shoulder. "It's a snaky path we got to walk. The wrong woman will ruin your life and get you killed—one way or another. But even if you get a good woman, if you out of control, you will kill her."

Leviticus took his hand away and laid it on the bar. "Life or death, young blood. That's the choice. Anyway you look at it; it's life or death. You choose."

Tony stood outside her window afraid that the crickets or a bush would give him away. He was hidden in darkness; the sun's heat was gone. He tossed rocks at Shirley's window and hoped that no one else would wake. It was a crazy thing to do—to get up out of his bed in the middle of the night, to get dressed, to drive across town, to sneak to her window.

Tony tossed more rocks and willed Shirley awake. It was something a kid would do—the kind of thing that parents had to be on guard against.

It was crazy, but here he was anyway. Tony's chest was heaving, and he was sweating. He stepped from behind the bush that shielded him and walked quietly until he was right outside her window. He rapped on her window. He whispered urgently. "Shirley!" Tony knocked again. "Shirley!" When she popped awake and saw him, she laid her hand over her heart. He put a finger to his mouth and waved her to come outside.

"Tony what are you doing h—?"

His kiss stopped her questions, and his arms held her. Shirley tried to think her way out of it. *My teeth aren't brushed. It's night and Tony shouldn't be here. This robe is so ratty. What if the kids wake up?*

Tony wasn't giving her time to protest. One arm was around her shoulders while the hand of the other arm rubbed her back. She held onto the front of her old pink chenille robe with both hands, closed her eyes, and surrendered to the embrace. The hand that was rubbing her back stole higher and removed the silk scarf that was tied around her head.

The more she surrendered, the more she felt the tightness she carried in her shoulders leaving her. Shirley wondered what was happening and where they were going. Just when she decided that she was going wherever Tony took her, he moved his face away from hers. Shirley opened her eyes to see that he was smiling. He kissed the tip of her nose, then nuzzled her neck. He still held her so close she couldn't move her hands. The hand that was rubbing her back now moved to play with her braids.

"I couldn't sleep." Tony bit her ear.

"Tony, this is *crazy.*"

He laughed into her ear. His breath was warm and it tickled her. "That's what I was just telling myself." He hugged her even more closely, squeezed her, then loosened his hold. He looked down into her face. "I couldn't sleep. I kept thinking and thinking and thinking. I just needed to see you."

"Tony?"

He used his hands to guide hers from her robe to around his waist. Then he placed the palms of his hands on either side of her face and kissed her again. His eyes were closed. "It seems like I've been waiting all my life to kiss you."

Shirley kissed him on his cheek.

"Wow!" The word was soft. "You kissed me back."

"Tony…"

He brushed her braids back from her face, then tilted his head to kiss her. He grabbed the collar of her robe with his hands. "Shirley." He kissed her again. The long kiss turned to short pecks. He talked in-between them. "I'm tired of talking…and trying to figure it out…I thought I would never see you again…but here you are like some dream…and I would be a fool to let this pass me by…to let whatever it is that scares me…or scares *us* make us pass this by."

"Tony, my teeth aren't brushed. And look how I look." She raised one of her hands to her hair, and he covered it with one of his.

"No more excuses, Shirley. Whatever it is, we can work it

out, right? Kids, jobs, church—whatever it is." He laughed. "Even teeth." He kissed her again. "I was lying in the bed saying this is crazy. When I had dreamed so many times hoping that I would see you again. Now here you are, and I'm sweating the details, baby."

Baby. Something in her broke, and she laid her head on his chest. "I'm just scared, Tony. I don't want to fight. I just...I don't have it figured out."

"We never figure it out. It never gets figured out. We're not supposed to figure it out. We live every day and we never have it figured out. We pretend to ourselves that we do—it makes us feel safe. But we don't." Tony talked into her hair. "I was praying and talking to God, asking Him to help me figure it out." Tony rubbed his face against hers.

"Then it came to me—we're never going to have it all figured out. If we wait for that day, we'll just be waiting. I'm never going to figure it all out about church or about women. You're never going to figure it out about why Danny died, or about when is the perfect time, or where is the perfect place to be.

"Just breathe, Shirley. We're never going to figure it out. We just have to be where we are and trust that it's the place that God wanted us and that He's taking care of us—all of it is part of His plan." He kissed her again. "We're not so old that we have to kill the mystery."

"I'm so tired." She could feel her knees weakening. Tony held her. "So tired. I just feel like I'm fighting so hard. Like I'm trying to hold it all together so hard. If I could figure it out and know what's going to happen, if I could control it, I wouldn't have to worry."

"We're never going to figure it out."

"I wanted everything to be settled about Danny, about the

kids, about where I'm going to be before..." Shirley pressed her face to his chest and cried.

His arms held her close. "I know it was God who brought us together—twice in one lifetime. If He can do that, He's got the rest of it in His hands."

They sat together on the steps. She trembled against him. He held her until she stopped crying and then he sent her to bed. "You sleep. I'll be here to see you off in the morning. We don't have to figure it out. God's got it all in His hands."

THIRTY-SEVEN

ex used his thin, little boy arms and helped Shirley push and shove to get her last piece of luggage in the car. The early morning sun was already burning her shoulders. She didn't know exactly where she and Windy were going or how long they would be there. Shirley touched her fingers to her lips. It was okay that Tony wasn't able to make it. He had work—she was going out of town, but life still went on. It was good enough that she had seen him last night.

Mother wasn't acting as though she had heard anything. But it was definitely good that *Ma Dear* didn't know that she had seen Tony. Mother's old friend would never let her live it down.

Mika stood beside the car holding a white-and-orange plastic jug of cold water and ice. Windy stood just outside the gate talking to her grandmother. Mother Johnson stood just inside holding a sack filled with sandwiches and fruit.

Ma Dear was on the sidewalk that led to the house, almost halfway to the porch. "You sure you two gone be all right? It just makes me a little nervous to think about the two of you traveling all the way to Illinois alone. Not really knowing where you going and everything."

"I drove here with the kids from Alabama, Ma Dear, and that's even farther away. We're going to be fine." Shirley sounded more confident than she felt.

Mother Johnson turned and nodded at Ma Dear. "They're gone be just fine. They're just taking care of a little unfinished business. The Lord has got His eye on them. Besides that, they got angels watching over them all the way there." Shirley thought she saw Mother wink at her. "And they got three ladies praying that ain't gone stop until they get back. What more reassurance do you need?"

Ma Dear fanned herself and looked at Shirley. "I know you gone be fine, I'm just being an old lady." She looked at the children and then smiled at Shirley. "Actually, I'm just pretending. I can't wait for you to leave 'cause me and the children got some good times planned."

Shirley looked at Ma Dear while she bent to hug Lex and Mika. "You're just being someone who loves me. And I can imagine all that you all are going to get into while I'm gone." She smiled at Mother Johnson. "Keep an eye on the children—all three of them—for me, please!" Shirley stood, took the cooler from Mika, and looked at Windy who was hugging her grandmother. "You about ready?"

Windy squeezed her Granny Mildred one last time, picked up her duffel bag, and headed toward the car. "Ready as I'm going to get, I guess."

By the time Shirley and Windy were packed into the car, the rest of the family was waving from the porch. *We're going to be fine. I'm going to be fine. I'm going to be fine, right, God?* Shirley put the car in drive and began to ease away from the curb.

"Shirley, wait!"

It was Tony.

She braked and put the car in park. Tony leaned in the window and kissed her on the cheek. He handed her a red rose. "I told you I was coming." He squatted beside the car. "You call and check in, okay? And if you need me, I know how to get to wherever you are." He looked across Shirley to include Windy. "You two be careful. Don't drive too far. Don't get too tired." He looked back at Shirley and pulled one of her braids. "We got stuff to talk about when you get home, okay, lady?" He kissed her again, but this time the kiss brushed the side of her mouth. "Take care of each other." Tony stood and waved as Shirley drove away.

Shirley and Windy didn't talk much along the way. Shirley thought of all the things that could go wrong. Her mother could have been moved. She might not be able to find her. Her mother still might not recognize her. Her mother might recognize her and not want to see her.

She wasn't hungry, but her stomach gurgled and whistled almost like the fourth of July, like her stomach did when Danny died.

Not much has changed since we left Alabama. Except we have less money. She reached into the purse that rested against her left thigh. The brown envelope was noticeably thinner. Nothing had changed, except that she had kissed a man—a man who was not Danny. Nothing had changed, except now she was on her way to do what she had thought would never be done. Nothing had changed, except that now she was linked—was sharing her search to find herself with someone at least as lost as she was.

The same group of envelopes, tied with pink ribbon, lay on the console between her and Windy. It was the same bundle that was on the seat when she, Mika, and Lex had left Alabama headed to California. She had not untied them in the time she had been in Tyler. They were memories she kept, but didn't want to see.

They spent the night in a chain motel in Arkansas. Shirley still didn't have much to say, and Windy seemed engrossed in her thoughts. Shirley climbed into her bed, the bundle of letters in her hand. Once she heard Windy's breathing change and Shirley knew the girl was asleep, she turned on the lamp next to her bed and pulled open the ribbon on the envelopes. The pink was lighter on the fabric that had not been exposed, so that there was a pattern. Shirley flipped quietly through the letters until she came to the one from her uncles, the letter that had come just as she and Tony were about to leave for the high school prom.

It had been a long time since she had allowed herself to think about her uncles. They had been so much a part of her life. Big Uncle, who was actually the younger of the two, but who was tenderhearted and kind, and Little Uncle, who was the thinker and the talker, had been central to her life growing up. She could not think of East St. Louis, or about going home, without thinking of them.

Her uncles had stood as her father when he was away in the military and away at war. Shirley remembered the joking and the arguments around the dinner table, Little Uncle controlling the television…but what she remembered most was something she had not recognized then, a certain tenderness in their eyes. It was rare, she knew now, among men. Despite their strength, there was almost a doelike innocence and kindness in their eyes.

The letter, written in Little Uncle's hand, had been hand-delivered. When she had seen it, Shirley knew that it would change her life. It was, however, a change she had put off for almost twenty years. Shirley removed the letter from the original envelope. The paper had softened and the creases were sharp. Her uncles had written to her from the maximum-security state prison in Joliet.

Joliet, Illinois
May 1975

Dear Shirley,

This is not the way to get reacquainted, is it? Everything in your life, your sweet little life, has been turned upside down. Your uncle and I, every time we see each other, talk about you. We worry over what we could have done differently. What we could have changed that would have made your life better. We worry about whether you are happy in Tyler—though we were both happy to find out that you were with Cousin Mavis. Grandpa Demosthenes would have been glad. "God never made a finer woman," he used to say.

Still, that does little to relieve our guilt. The only thing that helps us feel better is that every time we replay our choices, we always come to the same place: we did what we had to do. There were lots of people suffering in the sixties. It's just been ten years, and you probably don't remember a lot of it, Shirley. But there were riots in the cities, buildings were burning, and in a lot of places in the South (and in the North, for that matter) black people were living afraid. There was hope that things were going to change, that one day our children would be able to walk to school and not be afraid, that one day a black man would be able to voice his opinion and not be hung or silenced if it offended white people.

There was lots of hope, there was lots of talk, but— even though there were many people involved in the struggle—there weren't enough people able or willing to make the sacrifice to push for change. What your uncle and I knew was that change never comes without sacrifice and without struggle. It never comes without first changing people's minds. What we could see needed to be done was to expose to the light the filthy thoughts men had been having for years that made them comfortable hurting and oppressing other men.

Your grandfather Demosthenes always taught us— from the time your mama, your uncle, and I were children—if you see something that needs to be done, then you are the one to do it. We saw something needed to be done. Well, actually your Big Uncle saw it first, and I didn't want to get involved. But when we went home that time— I'm not sure you still remember—for your grandmother's funeral, even I couldn't deny it. We had all moved away to Illinois, and as bad as things were, there were still some things we didn't see. But when we went home, we couldn't deny that we saw something that needed to be done, so we did it.

I know, at the time, it might have looked to you as if we were leaving because of your mother. Shirley, if your uncle and I have cried over anyone more than you, then it would be your mother. I wish you had known her as a girl. She was always laughing and dancing. But life put strain on her she couldn't take. That time she went through—your daddy in Vietnam and all the burnings, the murder, the chaos that was going on around us—put pressure on all of us. It's hard to be normal, whatever that is, when the times around you aren't normal.

We didn't leave because of her; we left because there was something we had to do. You were our heart, Shirley. You still are. But there were lots of other children just like you who weren't safe. Something in the country had to change. If four little girls could be blown up in a church, then we knew no little children were safe. If a boy could be beaten and murdered and no one brought to justice, then we knew none of our children were safe. You weren't safe, even with us at home, if that kind of evil was able to walk around free with nobody challenging it. People were living in fear—black men, women, and children were afraid in their home; they were afraid walking the streets; they even had to be afraid in church.

Your daddy went to war outside the country to protect us here at home. Your Big Uncle and I fought for rights inside the country to protect us here at home. Our greatest sacrifice to the greater good was that we had to leave you and your mother alone to fight the wars that would make you safe. Your daddy went to Vietnam and lost his life, but that was a price that he was willing to pay to protect you, your mother, and the country. Your uncle and I went to fight injustice and we lost our freedom, but that was a price we were willing to pay for you, your mother, and for the country.

In all wars, though—even for the victors—there are victims among those who stay at home. Your mother was a casualty, Shirley. She wasn't the cause.

This is a long letter. Your Big Uncle and I have been talking about it for a long time—what we should write, what we should say. We don't know when or if we'll get out of prison. We've been accused of murdering two policemen. No one hears our voices saying we didn't do it—that we used words, not guns—when all the other voices here in Joliet are yelling the same thing. Your Big Uncle and I have peace about it, though. We would give up our freedom again to be able to make sure that the children are safe. We would do it all again.

You are probably about to graduate. We don't have any money to buy you a gift in here. We spent weeks talking about it—about what we could give you, what we could leave you. The greatest gift we thought (because you already have our love) would be peace.

Shirley, if you can, forgive us and make peace with what your Big Uncle and I felt we had to do. Shirley, your father was a good man and you know he loved you. Make peace with what he felt he had to do. Most of all, Shirley, make peace with your mother. Make peace with who she is. Remember how beautiful she was and how easily she laughed. Remember her cooking and how well she loved your father—all the things she did. But also don't be afraid to remember and make peace with the parts of her that are broken. Don't look away from those places; make peace with them.

The beauty of stained glass is not just the colors, but it is also the broken places where light cannot get through. I've been thinking a lot about that lately and that those windows reflect the beauty of what God does with us. He takes all our bright, shiny places and shines through them. But He *also uses our dark places, reshaping them and reforming them, so that when He is done—despite our dark places— our lives still shine.*

Everything isn't perfect, but your mama's life still shines. Find peace in that, Shirley. Look at her beautifully colored places and know that those same colors are in you. Study her dark places and see if the same ones are in you. But find peace knowing that if you cannot change your own dark places, God will find a way to use them, too. Our gift to you, Shirley, is peace and when you receive it, give it away to those you love.

We love you.

Your Uncles (Big and Little)

When she slept that night, she dreamed about riding her bicycle and falling down.

It happened so fast. Her ankle caught in the chain—there would be bicycle grease on her white socks and Mama might get mad. Shirley thought about Evel Knievel, then she was in the street and there were little rocks sticking in her hands, and her palms were bleeding. Little Shirley closed her eyes. If you didn't look, it didn't hurt as much. She didn't want to cry, somebody might see. She was on her stomach and couldn't breathe, but she knew it was just the wind knocked out of her—Big Uncle had told her about that. But the rocks on her knees hurt, and she didn't believe she could walk or get up. Shirley could only grunt.

Her mother's voice came to Shirley while she lay in the street.

People can think fast when they're in danger, Mama always said.

You know that's the truth, Little Uncle had agreed. They can do the impossible. Get strength from nowhere. *I even heard of a woman lifting up a car by herself when her son got run over.*

It hurt, but Shirley crawled to the side of the road onto somebody's grass. *Please, God, don't let anybody smash my bike flat as a pancake.* Shirley turned her face into the grass and cried.

Then there was Big Uncle. Without a word, he lifted Shirley, cradling her in one arm while he grabbed the bike with his free hand. It was okay to cry in front of Big Uncle; Mama said he had a tender heart. Shirley buried her face in his neck and wept while he told her it would be all right.

It was going to be all right. Somehow, after too many years, she was going to have to find the strength and the courage to see them.

THIRTY-EIGHT

he closer they got to Illinois, the quieter they got. Not that either one of them had been saying much since they left Texas. Windy was balled up almost into the fetal position; Shirley kept humming the lullaby she had been singing since she was a child.

"What is that song?" Windy raised her head. "I hear you singing it all the time."

"It's just a song I made up when I was a little girl. It helped me to go to sleep at night."

Windy brushed her hair out of her face. "Really? Sing it to me."

Shirley looked at the girl and wondered how she could have missed the resemblance—the almost white hair and the clear blue eyes. Maybe it was that Ken's hair, in third grade, was coated in dirt, and the eyes that in Windy's face were cool and clear were cold and angry in Ken's. Where his face and his look were hard, Windy's was sweet and quietly frantic.

Am I really doing the right thing? It was pointless, now, to ask the question. It was too late to turn back.

"Come on, Shirley, sing it to me." Windy turned in the seat

and smiled. Ken never would have smiled—he snarled. Shirley knew he would have been disgusted to ride in the car with her. How was it that the two of them—Windy and her father— were so different?

"I'm not so sure you want to hear me sing. I'm no Stephanie Mills or Pat Benatar."

"I'm really good at whining. I can make it miserable for you all the way there."

Shirley smiled. "It's not much. Just a little song." She began to sing.

Rock me, baby Jesus,
Hold me, baby Jesus,
Love me, baby Jesus,
So I won't be afraid.

Windy laid her head back on the seat and nodded, so Shirley sang it again.

Rock me, baby Jesus,
Hold me, baby Jesus,
Love me, baby Jesus,
So I won't be afraid.

Windy began to sing the little song, too, and she sang it off and on until they reached East St. Louis.

When Shirley pulled off of Highway 55, she followed Fourth Street to Broadway and knew she was home. "We'll find someplace to stay, then we'll go find the hospital, and then we'll find your daddy."

She was home.

Only it was Kansas after the storm. Nothing had prepared her, no one had told her how Dorothy must have felt returning from Oz. How not much, except an occasional street name, was familiar to her. Everywhere there were empty buildings, boarded up, and broken windows, as though some violent storm had blown through town. And liquor stores—there seemed to be a liquor store on every corner. The grocery stores where she remembered shopping with her mother and father were closed. There were just the ghost of signs—dirty footprints where there used to be neon letters. The city looked abandoned. And all the people were black.

Windy's head turned from side to side. She looked sad, confused, and disappointed. Her expression said she had been expecting and hoping for something more.

"It wasn't always like this." Shirley started trying to explain. "I can remember when it was a good place to be. There were people and cars and life all over." As they crossed over onto State Street, Shirley pointed out faded landmarks. "The public library used to be on that corner. And that big building over there used to be Sears and Roebuck. I don't know why it closed…there were always people shopping in there."

She pointed across the street. "And over there used to be the Rex-All drugstore. People used to really live here. It's hard to imagine now, but there used to be parades on this street. I remember seeing people happy and smiling. I remember holding my father's and my mother's hands and watching the bands march by. Bands used to come from other towns." Shirley shook her head. "People used to come from other towns to work here. People used to work in all these places. I don't know what happened."

The city looked like it had been murdered—as though someone had, with premeditated and malevolent intent, killed it.

The color was gone. It was like those despondent old grainy Depression era photographs—the ones where people looked grim and never smiled—that are tucked away in family albums. The pictures that people skip over because they are colorless and sad compared to the bright slick photographs of happier times. The city looked like the pictures that people only turned to when they were searching, when they were seeking to make sense of the present by excavating the past.

Shirley gave Windy a nod. "It will get better. When my family moved farther down State Street, things had already started to get a little bad here, but the other end was always fine."

But it wasn't fine. Whatever had poisoned the city, whatever bomb had exploded, whatever thing had choked the city had tightened its tentacles past Twenty-fifth Street. The fungus and decay had crept past Thirty-seventh Street and had choked all the schools and businesses along the way.

The main street, which had once been chugged with traffic, was now easy to navigate. A bypass that had been built now escorted people and traffic around the city.

Windy was pale, her eyes wide. "What happened here?"

Whatever happened to East St. Louis, whatever had killed the city, was creeping and deadly—even most of the grass was gone. All that was still green were the trees that were deep-rooted, trees that drank from silent, ancient, unseen streams. The rest had died. And no one seemed to be mourning. Maybe that had to do with the bypass that made it easy for people to pass by, that made it easy for people not to see, that made it guiltless for people not to care.

There was no real estate boom in Shirley's hometown. There were no men profiting from paper deals. There was no illusory speculation, no junk bonds, no contracts or shady arrangements and business pacts that netted them millions of faux dollars. Phantom dollars that they could cash in at banks to buy bigger houses, to finance businesses, to pay high-priced tuition, to pay for junkets and trysts, and to make more deals. No one overpriced the value of the land, or overestimated the men's earning potential so that they could qualify for more nonexistent money to buy more overpriced land. In what was left of her town, what was, was.

Black men holding on to the front of their pants, holding on to the last thing that made them men, stumbled back and forth on corners on which only white men used to stand, on land that only white men used to own. Gesturing at each other and at the few cars that passed, they seemed to be laughing and denying their own mortality, to be joking and holding at bay whatever it was that had depressed the land and devalued them.

The bypass might have been intended to corral and border the decay, but it hadn't worked. Decay had jumped the bypass and crept unchecked past Fortieth Street to Fifty-fifth.

On the corner of Fifty-ninth, Shirley pulled onto an abandoned lot and parked. She pointed at a fast-food fried chicken place on the corner. "I think there used to be a candy store there, or maybe it was a little five-and-dime, you know a little discount store." She waved her hand at the area around them. "All of this used to be green. There were always children going and coming from school. A crossing guard used to stand here, almost right where we're parked, and walk us back and forth across the street to school." She shook her head and laid her hand on the side of her face. "I can't believe this. I can't believe what has happened here." She pointed across the street and indicated farther down Fifty-ninth Street. "The school's down there. I guess it's still down there. That's the place where I knew your dad." Shirley looked at the clock on the dashboard. "I guess we better keep going until we find someplace to stay."

But she turned instinctively instead toward the place that had been home—down Fifty-ninth to Lake Drive. Shirley turned left off of Lake Drive onto Sixty-second Street and expected to smell pears and to see military, manicured lawns. Though she could not smell the fruity sweetness in the air, the street still appeared to be alive, though the yards were not as rigidly uniform. The park looked a little worse for the wear, but the street still looked hopeful, though there were no children outside playing. She slowed when they drove by her old house. It was painted brick red, but the same white picket fence bordered the house and the flower garden. The breezeway and garage were intact.

As Shirley sat staring at the house, she remembered her family eating dinner in the living room and her family laughing in the kitchen. "We used to live here. That was my bedroom." She pointed to the room, then continued driving down the street until she saw the lot with the large stone, the place she used to meet Sheri—or where Shirley imagined she used to meet Sheri.

"Don't cry, little girl. I know where you are." Sheri walked to the rock and took Shirley's hand and patted her on the shoulder. "I been way farther than this before. And I was watching you. I know where your bike is and your street is really close."

"It's almost dusk-dark!" All kids had to be home by dusk-dark, even bad ones. The little girl nodded—she understood.

"I'll walk you to your street, little girl," Sheri said, still patting Shirley on her shoulder. They held hands, and the little girl walked Shirley around the rock until she saw her bicycle on the path where she left it.

"There's your bike. See? I told you. You don't have to cry no more."

Shirley wiped her face. "I'm not crying. And I'm not a little girl. I'm as old as you."

"Come on, little girl. We better start walking."

Shirley pointed at the lot and the space where the large rock had been. "I used to play here," she told Windy. It made sense, her college professors had told her. She'd been a normal child living in tragic, unnatural circumstances. She had simply created a friend to comfort her, to be a sort of mother figure when her real-life family was falling apart. By choosing a name so similar to her own, the instructors had told Shirley, she was subconsciously reassuring herself that if her family abandoned her, she could take care of herself.

She could take care of herself. *"I told you. You don't have to cry no more."*

"Sixty-third Street!" The excitement in Windy's voice brought Shirley back. Windy was pointing at the street sign. "I remember hearing something about this street. I'm not sure what, but I'm sure that I heard the name. Maybe this is where my daddy lived!"

Shirley shook her head. "No, they lived in another part of town, closer to the school." There was no point in describing the place where Ken and his relatives had lived. Windy would see it soon enough. "This is not the place."

As they drove back toward State Street, Windy turned to look behind her. "I'm sure about the street name, though. I *know* I remember something about that street name."

THIRTY-NINE

They didn't find a hotel until they reached Belleville. Though it wasn't as severe, whatever was infecting the city had made its way to the Belleville border, then stopped.

They unpacked, and then Windy flopped across her bed. "I've been thinking…I've been wondering what we came here for."

"You're not saying you want to go back. We came all this way to see where you came from, to maybe find your father. You're not saying you want to go back?"

Windy walked across the room and turned on the television. "We got cable." She flipped the dial until she came to a music television channel. She stared at the television for a moment, and then looked back at Shirley. "I'm not saying I want to go back. I was just saying."

Shirley nodded. There wasn't much to say. "I think I'm going to call and check in with Mother Johnson."

Inside the telephone booth, Shirley laid the roll of quarters she had been able to get at the front office on the little shelf. If she were honest with Windy, she would tell the girl that she wanted to go back to Tyler. That she wasn't sure why they had come. If she were honest with Windy, she would tell the girl that there had been a weight on her chest since they had turned off the highway and crossed the bridge into the city.

After all these years, what was she supposed to say to her mother? What was she supposed to expect? What was the point? The truth was, Shirley would have been relieved and ready to go herself if Windy had only shouldered the blame. Any excuse would have been excuse enough to leave.

She peeled the roll open, deposited the quarters, and dialed. "Hello, Mother." She told Mother Johnson that she was fine. Windy was fine. Everything was going fine. Mother Johnson didn't question her. "All right then, baby," Mother said. When Shirley spoke to Mika and Lex, she told them that she was fine, Windy was fine, and everything was going fine. "I miss you," she said and then hung up the phone.

Shirley picked up what was left of the quarters, opened the door to the booth, and then stopped. She closed the door, turned to put quarters in the slot, listened for the dial tone, and then dialed Tony's number. Before it rang, she hung up the phone. The quarters clanked into the change cup. She didn't need to call him. It was silly. She turned to leave, then turned back again. She replaced the quarters, took a deep breath, and dialed. Maybe he wouldn't be home.

"Hello."

She cleared her throat. "Hello, Tony?"

"Hello, baby. I was hoping you would call."

Baby. Tony seemed to have just settled into it, to have made a decision that he was having a relationship and to make himself at home. "Are you home? How's it going, baby?" He sounded so comfortable, as though he had been saying it all along.

"I'm fine. Windy's fine. Everything is fine."

"You don't sound fine. I don't hear fine in your voice." It sounded as though he was sitting down. "Come on, Shirley, tell me."

"It's nothing," she said. Then she began to tell him about the city, about the death, and about how it made her feel. "I'm afraid my home is dead—you know? That the town is dead." She told him about the house and her old street. Shirley told Tony about rereading the letter from her uncles. "I'm going to try to go see them. Joliet is a good ways away, but I'm going to try. I think I needed to be here to really understand the letter—I've been carrying it with me for years—and to remember. It was good to make it here, but now I'm asking myself why I even came. I mean, my uncles could be dead. I just don't—"

"I thought you went to see your mother. To try to get some things straight with your mother."

"But why? That's what I'm asking myself. I mean, I haven't seen her in years. I've moved on. She's living her life. She may not even be aware that…she may not even be aware. Who knows if she can carry on a coherent conversation? I mean, what am I expecting of her? Why even put myself through this?" She took a deep breath. "And I think Windy is asking herself the same thing about her father.

"What is it going to change about who I am when I see her? How is it going to help me to see her wrapped in a white sheet staring into space or slobbering or doped up on drugs?"

"I think you won't be able to answer any of those questions unless you go. It might be that you made this trip for nothing—I don't think so, but you won't know for sure unless you go to see her. Shirley, I know this has to be hard for you. I can understand you feeling afraid—"

"I'm not feeling afraid!"

Tony paused before he spoke. "Sure you are, Shirley. You have to be feeling afraid."

Shirley scuffed the toe of her shoe on the floor of the booth. "I'm feeling afraid."

"We don't have all the answers up front, right?"

She couldn't answer, she just held the phone.

"We don't have to have all the answers, right, Shirley?"

"Right."

"We don't have to have them. We just have to be brave enough to try, to search for the answers. And we have to trust that whatever it turns out to be, in some way it's going to be for our good."

"Yes, doctor." She laughed softly. Shirley took a deep breath. An operator recording interrupted to ask for seventy-five more cents in coins. "I have to go, Tony. Thanks...thanks." She hung up the phone.

Mika and Lex were in the bed. It had been a long day, but a good day. Mother Johnson laughed to herself. Ma Dear had hollered out loud when she saw Tony Taylor kiss Shirley on the cheek. Mother Johnson had grabbed her arm and shushed her. "I knew it!" Ma Dear had squeaked out. "I knew it!"

She knew Ma Dear really would have really been yelling if she had known that Tony had come by just the night before.

"Lord, you're working it out. Everything is going to be all right."

Mother Johnson fell asleep lying in bed on her side and praying. When she dreamed, she dreamed about Shirley. She also dreamed about a fight going on in heaven. Everywhere that Shirley walked underneath heaven, in the dream, there were eyes that watched her from the shadows. Above the shadows, there was great light in heaven, but there were also the shadows. Mother Johnson couldn't see the body in the shadows, only the eyes. But she knew without knowing that the eyes wanted to draw Shirley into the shadows, to keep her from walking in the light.

But greater than the shadow that tried to hide itself away, was the light.

There was another figure whose eyes watched Shirley— this one watched from the light. It was hard to distinguish the details of the figure because the light was so bright, but Mother could see that the figure wore a luminescent belt, breastplate, helmet, and shoes. The figure held in one hand a brilliant, blazing shield, and in the other a burning sword with two edges.

The shape in the darkness, the eyes, said nothing. But the shining figure bent to whisper in Mother Johnson's ear. "Fear not. Pray always," the glorious warrior said. "Stand and always pray."

The voice was so loud it startled Mother Johnson awake. She looked around the room and listened, unsure if the children had heard the voice. *Fear not. Pray always. Stand and always pray.* Mother Johnson fell back to sleep thinking she would have to gather the praying women—Mildred and Ma Dear.

FORTY

By the time Windy awakened the next morning, Shirley was already dressed. Shirley fingered the money in the brown envelope. Every day it was getting thinner and thinner. "Did you sleep well?"

Windy wiped her eyes and nodded. "Yeah." She yawned. "I'm hungry."

Shirley tapped her finger on the envelope, which was tucked in the side of her purse. "Okay. We should be able to find something around here." She faced Windy and tucked one of her legs underneath her. "The way I see it, we have about three days to do whatever we're going to do. I've got two uncles that I would like to make contact with—I'd like to try to see them. They're at a prison in Joliet." It surprised her how easily that slipped off her tongue—*at a prison in Joliet*. She'd never mentioned it to anyone; she had never wanted to explain. Now it was just fact—there was no disgrace or embarrassment attached.

"Joliet is a few hours from here. And I don't know how I'm going to do it, but…I don't have to have it all figured out; I just have to try."

She made herself smile as she shrugged at Windy. The city

was gloomy and, most likely, things would not be well with her mother, but she had to hold on. Shirley knew all too well how easy it was to slip into the shadows, to surrender to the grayness around her. She was going to hold on…she *had* to hold on, even if all she could do was to force a smile.

"Then, I need…I've got to…I need to see my mother." Shirley felt the weight return to her chest. "She's at a hospital in town, so that should be pretty easy." Maybe if she talked fast enough, Windy wouldn't know how troubled she was. "You can stay here and rest while I'm visiting her—you know, there's no need for you to be running all over the place." She smiled again. "Then I'll take you up to the school, and maybe we'll find someone who can help us…help you get in contact with your dad."

Windy sat up in bed. "So you got this all figured out?" She pulled at a clump of her hair. "It's like some kind of tour or something." Windy stretched. "But I don't see how we're going to get all this done in three days."

"Well, we don't have much choice. That's about as far as we can stretch what we have." Shirley tapped the brown envelope. "Whatever we do, we have to get it done by then."

Windy got up and turned on the TV. "If it's got to be three days, then it's got to be three days. And really, if we're running out of time, I don't have to try to find my daddy. You can just drop me off in Oklahoma on your way back home. I'll be fine. Everything will be fine." Windy's eyes began to blink and she waved her hands excitedly. "I'm sure my family is just waiting for me. They never wanted me to go in the first place—"

Shirley opened her mouth, about to debate Windy about the facts. Before she could speak, though, Windy sighed. "Well, really, you know what's really going on, don't you?" She flopped down on the bed and hung her head. "I don't know what's going to happen. I don't know where I'm going to go. I just…"

Shirley nodded. "We just have to try."

While Windy bathed and dressed, Shirley picked up breakfast, then drove back to the hotel. She stopped at the pay phone with a fresh roll of quarters—she was personally going to keep the U.S. Mint in business. It made sense to call Joliet Prison before the two of them—or before she—drove to Joliet. Shirley got the number from information and called.

"May I help you?" The woman on the other end of the line sounded as though she really didn't want to help. Her nasally tone sounded as though this was just one more communication that interrupted her daily routine of waiting for breaks and her lunch hour. "*Hello?* May I help you?"

"Well, actually, I'm hoping that you can." Shirley told the woman her maiden name—Shirley Ferris—and the names of her two uncles. "I believe they're in your facility."

"Do you know for certain that they're here? There are many correctional facilities in the state of Illinois. There's no way I can find them if they aren't here."

Shirley bit her tongue so that she wouldn't say what she wanted to say, because if she said what she wanted to say, she was never going to talk to her uncles. "Well, I have a letter that indicates that they were in Joliet."

"All right then. Is it an official letter?"

"No, it's from one of my uncles."

"Well, it may not be official at all. And they may have been here and then moved on to other facilities in the system. What is the date on the letter?"

"Well, it's dated 1975—"

"Nineteen-seventy-five! Well, there's certainly little or no chance that they're still here—if they ever were here." The woman blew air into the receiver as though she were exasperated. "I really want to help you. I try to help people all the time. But you're really not giving me very much to work with." She blew again. "Do you have a name or names?"

"Yes, I do—"

"I also need their birth dates and race, if you have that information."

Shirley forced herself to be patient. "I have the race, and I believe I can approximate the dates."

"I'm sorry, but we have to have the exact dates. I can't help you without the exact birth dates. I'm sorry." The woman didn't sound sorry.

"Well, will their prison identification numbers help?"

"You have their numbers? Well, if you had said that first, I could have already checked for you."

Shirley wouldn't let herself scream. "Well, I'll give them to you now." She read the numbers to the woman.

"I'm going to put you on hold and check. I'll be just a moment. Please hold."

Please hold? Please hold! No, please don't let me put my hands around your throat! Why did people have to make helping so hard? Why were people like this woman getting paid to make life more frustrating and complicated for people that only wanted a little help?

While Shirley waited, the pay phone recording played asking her to feed the phone more quarters, and she did.

The woman came back on the line. "Miss Ferris, those two prisoners are *C*-numbered. They're here, but their sentences are indefinite."

"What does that mean?"

"It means they weren't sentenced to a specific number of years. Their sentences are indefinite. They can be held for an indefinite number of years; they also might be released at any time."

"But not within the next three days."

The woman sounded even more exasperated. "No, I wouldn't think so. Is that all?"

"No. No, could you tell me when visiting hours are, or if there are certain days when I can visit?"

"Well, first your name has to be on the visiting list."

Shirley nodded as though the woman could see her. "All right, so how do I get on the list?"

"The inmate has to request that your name be put on the list."

"But they don't know I'm here. They haven't seen me in years."

The woman had hit the repeat button. "The inmate has to request that your name be put on the list."

Shirley took a deep breath. "Okay. How do I get them to request that I be put on the list?"

"We suggest that you write to the inmate; then they can request that your name be put on the list. A simple investigation will be done; then your name will be added to the list. It takes approximately two weeks."

"Two weeks! I only have three days."

"It takes approximately two weeks, ma'am. The inmate has to request that your name be put on the list; there will be an investigation, and then it has to be approved."

Shirley could feel her heart beginning to beat more rapidly. She added more quarters to the phone. "Is there some other way? Can I call them?"

"Inmates may make contact by telephone, but they can only call collect. However, in order to be granted permission to call, the person that the inmate wishes to contact must be on their approved contact list."

Shirley shifted her weight from foot to foot. "How do I get on the telephone contact list?"

"We suggest that people wishing to be added to the list contact the inmates by mail. Once contacted, the inmate may request that you be added to the list. An investigation will be completed; if approved, the person will be added to the list and the inmate may call—but only collect."

Shirley put one hand over her heart. "And how long does it take to be added to the telephone contact list."

"Approximately two weeks."

Shirley slapped herself on the head. "Lady, I only have three days. I'm only going to be in Illinois for three days. I haven't seen my uncles in almost twenty years. I just need to see them or call them. I just want to visit, for goodness' sakes!"

"I'm sorry, ma'am. In order to visit or call, you must be on the inmate's approved contact list. The approval process takes approximately—"

"Yes, I know. It takes two weeks! *Two weeks!*" Shirley hung up the phone. Picked it up to call—she didn't know who—and hung it up again. She picked up the receiver, tapped it against her forehead, then slammed it back into the cradle.

"God?" She walked back to the car.

"I thought you had left or something." Windy was towel-drying her hair. She tossed the wet towel on the sink and walked into the room to peek in the food bag. "Great, I love these little breakfast sandwiches." She picked up a cup from the carrying tray. Windy lifted the lid and sipped. "Yuck! This is cold!"

Shirley could feel her temples pulsing. She forced herself not to scream. "Windy, just don't say anything about it, okay. Just don't say anything."

They pulled into the empty parking lot of Morrison Elementary School. The building was essentially the same. Shirley walked with Windy and pointed out the cafeteria and the playground.

"This was the boys' side, and this was the girls'." She showed Windy the asphalt lot where they took P.E., and then she pointed out her third-grade classroom—Mrs. Canada's classroom—where she had tried to teach Ken, Barbara, and Misty to read. "I was just a little kid." She shrugged at Windy and smiled.

Every smile was an effort, but she was not going to surrender. If she couldn't see her uncles, then they were going to see the school. She was going to keep putting one foot in front of the other until she and Windy had done what they came to East St. Louis to do.

Shirley pointed at the cloakroom window. "I didn't know what I was doing. Probably someone trained could have taught them to read."

Windy looked at her. "But that's why you were teaching them, right? Because the teacher couldn't teach them. Do you think something was wrong with him—with my father—that he couldn't read?" Windy stared at the classroom windows as though they would tell her something she didn't already know. As though, if she looked hard enough, they would tell her who she was and where she was going. "Will you take me by the house, where they lived? You know…what was it, Cootie Town?"

Shirley drove and tried to remember where the bus had driven when she was a girl, how they got to the place where Ken, Barbara, and Misty lived.

"That seems like a mean thing, you know? To call them that. I wonder what my daddy felt like being called that. I wonder why he let people call him that—a Cootie. I would never let anyone call me that. Especially not my kid—never!"

Shirley didn't know what to say. It *was* mean. And she had thought for years how the kids must have felt, what they thought of their childhood moniker when they became adults. Probably the same thing she felt about the names she was called.

"Why did it have to be me? Why did I have to be the one raised without a daddy?"

"Windy, you don't know how many times I've asked myself the same thing. I don't have all the answers—I'm not God— but I wonder sometimes if it might be the only way to break a destructive family pattern." Shirley shrugged. "I don't know."

"Why didn't somebody do something to help? Why didn't somebody try to help them?"

She didn't have an answer, so Shirley drove in silence until she had exhausted her memory and any time they had to search for Windy's father's old home.

Windy used her hands to tousle her hair, to air it so that it would finish drying. The air blowing in through the car windows helped. "So you mean you're not going to be able to see your uncles? Good thing you called before we drove way up there."

Shirley's lips and jaw were tight. "Good thing."

"So what are you going to do?"

"Well, I'm not going to see my uncles. I can't even call them." Shirley flipped on her turn signal, checked her rearview mirror, and changed lanes. "So I guess, I'm going to try to see my mother. The way things are going, we won't need three days. I don't think I'm going to be long with my mother. You can probably wait in the car. I'll run into the hospital, see her, and then I'll run back out."

"But you haven't seen her in years. How are you going to see her that fast?"

Shirley looked straight ahead. "It's hard to explain. But the bottom line is she probably won't even know I'm in the room."

"So, why are you—?"

"Why I am bothering to go see her? I've been asking myself that. Other people seem to think it's going to make my life a bowl of cherries—my uncles, Mother Johnson, Tony…I thought God sent me a message that I needed to see her. But it's not like my life is not together. I'm happy." She threw one hand in the air, then slapped it back on the wheel. "I'm content where I am. As a matter of fact, I think I'd be more content if I wasn't here." Shirley could feel tension creeping up her shoulders. "I'm here, though, right? So, I might as well go through with it."

She shook her head. "I'll get in; I'll get out. It'll be over."

The drive back through town, back through East St. Louis, was no less depressing. Nothing had happened overnight to magically transform the city. Shirley was ready to do what she had to do and go. They drove down State Street and made a left onto Eighth. The town looked hopeless; the trip was looking hopeless. There was nothing to smile about…

Except on one corner, after she turned, Shirley saw two

little girls. Each little girl held in one of her hands the end of a jump rope. They wore rompers that tied on the shoulders—one girl wore orange and the other girl wore blue. The two little girls turned the rope in time and jumped together while they sang.

"*Miss Mary Mack, Mack, Mack,*
All dressed in black, black, black,
With silver buttons, buttons, buttons,
All down her back, back, back."

And farther down the block, three little boys ran through a lot laughing and kicking a soccer ball. *There were no children yesterday. I didn't see any children yesterday.* She was desperate for any prospect, any good news, so Shirley smiled.

"Well, we have a psychiatric unit, but we have no one by that name here. How long ago did you say she was here?" The sister's expression—the plaque on the wall of St. Mary's Hospital said that she was with the order of The Poor Handmaids of Jesus Christ—was full of charity and concern.

There was no point in heaping her frustration on the sister. "It was 1968. My mother would have been admitted in 1968."

Windy stood next to Shirley, wrapping a strand of her hair around her finger. She had objected to being left in the car.

Sister Pietra shook her head. "This is a short-term care facility. Your mother would have been dismissed not long after she arrived." She looked hopeful. "Perhaps there are other relatives who might know where she is?"

"No, no one else. My uncles were sure that this was where she was."

"It may be that she got help here and that she's out doing

well and taking care of herself. Many of our patients go on to facilities where they live at home, but they are able to go and come for treatment on an outpatient basis."

Shirley shook her head. It was too much to try to explain.

"Well she may have been admitted here. In fact, she may have been readmitted at one time or another, but the unit is not intended to provide long-term care. The intent is that people come here, are helped or stabilized, and then directed to where they can receive any additional care they might require. To be honest, with all the health care cuts, we couldn't afford to keep them long-term even if that was our mission." She shook her head. "There are so many souls that need help, and we have so little to help them with.

"Unfortunately, at the time that you mentioned, we weren't keeping records as stringently as we are now. The records that we have are in archives. But I can assure you, your mother is not here." The sister reached out to pat Shirley on the hand. Her blue eyes looked deeply into Shirley's. "Don't give up hope."

Don't give up hope? No, she was about to give up the whole trip. This whole thing was a pipe dream. She was running after something that didn't exist. She was reaching for something that was always going to be out of her reach. Why did she let people get her all excited? What was she hoping for? Things were good enough. She knew to leave them alone. She was wasting money. She was wasting time. *Don't give up hope?* She was throwing in the towel.

As Shirley and Windy walked away, Sister Pietra called out behind them. "Alton State Mental Hospital. You might try there. It's called the Alton Mental Health Center." Shirley stopped and turned to listen. "They are not far from here and they do provide long-term care. We've discharged patients there. You might try there." The sister waved hopefully. "Don't throw in the towel."

The afternoon was hot. Shirley's shoulders were tight, and she was frustrated. "What if we call it a day? I think—I think I just need to get something to eat and lie down." They stopped at the fried chicken place on the corner of Fifty-ninth Street. Shirley got fried chicken, fries, and rolls for both of them. In each hand she carried a large cup of ice-cold red soda. It was time to drown her sorrows.

Windy was quiet. She stared out the window.

"I guess I should tell you what's going on." Shirley tried to think of a way to make it sound normal, but there was no way to do that, was there? *My mother had a nervous breakdown. She spent time in an institution, in a hospital.* It didn't sound quite as glamorous as, say, the Betty Ford Center. "When my father died, my mother had a…a breakdown. They took her to a hospital and they took me to some kind of hospital or clinic—you know, for people who come *unglued.*" Shirley wiggled the fingers of one of her hands in the air. She tried to poke fun at the word, but it wasn't working. "Mother Johnson came here and got me and took me to live with her. No one knows where my mother is. Of course, you were with me today at St. Mary's, so you know that. But that's why I'm here. Like Lassie, I'm trying to find my family, trying to find my way back home."

They finished eating and tossed the boxes in the trash. Shirley wiped the grease from her mouth and from her hands. It turned the yellow napkin she held almost transparent. There was something comforting and predictable about fried chicken and grease—there were at least a few things in life you could count on. If you got fried chicken, you got grease.

Shirley stretched out across her bed. She was going to lose herself in the most mindless thing she could find on TV. She stopped at a video music channel when she saw Tina Turner— sporting a leather jacket, high heels, and a head full of spiky red hair—wailing, "What's Love Got to Do with It!"

She turned to talk to Windy and accidentally kicked the telephone book that lay on the shelf of the table mounted between the two beds. "Windy, I'm counting on you. I want you to find something on TV so bad, so boring, that I just get happy." Shirley raised her fist in triumph. "I'm counting on you, Windy. Your mission, should you accept it, is to numb my brain. To find something so bad on TV that I just pass out." She swung her legs around and kicked the telephone book again. "Find me something that is going to put me out of my misery." She lifted the book and pounded it on the bed. "I need something that is so powerful in its horribleness that it's going to make this day seem worthwhile"

Windy giggled. "Okay. You got it!" Both of them seemed to be feeling better. Maybe grease really was the answer.

"I'm desperate for deadening entertainment. I'm so desperate I'm going to read this phone book." Shirley began to flip through the book. She closed it and laid it on her lap. She pointed at the screen and forced herself to laugh at the program Windy had found on the television.

Using her thumb, she feathered the pages of the book. *I might as well look up Alton while I'm sitting here.* She found the number for the Alton Mental Health Center, reached for the phone, and called. She talked to Windy with the phone cradled against her ear. "It's a local call. I might as well call and find out the rules before we waste time going up there." She dialed and waited. There was a busy signal. She picked up the phone to put it aside, then stopped.

There had to be other mental health centers in the area.

FORTY-ONE

*M*other Johnson, Ma Dear, and Mildred formed a prayer circle at the kitchen table. Sunshine from the window lit the table, their hands, and reflected a glow on their faces. With a cup of tea sitting in front of each one, they held hands.

"The dream was so real, I could have reached out and touched it. And I heard it so real, it woke me from my sleep."

Ma Dear nodded. "It's something how God can call us to prayer."

Mildred squeezed both their hands. "I've been praying since they left. Really I was praying *before* they left—and I know both of you were praying, too. But you're right, Ma Dear. There's something special about praying together, praying as one."

Mother nodded. "In the dream, I just saw darkness trying to overtake Shirley, trying to keep her from the light. But my goodness, the angel of the Lord was standing there on guard and ready to fight. And His word to me was to pray. Soon as I got it, it come to me that I needed to call you two to form a prayer circle, a prayer chain. A three-cord rope is not easily broken."

Ma Dear shook her hands loose and they began to flutter like butterflies. "Glory to God! I feel something moving up in here. God is working powerful. Great God from Zion, we ain't never doubted that You got these two children in Your hands. Now, Lord, show up strong on their behalf. If the situation looks impossible, God, with a wave of Your hand, You can make it possible. So do it, Lord."

The three woman anchored themselves together again, and Mildred spoke up. "Lord, my granddaughter is on a journey to find—to find peace, and to find a place to lay her head. I don't know how You're going to work it out. I've been crying. You know that. I just can't figure any of it out—how she got here, how You had Mother Johnson's Shirley bring her here, or even why she wanted to find me. I can't see with my eyes or my mind how her going to look for her dad is going to put any of this puzzle together. You know I'm not really one to pray this way, to pray out loud or with other people. But I'm so grateful that You have put these sweet women—both of these sweet women—in my life to help me pray for Windy and to pray for me. Open doors that need to be opened, sweet Jesus, and please close those that need to be shut. Thank You."

Mother Johnson bowed her head low. "God, I know You got power. You don't need nobody to prove it to me. When everybody thought I was dead, You raised me up. So here I am sitting before You right now, just like Lazarus. I got my right mind and I got a double portion of health and strength. I know ain't nothing too hard for God! Nothing! You sent me word to pray, to stand and pray. So, here we are, Lord.

"You go ahead of those children and make the way. Any ugly thing that tries to hinder what You have for them, Lord, I pray that You would bind that thing here on earth, just like

You bound it in heaven. Lord, and I want You to loose Your power here on earth just like it is in heaven. Hallelujah! God, I know You setting everything in order. You making the rough places smooth; You bringing down the mountains and exalting the valleys. Ain't no doubt in my mind who You are and what You can do." Mother Johnson laughed out loud. "You just come on in here, Lord, and do what You feel like doing! We ain't gone tell You how, where, or when. You got it worked out, and when it's all said and done, we know You gone get the glory! And You know how old women are, sweet Jesus! We won't be able to keep it to ourselves."

Ma Dear giggled. "Oh, you praying now, Mother."

She squeezed Mother Johnson's hand. "And, Lord, while You at it, don't let this prayer just help our children. But, Lord, help all the women and chirren that don't have a place to go, that's lost in the world. Lord, help the men that's trying to find their way back to You, that's trying to learn how to be mighty men of God for You. Lord, while You at it, those that are in prison—whatever kind of prison it is—set them free. Lord, those that need healing, You know I know You can heal; do Your thing. And, Lord, those that have had the enemy, the devil steal from them—it don't matter if it's joy, if it's love, if it's peace, if it's finances, if it's health, if it's beauty, if it's faith, or hope—Lord, You the One that can make it right. Lord, for their shame give them double. For the confusion and worry they have suffered, give them a double portion right here, right now, on this earth. Let them see the goodness of the Lord in the land of the living."

Mildred rocked from side to side. "Sweet Jesus, give them double for their trouble. And, Lord, give us peace among men. Give us new hearts, Lord. Take away our hard hearts that hate one another, that judge one another, and please, sweet Jesus, give us new hearts of flesh. No more racism, no more greed, no more mean-spiritedness—sweet Jesus, let us be one. Lord, heal the land. Open the eyes of the blind. There is no one else faithful, no one else we can count on. Change us, Lord, and let the change begin with me."

Mother smiled. "We love You, Lord, and all these things we ask in Jesus' name, the name above every name. Amen."

Lex rolled his Nerf football around on the bed with one hand and tugged at the bottom of Mika's shirt with the other. "They're praying out there again."

"I know, Lex." Mika sat on the edge of the bed reading a book. "Come on, let's pray, too."

The two children bowed their heads. "Okay, you go first, Lex."

"No, you, Mika, you're the oldest. Mommy left you in charge."

"She didn't say I had to pray first, Lexington—Oh, never mind. I'll do it." She held her brother's hand. "Dear God, thank You for everything. Please take care of our mother and Windy. Let them have a good trip. Let them be happy and bring them home safe. God bless everybody—Mother Johnson, Ma Dear, Miss Mildred. Bless everybody. Oh, and don't forget Mr. Tony."

"Thank You, God. And don't forget my puppy. In Jesus' name, amen." Lex frowned at his sister. "Okay, now, Mika, let go my hand."

"Good afternoon. Chester Mental Health Center. May I help you?"

Shirley wasn't quite sure who to ask for or what to say.

She dropped the telephone book and began to twist one of her braids around her finger—she was turning into Windy. "Actually, I was just going through the telephone book and I saw the number for your facility." That was a good start—she was sure the man on the other end was going to think *she* was rational. "I'm trying to get some information."

"Yes."

"It's a long story."

"Yes."

She told him who she was and that she was looking for her mother. "The sister at St. Mary's suggested that I contact Alton. I called Alton, but the number was busy. So I saw that there were other centers—I could tell from the zip code listing that yours was also close to East St. Louis, so I thought I would call thinking that maybe you could tell me how the system works and give me some direction, or maybe it will turn out that my mother is at Chester, because I guess it's as likely that she's at Chester as it is that she's at Alton."

The man on the other end paused and then spoke. "Most likely the nun referred you to Alton Mental Health rather than Chester because our facility population is male only. In addition, Chester is a maximum-security center, so unless your relative committed a crime, it is unlikely that he would be here. But because the relative you seek is a woman, as I said before, that point is moot." He cleared his throat. "It might be, though, that if you give me a little more detail I still might be able to help you in some way."

"No, I...no, that's all right. Thank you for your time."

"Are you sure? I don't like feeling that I haven't helped you. I know your search must be frustrating, but if we talk, I might be able to help." He chuckled. "In fact, if I don't help you, I am sure that I will be plagued with great guilt. I don't normally answer the phones, but I assured the receptionist that I could handle the task. I hate to think, that in my first at bat, I have struck out." He cleared his throat again—it must have been a nervous habit. "Let's start again. First, you will tell me your name, then I will tell you mine, and we will see what I can do about helping to solve your dilemma."

Windy had her eyes glued on the television, but Shirley was sure that she was listening. Not that it mattered, there was nothing that she didn't already know. "My name is Shirley Ferris and I used to live here. Well, I lived in East St. Louis. I've been away for some time and I'm here—I've driven from Texas—to find my mother."

"Good. Good. I'm Father Connelly, and I'm the chaplain here at Chester."

Alton was the first place to check, he told Shirley. There should be some record of her mother somewhere. There had to be. Eventually, she would pop up in the system, either as a patient, or as someone who had been discharged. "But try Alton first."

"Thank you, Father. I was hoping to talk to my uncles, thinking they might know where she is, but I only have three days and that's not enough time to make arrangements to see them."

"Has it been long since you've seen your uncles?"

It had been longer than since the last time she had seen her mother, she told him.

"Well, I would think you should at least call them and speak with them before you leave. You've come such a long way. It would be a shame not to speak with them." Father Connelly cleared his throat. "Whatever happened with your family, I can't imagine that they would be so hard-hearted that they couldn't make a way to at least speak with you in three days' time."

"Father, you don't understand. They're in Joliet. They're in prison in Joliet." Father Connelly listened patiently while Shirley told him how her uncles were incarcerated. Then she told him the story of the telephone and visitor contact lists for prisoners. "It takes two weeks, either way. And I don't have two weeks."

"Joliet, you said?" The priest cleared his throat. "There is sometimes a certain amount of brotherhood amongst chaplains. Let us pray and see what the Lord, you, and I together can do." Shirley gave Father Connelly her number and promised to sit tight near the phone.

Shirley didn't remember falling asleep, but the phone awakened her—slightly.

Windy answered. "Well, I'm not sure. She's asleep. Let me see." Windy shook her shoulder. "Shirley? Shirley? There's a call for you. Can you take it?"

Shirley floundered on the bed and almost dropped the receiver when Windy handed it to her. "This is the Telecommunications System with a collect call for Shirley Ferris, will you accept the charges?"

"What? Yes? What?"

"You may go ahead, sir. Your party is waiting." The operator clicked off the line.

Shirley could hear someone breathing on the other end, but no words. "Big Uncle is that you?" She held her breath. "Big Uncle?"

The man's voice was barely above a whisper. "Shirley? Shirley? Is that you?" The depth of the voice was thicker, but it was the same voice that had carried her home when she had fallen, when she had failed at riding. Big Uncle's voice pushed from his chest. There was an edge to it that said that he was tender, that he wanted to laugh, but there was no mistaking that he was a man. Her uncle was silent again. Shirley could tell he was fighting not to cry.

"How did you get through? They told me two weeks…"

"That priest of yours talked to the chaplain here. The good rev here got to checking things out—he's good man. He didn't have to go out of his way, but he's always square with the men in here. He got word to me. Me and Little had your name on the lists all the time. Every time we see each other, me and Little talk about you. 'Someday we're going to get the chance to talk to her.' I guess we never really thought someday would come."

Shirley wept. There wasn't enough time to allow her to talk her way through everything. He wasn't allowed enough time outside of his cell. So she told him about the children and about Mother Johnson.

"So you married, now, and living in Tyler."

"Not exactly, Big Uncle." She told him about Danny and how he had died. "I'm trying to find Mama, Big Uncle…I'm going to see her. She's not at St. Mary's anymore. They don't have records. I don't know where to look, but the priest that helped me get in touch with you, he tried to help me. But I don't know where to look."

He told her everything he knew, the names of people and of streets—most of which she no longer remembered.

"I know it's hard, but it's a good thing you doing, baby. It's going to be good for you and for your mama…it's sure been good for me just to *hear* you. It's been like talking to an angel." His voice sounded like he was choking, until he cleared it. "I got to go, honey. Okay? I'm going to get word to your Little Uncle when I see him. Don't worry, baby. Don't give up. Everything's going to be all right."

FORTY-TWO

*I*t was impossible to physically gain access to the Alton Mental Health Center. Shirley and Windy tried. The buildings were surrounded by trees and bushes as though it was a library campus, but it was an illusion. The Center's doors were not open.

Back in the hotel room, she called again.

"Alton Mental Health Center. May I help you?"

"I'm trying to locate a patient, Geneva Ferris."

The receptionist was unemotional. "May I ask who's calling?"

"I'm her daughter, Shirley Ferris. I've been trying to find her. She was once in the psychiatric unit at St. Mary's, but we lost contact. I'm here from Texas trying to find her. Someone at St. Mary's suggested I try Alton. Can you tell me if she's a patient?"

"Just a moment, please." There was still no reaction from the woman that Shirley could finger.

She held as asked, and heard a series of telephone connections, until, at last there was an answer.

"May I help you?" It was another woman.

"I'm trying to locate Geneva Ferris. Do you know who she is? Is she a patient?"

"May I ask who's calling?"

"My name is Shirley Ferris, and I'm trying to locate Geneva Ferris."

The woman's voice sounded guarded. "How do you know Geneva Ferris? What is your relationship?"

"It's really a long story." And she didn't want to go into it just to be disappointed, just to be told that her mother wasn't there, or to be told that there were rules that would prevent her from ever knowing. "Look, I'm here from Texas. I only have a couple of days left. I've been trying to find my mother—I've been trying to find my family. I know you're busy. I know you have rules. I just…I just…"

Shirley could hear papers rustling in the background. "If you could give me just a little more information, Ms. Ferris. We have to have a certain amount of basic information to pulse the system. You know how it is; the wheels grind slowly."

"Right. I know about that. Slowly, yes. It's just that I don't have a lot of time. If she isn't in Alton, I'm not sure where to look. But actually, my married name is, or was, Mills. Ferris is my maiden name. My mother's maiden name is Johnson."

"That information is very helpful, Ms. Mills. Should I call you *Mills* or *Ferris?*"

"It doesn't matter, I just need to find my mother. She probably won't even recognize me…"

"When was the last time you were in contact with your mother? Have you visited her here at Alton?"

"No, like I told you before, the last I heard she was at St. Mary's. I was a little girl—it was some time ago—1968. My father died, my mother's brothers left the state, my mother had a breakdown, and I was sent to live with a relative in Texas. The last time I saw my mother, she was…I don't think she recognized who I was. I don't think she would recognize me now. Of course, she wouldn't; it's been so many years. Anyway, I went to St. Mary's to try to find her. A sister there, Sister Pietra, suggested that I try Alton. I also tried calling Chester—"

"Chester only houses men."

"I know. That's what the chaplain there, Father Connelly, told me."

"You said your uncles left the state. Do you know where they are now?"

"Actually, they're here now. Not far away. They left Illinois, and I'm not sure of all the details, but they came back to work here—I believe in Chicago. But they're here. They're both in Joliet…I know this must all sound crazy to you." Shirley gripped the phone receiver. "You know what, Mrs.—I don't know your name."

"Janet Smith. I prefer Ms."

"You know what, Ms. Smith? I'm taking up way too much of your time. Too much time has passed. I should have done this years ago. It's just too late."

"Sooner might have been better, but you shouldn't give up hope, Ms. Mills. Things always have a way of working out. Now, if you could give me three last pieces of information. I need some way to contact you should we get disconnected or should my research turn up information that might be helpful to you. Do you recall the last address at which you resided with your mother? And what was your father's first name?"

She had come this far. She might as well play it out to the end. Maybe, since her mother wasn't there, Ms. Smith might be able to suggest to her the next place she could look. "I'm staying at the Rodeway Inn. We lived on Sixty-second Street in East St. Louis. I…we—I'm traveling with another woman—drove by to see the house. I guess it was day before yesterday. Oh, and my father's name was Calvin."

There were more papers rustling. "Excuse me just a moment, please." Shirley waited for the phone to click, to be put on hold. Instead she heard footsteps, a door close, and then Ms. Smith returned to the phone. "I'm sorry to put you through this, Ms. Mills. I'm sure this has been difficult for you. I know that all of the information you gave me…just reciting it must have been difficult for you. I appreciate your patience.

"You have a very involved family history. But you understand, we have to protect the privacy and the security of our patients. We have a legal and an ethical responsibility to protect their rights. Unfortunately—or fortunately, some would say—Geneva Ferris isn't here."

FORTY-THREE

What was all this supposed to be about? Shirley closed her eyes as the pressure on her chest pushed her down on the bed. She held the telephone receiver to her chest.

Why was this happening? Why was she here? This wasn't the way things were supposed to happen. She was supposed to ask God for help. He was supposed to tell her what to do. God was supposed to do the good thing—He was supposed to open the door. If this was what she was supposed to do, it should be easy, shouldn't it?

She cried all the tears that she had held back. She let out everything she had swallowed or shrugged away. *You're never alone.* What did that mean? *Fear not.* What was the point of all this? If ever she could use an angel, now was the time.

Shirley could hear Ms. Smith's muffled voice coming from the phone. "Ms. Mills? Ms. Mills? Are you there? Ms. Ferris? Ms. Mills?"

Shirley slammed the phone onto the receiver cradle.

Windy sounded frightened. "Shirley, what's wrong? Are you okay? What's wrong."

I didn't ask to come here, God. I didn't want to come. I came because I asked You for a sign. I could have been with my kids. We could have been on our way to California, instead of here. Why here? Why did You bring me here to do this to me? You told me You wouldn't make me ashamed. You told me I wouldn't be confused. Why did You make me hope? Look what I've been through, and just when I dare or even take the chance to hope…I would have been better without the hope.

Shirley rolled on her side, still weeping. Windy stood over her and touched her shoulder. "Are you okay? Do you need to talk?" Shirley shrugged Windy's hand away and turned her face to the wall. She willed herself to sleep.

When she slept, Shirley dreamed she was a little girl. The house in Tyler was silent except for the creaking of Mother Johnson's rocking chair.

"Come crawl up on my lap, Shirley." Mother Johnson circled her arms around Shirley's waist. "Baby, I want you to hear me now, and really, really listen. Mother may not be able to tell you all this some other time, so you need to listen right now. Maybe this is just for you, or maybe it might be for Sheri—you might have to carry the word to her someday, but I feel like I've just got to tell you." Mother rubbed her hand in circles on Shirley's back.

"You know what I hear in your story, baby? Heartbreak. A broken heart. And you know how I recognize it? Because I walked with heartbreak all the days of my young life. Everybody has a different story of how they got the heartbreak. But when you've had it, you recognize it; you know the symptoms."

Shirley felt like she could not breathe.

"In my house, my mother was a lovely woman, a beautiful woman. But somewhere along the way I do believe she got deeply

hurt or got frightened. And I think that what she told herself was she was going to make sure that there was no more heartache or storms in her life. So she wouldn't let anything that even looked like a storm come into her life. Of course, that also meant that she couldn't love. Because everyone wise in love knows there ain't no such thing as love that doesn't have any storms.

"You're too young to understand all this now. But if you got love and you got no storms, you got a play act or a movie, but not real love. 'Course on the other hand, if all you got is storms, you don't have love—you got drama.

"Keeping the storms away means you can't love much of any-body. You can do what looks like love—smile, wash clothes, tidy house, go to church, bake cookies, sing Christmas carols—but you can't let anyone touch your heart, so it's not love. Trying to keep the storms out of your life will run you crazy, 'cause you can't fight God, and He's the one that allows the storms to come.'"

Shirley squeezed her eyes shut and whimpered. And she imagined the trees outside of her window of her East St. Louis home. She could see and hear the tree limbs that brushed against her window when the rain and winds came.

Mother stroked Shirley's hair and hummed the chorus of a lullaby in her ear. "'Hush, little baby, don't say a word. Mama's going to buy you a mockingbird...'" She rocked her—back and forth, back and forth, until Shirley quieted.

Then Mother Johnson began to tell her story again. "So because she was heartbroken, my mother gave us everything but her tender, wounded heart. And anybody wise in love knows that the one thing children—or people for that matter—can't hardly live without is love. We all looked pretty on the outside—fed, clothed, and polished. But we were messed up on the inside. See, Mother didn't intend to harm us—she probably went to her grave not ever really knowing it—but trying to keep the storms away on the outside, trying to do what she thought would keep her and us safe, just kept storms brewing on the inside of us."

Shirley could feel herself in her bed, feel how she'd curl into a ball, pillow over her head…

"It's sad what heartbreak will do. It made me ashamed. I didn't want anyone to know that my mother wouldn't love me. I tried to figure out every day what it was I could do that would make her let me in her heart—I figured there must be something wrong with me. And I tried to keep people away so they couldn't come to my house and see that she didn't love me, because then they'd probably see that something was really wrong with me."

Mother cuddled Shirley closer to her and rubbed her chin along the top of Shirley's head. "So I know heartbreak when I see it, all right. I know the look of people starving for love, starving to give love. But you know, Shirley, that's what makes me love the Lord. When no one else loved me, I could feel Him holding me while I cried at night."

Shirley raised her head and looked into Mother's eyes. "Baby Jesus. You, too?"

Mother nodded. "Me, too. And, Shirley, He did something special for me. He healed my broken heart. One day, even if no one else loved me or let me love them, I knew His love was enough." Mother touched her finger to the heart place on Shirley's chest. "And I never heard anybody preach about it in church, but one day I was reading the Bible and there it was. God will heal our broken hearts. He wants to heal our broken hearts." She wagged her head. "It was beautiful medicine to my eyes, ears, and heart."

Little Shirley thought about the song that she hummed at night.

Rock me, baby Jesus,

Hold me, baby Jesus,

Love me, baby Jesus,
So I won't be afraid.

Mother Johnson hugged Shirley closer. "So I started praying to Him about my broken heart. I cried to Him about all the hurt and shame and confusion in my life. I begged Him. And I don't know what happened or when it happened, but one day I didn't hurt anymore. The pain just went away." Mother snapped her fingers, then put her arms back around Shirley. "So when I'm crying to the Lord—you know, like at church—and people think I got troubles, what they don't know is that I'm crying because He took my broken heart away, rolled it away like a stone. And He gave me a new heart."

Mother Johnson toyed with Shirley's braids. "Shirley, somebody in your life, or Sheri's life, maybe both…somebody was afraid of storms. And they were trying too hard to keep control of their lives, to keep pains and storms out of their lives. Trying so hard that they left somebody else with a broken heart. What they didn't know is that God is also God even in the storms. They didn't know that thunder comes when God is creating—be it peace or love or joy or families. They didn't know that God's storms won't kill you, and that out of the storm, God brings deliverance and order—divine order."

She rocked Shirley. "You know, I can't make all the hurt go away. I can rock you and rub your back. I can tell you everything will be all right. But I know Someone who can make it go away. He can heal broken hearts. I'm living testimony. If He healed my heart, Shirley, I know that He can heal yours. And you remember that I told you so."

Mother Johnson took one hand and lifted Shirley's chin. She looked deeply into Shirley's eyes, and Shirley felt something inside of her tremble.

"Now I can't tell you that everything was perfect. I been through a lot and I got scars to prove it. But God gave me more love than I could have ever imagined. The scars I have, I just use them now to prove to other people that they can be healed. God gave me joy. And nothing—He won't ever let nothing separate me from His love. 'Cause God is a good God. He is a mercy God.

"You been through a lot today, baby. You been through a lot in your short life. But, Shirley, you need to know that this world is not a place for the fainthearted. But you need to know that the Lord is with you and He is going to make something beautiful out of all the turmoil you been through. You remember I told you so."

Shirley pulled her chin away, closed her eyes, and began to cry. Mother Johnson adjusted Shirley's position on her lap. "I don't understand it all, baby. Why anybody has to suffer."

Mother nuzzled Shirley's head with her chin. "I know all you can see around you now are shadows. And in the shadows it feels like you're all alone—like you're in a thick, dark fog, and there are monsters lurking in the darkness waiting to do you harm. But you remember this if you don't remember anything else I say: God is walking with you in the shadows. You have to learn to find Him, to hear Him in the shadows. You have to learn to recognize His touch. When you're lost or frightened, don't be afraid to cry out to Him. He knows the voice of His sheep. He'll walk with you, and He'll direct you; He'll correct your path. Believe me, I know. No matter what darkness He allows you to walk into, He intends for you to come out. And you remember that I told you."

Shirley pulled away from Mother Johnson's hand and spoke between sobs. "But I don't know how, Mother. I don't know how to call Him. I don't know how to find my way."

"Always remember that you are stronger than you think you are. You're in a battle, Shirley. You're a little girl, but it's still a battle.

And the Lord would not have let you enter the battle if He did not know that you are strong enough to win. You fight and win by keeping a pure and forgiving heart. Forgive and forget the hurts that you suffer, no matter who does it. You win by praying to God. You win by doing what you hear me and Ma Dear doing—praying just a little bit of God's Word. And if you don't know what else to do, you win by crying out His name. Cry it out loud as you can. Sing to Him. Shout to Him. Beat something. Tell Him you believe and beg Him to come near. Beg Him to walk you out."

"But, Mother, I don't think I can. I don't think I know how. I'm just scared!"

"Shirley, someday…someday just when you need it, you're going to remember what I'm saying to you now. You remember, no matter what it looks like—no matter how much it looks like midnight, no matter what stirs in the shadows—you are never alone. You are never, never, never alone. Your mind may be too young, but I want your spirit to understand—you have forces at work for you—God's army, in a kingdom that you cannot see. There are forces that are just waiting for you to pray, for you to beg, so that they can—at the direction of the Lord—come to fight against things in your life that are too big for you to fight. They are willing to do whatever is necessary to bring you out, so don't give up. You got to pass through the shadows to get to the light. Pray. Don't ever give up. Pray. Don't you ever give up, Shirley. Pray!"

Then the scene changed in her dream. Shirley was standing in the midst of shadows, in darkness. When she turned she saw the presence. It was the angel. He was wielding a sword of light that cut through the shadows, through the things that lurked there. As he fought, Shirley could hear him speaking, "Fear not. You are never alone. Don't be afraid."

Tony Taylor sat hunched over the bar, nursing his third ginger ale. He couldn't stop thinking about her. He couldn't stop thinking about Shirley.

She was a big girl. Shirley was a strong woman—she'd always been strong—and she didn't need someone running after her and trying to watch over her. Shirley was independent, which was part of what he found attractive about her, so it was foolish to waste his time sitting at the bar worrying.

Shirley was fine. She was safe and everything was under control. Only she hadn't sounded under control when he had talked to her the other night. She had sounded tired and scared. That's probably what had his mind going.

But the truth was, Shirley didn't need a knight in shining armor. He knew that. He was just an old-fashioned throwback. He had been by to check on the kids and to visit with Mother Johnson. Everything was all right. He needed to get his imagination under control.

Only Tony couldn't shake the worry.

"What's up, young blood?" Leviticus Lamentation Jones's slap on the back brought Tony back from his thoughts. "You sure throwing down your poison, there. What's going on?"

God, take good care of her and bring her home safe. Tony said a silent prayer before he turned to talk to his old friend.

FORTY-FOUR

The pounding on the door woke her.

"Ms. Mills? Ms. Ferris? Are you in there? Are you all right?"

It was a woman's voice. Shirley pulled the pillow over her head. *Go away. Just leave me alone and go away.*

"Ms. Mills? Are you in there?"

Windy sat up rubbing her eyes. "What is that? Who is that at the door?"

The knock on the door changed. It came from higher up on the door. The rap was sharp, authoritative, and insistent. She could hear a man clearing his throat. "Please open the door. If you don't open it, we're going to have to get the authorities to open it." It was Father Connelly.

The other voice, the female voice, must have been Ms. Smith. Shirley pulled the pillow off of her head and threw it against the door. "What do you want? Just leave me alone."

Father Connelly spoke again. "We need you to come to the door now. Once you answer the door, if you want us to leave, we will. But we need you first to answer the door."

Windy's blue eyes were large and round and her voice sounded frightened. She whispered, "Shirley, I think we need to answer the door. Do you need me to do it?"

Shirley closed her eyes and exhaled. "No, I'll do it." She swung her legs out of the bed. "I've given up; I can't find her. I just don't know what else they want." She walked to the door and jerked it open—but just to a crack. "Yes?" She squinted and held her hand over her eyes to block the sunlight.

Ms. Smith—she was small with gray-streaked black hair—spoke first. "I tried to call you back last night. I was so worried when you hung up the phone. I didn't know how to reach you. I couldn't find a Rodeway Inn that had a listing for you. I was going crazy. I knew how desperate you were to find your mother—I just kept praying that you wouldn't lose hope. Then I remembered that you had mentioned talking to the chaplain at Chester. Father Connelly had the number and, because of him, I was able to find you."

Father Connelly nodded. "We have something we think you need to see."

"You hung up so quickly. I was trying to tell you, but you just hung up the phone."

Shirley just wanted to lie back down. "I'm fine. Everything is fine. I'm just tired and I want to go back to sleep. So I couldn't find my mother. I got to talk to my uncles—one of my uncles. And that was good enough. I'm not going to lose my mind about it. I haven't seen my mother in years. Really, there was no point to it. She wasn't coherent enough to even recognize me anyway. It's been a lot of years, and I've survived. I'm going to keep on surviving. So you don't have to worry." She looked at Ms. Smith. "I'm not going to do anything desperate. I'm just going back to sleep."

Father Connelly's face was set. "We really wish that you would come with us."

Ms. Smith nodded. "You have to come."

When Shirley and Windy were dressed, they left the room and walked to the hotel parking lot. The shower helped, but Shirley still felt tired and ready to return to the room.

Father Connelly stepped from his car and waved to them. "My car is big enough, why don't we all ride together."

Ms. Smith shook her head and shrugged constantly. "I felt so badly that our conversation ended the way it did yesterday. I know how desperately you wanted to find your mother and how disappointed you were that she wasn't at Alton."

Shirley turned her head and stared out the window while Ms. Smith talked.

"I'm so glad you mentioned Father Connelly and that he agreed to help me. I just felt that it was so important for you to see this."

"Yes, she was quite distraught." Shirley turned to look at Father Connelly. "It is my pleasure to help." He looked briefly at Shirley, then he looked at Windy in the rearview mirror. "And what is your name?"

"I'm sorry, Father. I didn't mean to be rude. I'm just tired." Shirley covered her mouth and tried to stifle a yawn. "This is my friend Windy."

Father Connelly looked at Windy again. "So are you from this area?"

Windy shook her head. "No, I'm from Oklahoma. That's

where I'm on my way back to when all this is over."

"I see."

"I just thought it would give you so much hope to see this."

Ms. Smith continued talking, and Shirley closed her eyes, leaned her head back on the seat, and fell asleep.

When she awakened, they were parking in front of an old red brick building in an aged neighborhood. The outside of the building had been refurbished and the front sign read *Holy Angels Homeless Shelter.* On the sign, there was a picture of an angel with a sword and shield.

Ms. Smith talked as they walked up the steps and to the door. "When we release people from long-term care facilities like Alton, or from the psychiatric units like the one that used to be at St. Mary's, the people often transition through shelters like this one. This facility is funded, in large part, by the generosity of Catholic Charities of Southern Illinois. There are other funding sources, but the beauty of Holy Angels is that all kinds of people work together here."

They stepped inside the door onto hardwood floors. Ms. Smith looked around them as they walked. "There is a Baptist preacher who comes to minister to the women and to teach Bible studies each Thursday night. And those Bible studies, just like this shelter, are open to all people, regardless of faith. Holy Angels also has a nun, a social worker, who has renounced her vows. Her order left the area, but she stayed so that she can continue to work in this shelter and serve this community that she has come to love." Ms. Smith turned down a hallway. "I'm going to stop talking and let you meet her." She stopped outside an office doorway and nodded in Shirley's direction. "This is the woman I called you about—Ms. Ferris-Mills."

A middle-aged woman stood, stepped from behind her

desk, and extended her hand. "Paula Schultz. Welcome to Holy Angels."

Paula Schultz took long, commanding strides, though she stopped to hug women and children that passed. "God moves in this place. Women and children come to Holy Angels with all sorts of labels—prostitute, drug addict, schizophrenic, bipolar—some of them overmedicated. When they arrive, they believe that they are what they have been labeled. However, we believe in the Holy Father as a merciful healer. We offer them love in exchange for their labels. We see ourselves as repairers of the breach, as the ones charged to rebuild the desolate cities. At Holy Angels, we do it one soul at a time."

Shirley and the others followed her down a long hallway. "Within the short time that they are here, we see broken people transformed. They realize that their labels are not who they are, but something that they may have done." She led them up a set of stairs, stairs made from aged deep brown wood, smoothed from years of polishing and feet ascending. "They embrace themselves as beautiful women, God's own handiwork created in His image." They continued climbing. "Most of them are discharged and leave here to move into their own homes or apartments. They get jobs, begin or restore their families. They miraculously become fully functioning members of the community."

She laughed softly. "But once they are here, we don't seem able to get rid of them."

Paula Schultz walked up two more stairs, down a short dark hallway with white painted walls, and then laid her hand on the knob of a bright red door. "They leave here restored and transformed and they return to plant the seeds of love and healing that they have received into the lives of others." She turned the knob and walked inside.

FORTY-FIVE

❧

*I*nside the room with the red door, a middle-aged woman sat in a bright yellow upholstered chair. Her head lolled on her neck, but she stared straight ahead at the single-paned window in front of her. She was wrapped in a white sheet—which she clutched to her chest—that completely covered her, except for the red terry cloth slippers she wore on her feet. A woman, wearing a pink dress, walked in and out of view, attending to the woman in white.

Paula Schultz waved to Shirley and the others. "Come in." She took Shirley's hand and held it. "I have someone I want you to see."

Shirley walked closer to the woman sitting in the chair. Paula pointed at the woman in the pink dress. "I believe that you two should get acquainted."

Shirley frowned. The woman in the pink dress looked vaguely familiar.

"Shirley, baby, is that *you?*"

Shirley Ferris-Mills and her mother, Geneva Johnson-Ferris, sat together in a prayer garden behind the shelter. Sometimes, they were arm in arm. But often Shirley simply fell into her mother's arms like a little girl. "Mama," was all that she could say.

Over the hours that they were together, Shirley learned that her mother had been at St. Mary's in 1968. "I was so gone, Shirley, I don't really remember when I left." At some point she had been transferred to Alton. "It wasn't that long ago that I left there. Ms. Smith was my caseworker. She got me released to Holy Angels."

She hugged Shirley. "I thought I was never going to see you again. By the time I was well enough to begin to piece together what had happened, I couldn't find you or your uncles. I looked for you for years, but it never occurred to me that you might be in Texas." Mama smiled. "I should have known, though. Mother Johnson has always been a wonder." She rubbed circles on Shirley's back. With every circle, she felt lighter, she breathed more deeply.

"I tried to find my brothers, to make it up to them, to apologize. I was making myself more sick worrying. Finally I just surrendered it all into God's hands. I stopped trying to figure it out—I stopped expecting to know and control the plan ahead of time. When God was ready, if it was part of His plan, He was going to work it out.

"I think that's what made me sick in the first place, Shirley—trying to control things I couldn't control. So many nights I've thought about you and wondered what I taught you. I know I taught you some good things—your daddy and me. But I've been praying that God would rewind and undo those things that are not good.

Her mother continued to rub her back. "There were so many things going on in the world. People were so afraid. There was war in Vietnam and children being murdered in churches. There were riots and confusion. When everything is working well in a family, the world falling apart outside puts a strain on them." Shirley's mother cleared her throat. "When the family is strained, terror outside of their door just adds more pressure. I was like a lot of people, Shirley; I needed help and I didn't know how to ask. I thought it was weak to ask."

Her mother began to stroke her hair. She asked Shirley about her life.

Shirley told her mother about her children and about her husband that died in Germany.

"It's a sad thing," her mother said, "to lose someone that was a part of you. It's like a piece of you dies. It takes a while to heal. You can't imagine living without that person. It just seems easier to give up. It almost seems loyal somehow to put your life aside. But don't die, Shirley—live. You hear me? Don't die, Shirley—*live!*"

Shirley lifted her head to stare into her mother's eyes. It was more than she could ever have imagined, to hear the woman she had thought utterly without hope commanding *her* to live.

"I'm whole again, Shirley. Actually, I'm better than I was before. It's like a fairy tale, isn't it? I have my own place. I have a job, and I come here to spread the blessing that was given to me. I come to show other people—other walking dead—how to live.

She touched Shirley's face. "Now I have my daughter *and* my brothers. Mother Johnson is right, God is a mercy God. We have time to get to know each other; you have time to get to know who I have become. And grandchildren! I never imagined such a gift. No matter where you go, Shirley, I believe the Lord is going to help us repair what has been broken. Distance and time are nothing in the Master's hands." Shirley's heart pounded, tears covered her face. She was speechless. She kept searching her mother's face—the miracle was hard for her to believe.

"Baby, it might be too late. And this may not mean anything to you, but I promised if I ever got the chance, I would say it."

Shirley wiped away tears as her mother spoke.

"It may be too late…but I'm sorry."

Like a little child, Shirley enfolded herself in her mother's arms. She didn't know she needed the words until she heard them. "Thank you, Mama. Thank you!" Shirley and her mother were silent then, except for an occasional escaped sob while they held each other, rocking back and forth.

"Shirley, most of the things I did wrong, I did because I just followed what I had seen people do before me. Kind of like a pattern, you know? But you don't have to follow the pattern, baby. None of us have to. You can change things. We can all change."

When they walked back inside, arm in arm, Windy was standing by the front door with Father Connelly. Her eyes were red-rimmed and her face was pink. Shirley was sure that her own face was glowing—it felt warm, and it was as though she were floating on air. But she felt ashamed now because in her own joy, she had forgotten about Windy. Windy who had been unable to find any real piece of her life, any real connection to her father.

"Windy, I'm sorry." Shirley smiled at her mother, then moved to hug the girl, who continued to cry. "I spent so much time moaning about my own family, I haven't been such a good friend. It seems unfair for you to come all the way here and then return home with no answers."

Father Connelly nodded. "God works in mysterious ways."

On the way back to the hotel—after they had said their good-byes to Shirley's mother and to Paula Schultz—they dropped Ms. Smith at the gate of Alton Mental Health Center. Shirley squeezed the woman and thanked her. "You gave me back my life; you gave me back hope."

While he drove Shirley and Windy to the hotel, Father Connelly smiled at both of them. "So many of my friends in ministry ask why I choose to labor in the prison system. I tell them that the men are hungry. It's my pleasure to offer them Christ. When I saw Windy, I was struck by a startling resemblance she shares with one of our inmates. The startling blue eyes and the pale blond hair—I just could not believe they were not of some relation."

Windy grabbed Shirley's hand and began to cry again into the handkerchief that Father Connelly had given her. Shirley's mouth dropped open. She gasped for air—it was good news she was not prepared to receive.

Once they were at the hotel, Windy went into the room, while Father Connelly finished his story. "Of course, when Windy told me that she was from Oklahoma, I thought I must have been mistaken. It was when you were with your mother that the two of us—Windy and I—were able to talk, and I put two and two together. The inmate in question first came to the attention of the prison system with what seemed like some minor infractions. However, it became apparent that he had some more serious illness that led to him being committed to the Chester facility. Her father, Ken, is an arsonist, you see. As a youngster, he set several fires in this area—actually in East St. Louis near the Fifty-ninth to Sixty-third Street area— mostly residential, that led to some loss of property and possibly life. Ken found his way in and out of the juvenile system, until he progressed to larger blazes and found his way to Chester."

The priest shook his head. "I would have hesitated to tell Windy about her father, since she is with child, except that it is important for that very reason. I have come to understand more and more each day that there really is nothing too hard for God. Ken was quite resistant when I first began to speak with him. But it is he who in the last few months has sought me out and asked me if I could help him find his child.

"I would say that we shouldn't expect a miracle, but as you well know—there is nothing too hard for God."

Shirley held the telephone receiver to her ear. She held on tightly, so much had happened, she might otherwise float away. "Yes, Mother Johnson, I'm fine. You won't believe how God worked everything out. I still can't believe it, and it happened to me." Shirley promised to give them all the details when she got home. "I'm just too tired right now." She blew telephone kisses to Mika and Lex. "I miss you guys so much!"

"We miss you, too, Mommy!"

"I've got so much to tell you. I can't wait to see you. I'll be home soon."

Shirley hung up, then stood in the telephone booth, armed with quarters, trying to get the courage to call. It was silly; the man loved her. It was silly to be afraid of something so sure. She inserted the quarters and dialed.

"Tony?"

"Shirley! Where are you? I've been thinking about you—man, I'll be glad when you get home. How did everything turn out?"

"Good. Miraculously! I'm really too tired to talk. But, Tony, I just wanted to thank you for…for propping me up through all of this. And…and for being a friend." Her voice lowered. "I love you." She slapped her hand over her eyes. "Okay, there I said it. It's out."

Shirley could hear a smile in his voice. "You are a funny girl." He paused. "I love you, too." Tony cleared his throat. "So when will you get home?" He spoke quickly, as though he were trying to change the subject.

"Tony, I'm so tired. I don't know how Windy and I are going to make it back. If I could have anything I want, I would have someone come and drive me home. You know any available knights in shining armor?"

Tony paused and then laughed. His voice sounded excited and relieved. "Hang up the phone; I'm on the way."

Shirley lay across the bed. It was probably pointless to try to sleep. So much had happened…things she never expected, things she was too afraid to believe, promises she thought would never be answered.

Thank You, God.

She toyed with the pink ribbon of the bundle that lay on the bed next to her. She'd faced everything else, she might as well clean the slate.

Shirley untied the ribbon and removed the brown envelope with recollections from Danny's memorial service. She hadn't read any of it yet. She hadn't been able to. But she was strong enough to read it now, to look at the pictures, the program.

There was a clipping from the newspaper *Stars and Stripes* about a serviceman—Danny Mills—and a woman that were killed during a bombing at their Air Force base where they worked. The article detailed that they were standing together near a window and were the only people in the office killed.

Inside the memorial envelope there was a handwritten letter of condolence from Danny's commanding officer. He talked about what a good man Danny was and how he was laughing with a coworker, the woman who passed away, at the moment just before he died.

Also inside was a smaller, folded piece of paper. She opened it and recognized Danny's handwriting.

Shirley,

I know you are falling off your chair. I never write. But I couldn't hold it anymore. There's a woman in the office where I work and some of the guys told me she's from East St. Louis. She looks to be about your age. And guess what? Her name's Sheri! Spelled just like your Sheri. So I was thinking, how many Sheri's could there be from East St. Louis? Maybe she really was real after all, Shirley. Wouldn't that blow your mind?

It would be a nice gift to give the girl I love, huh? So, anyway, I'm going to go over to her desk—she sits near the window—and ask her. What have we got to lose?

Love you.

That was the last thing Danny wrote. He didn't even sign his name.

Shirley dropped the letter. It was crazy. It couldn't have been Sheri. Shirley felt perspiration on her forehead. She sat up and pushed aside the brown envelope and its contents. *I shouldn't have opened it. I should have left well enough alone.* There were too many questions…questions she thought were settled before she opened the envelope.

We can't know everything. We can't know it all… Tony's voice came back to her and soothed her.

Shirley forced her breathing to slow. She willed her heart to slow its pace. If it were her Sheri, if Shirley had not dreamed her after all…then she had the strength to say good-bye to both Sheri and Danny. Shirley wasn't a little girl anymore. The fear was gone.

Shirley smiled. Even if Sheri *never* existed, Shirley now had the courage to say good-bye to the make-believe friend who had comforted her. It was okay to remember Sheri and Danny and to treasure their memories. It was okay to feel the sadness of losing them. It was part of her being able to walk forward into the promise that lay ahead of her.

If I could see Sheri again, I would tell her. I would tell her that what happened at her grandmother's house had very little, if anything, to do with her. I would tell her that her grandmother probably didn't even know. That she probably didn't do it on purpose. That her grandmother probably had other things that tormented her. I would tell Sheri how they did not believe me—did not believe me about her. We would laugh and talk about how they poked and prodded me. How they did not believe me. How sometimes even I wondered. I would tell her that, despite everything, I made it—I did shine.

I would rub her shoulder, if I saw her again, and tell Sheri to rest.

Shirley lay back on the bed and before she went to sleep, she prayed for rest and for peace, then she said good-bye.

FORTY-SIX

indy sat on the edge of Shirley's bed and rubbed her hands over Shirley's chenille bedspread. Her hair was still white-blond, but the spots that were colored seemed less startling, less fluorescent. Shirley smiled at Windy. To tell the truth, everything about the girl seemed calmer. For weeks now Windy had seemed less frenetic, less frenzied. Purple toenail polish still showed beneath the sandalfoot pantyhose the girl was wearing, her hair was still stiffly moussed into spikes—but her gaze seemed less guarded and anxious.

Shirley kept putting items in her carryall bag as she listened to Windy talk—stockings, deodorant, shoes—so that she could still make it to church. Mika and Lex had gone ahead with Mother Johnson, but there was so much left to do. She turned to the closet and the dress hanging there. Shirley unzipped the garment bag that covered the dress and peeked inside; everything was perfect.

Calm down, Shirley. Don't start sweating! She glanced in the mirror at the new hairdo that was part of announcing her new life. She needed to move quickly, but she definitely didn't need to sweat. Who knew if, where they were going, there would be easy access to a beautician to fix her hair?

She looked from the garment bag back to Windy, whose stomach was round beneath her pale, mint green dress. There was no doubt—the baby was coming soon!

Windy looked back at her and smiled. "I never thought I would see this day come. Here you are packing to leave—" she patted her stomach—"and I'm unpacking to stay. You and the kids are moving out. Me and my grandmother are moving into our own little place." Windy rubbed the bedspread with her other hand. "My daddy's so excited about his first grandbaby." She stopped talking and looked down with a sigh.

Shirley took a step toward her, but then Windy smiled as she looked up again. Shirley thought she saw tears in the corners of the girl's eyes.

"I still can't believe that I saw him—that I saw my daddy. I never imagined I would be seeing him in some place like that…a prison hospital. The bus ride back there was so long, and I kept telling myself I was going to get off the bus and come back—that I was wasting my time."

Shirley imagined the priest in his dark coat escorting Windy's small, rounded figure through heavy iron doors that slammed shut behind her. She imagined the girl sitting alone in an institutional-green painted room on a scraped, scarred chair. Windy's gaze said that though she was sitting on Shirley's bed, she was back in the cold, sad room with her father. "But when I saw him, I forgot where I was…that I was sitting on a little stool and talking to him through Plexiglas." Windy shook her head. "He was in chains, but all I could see was his eyes—my eyes. And his hair—my hair."

She focused directly on Shirley. "It was so weird, but good

weird, you know?" She took a deep breath. "I don't even remember most of what we said. It was like I was in a fog. But I remember feeling like I was seeing myself in him, and I remember him saying, 'So, you're my little girl?' He didn't say too much more than that." One tear fell from the corner of her eye and made a tiny meandering trail on her cheek. "I never thought I'd hear that, Shirley. I never really thought I'd ever hear my own daddy call me his little girl." Windy patted her stomach again. "Maybe after I have my baby, we'll be able to go see my daddy again."

Shirley smiled and nodded, not sure what to say. "Maybe." So much had happened in the past few months. "With all the stuff that's been happening to the two of us—really to all of us—I guess we better learn to expect happy endings." Shirley shrugged. "It doesn't take any more energy to hope for something good than it does to forcing ourselves to settle for bad things, does it?"

Shirley paused. She strained to hear. Was she hearing what she imagined? Yes, there was whining coming from the kitchen. She yelled into the kitchen. "You're just going to have to wait, Roscoe. We'll be back to pick you up after church." There was still too much to do. She couldn't spare more time for him.

Windy laughed. "Roscoe?"

"That's what Lex named him." Shirley grabbed a tissue from the box on the dresser and dabbed around her hairline. "Ever since we got back from East St. Louis, Lex has been praying and praying. But you know that." Windy nodded. "He and Mika have worn a groove from their bedroom to the prayer house." Shirley motioned for Windy to move over and then sat down beside her. "He has just been determined. Well, a few weeks ago, we started noticing the dog that belongs to the man across the street trotting up the driveway and cutting through Mother's backyard. Poor thing, it looks so old."

Windy laughed. "You're not kidding. Does the dog have any teeth left?"

"That poor animal. She's looks like she's had enough puppies for three or four dogs. Her stomach was almost dragging on the ground, but I just thought… Anyway, Mother said the dog had never been over here before. 'She's looking for some place to drop those pups.' I should have known." Shirley dabbed her forehead. "Well, one night we all woke up when we heard this kind of groaning sound, then this kind of mewling, yipping sound."

Windy touched one of her hands to her cheek. "Oh no."

"Oh yes! Right up under Mother's house. I guess that dog crawled up underneath from the old porch out back. When we told the man across the street and he came to get his dog and the pups, he offered one to Lex and Mika." Shirley jumped from the bed and began to dance around, mimicking Lex and Mika. "You would have thought they found the pot of gold at the end of the rainbow."

Shirley dabbed her hairline again and sat down. She was going to have to remember to be calm…to stay cool. "There was only one puppy out of the whole litter that was black and white. When Lex saw him, he hollered, 'That's the one!'" Shirley laughed. "Actually, both of them hollered—you know Mika and Lex." She turned to look toward the kitchen. "They already have the little thing spoiled."

She turned, looked at the window she and Windy faced…the window she'd looked out all the years she lived with Mother Johnson. Leaving was bittersweet. She looked down at Windy's soft hands and squeezed the one nearest to her. "I'm glad you found home." Shirley rubbed the top of Windy's hand and covered it with her own. "I'm happy it worked out for you. Who would have ever thought?"

Windy nodded. "Who would have ever thought?"

Shirley smiled, glanced at the clock on the nightstand, then stood. "We better go."

When they pulled up to the small church that Mother Johnson had attended for all the years that Shirley had known her, Shirley was glad that someone had thought to reserve a space for her. The grass-covered yard that served as the church's Sunday parking lot was jam-packed with cars. The cars looked to be all around the church, except for a small space in the front. It seemed as though the early arrivals had made nice, neat rows. Apparently the later arrivals were angled in all directions—wedged in wherever there might be even a hint of a parking space.

She and Windy opened the doors of Shirley's small car—which was stuffed with bags and suitcases—then hurried across the bit of yard between them and the church. Passing the remains of an old water pump, they climbed the red brick steps, and slipped inside the church onto the last pew.

Windy leaned over and whispered to Shirley. "One good thing about being at your church this Sunday, at least I can come here and not have to hear my grandmother asking me over and over, 'Are you going to join this week?'" Windy smiled, her eyes looking in the direction of the woman who was up front, reading the directions. "She loves me. But every Sunday, it's the same thing." Windy spread her hot-pink-frosted fingertips wide. "I just need time, you know?"

The woman sitting next to Windy—an usher with blue-black

hair smoothed severely straight underneath a white lace cap that looked like a doily, that matched her white nurse's uniform and shoes and her white gloves—leaned forward, as though to be sure both Shirley and Windy could see her. The woman pointed at her usher's badge, lifted an index finger to her lips, and scowled. Shirley felt caught, like a kid again. Her face got warm and she began to perspire. She pressed the tissue she had stuffed in her coat pocket to her hairline. It was cool outside; she needed to think cool inside. Appropriately chastised, she turned her attention back to the pastor, who had taken his place at the front of the church.

Reverend Howard had been pastor of the church for years. With the authority that comes with purpose and the familiarity that comes with more than thirty years' service to the same flock, he paced back and forth in front of the congregation as he read from the Bible. "As Jesus was getting into the boat, the man who had been demon-possessed begged to go with him. Jesus did not let him, but said, 'Go home to your family and tell them how much the Lord has done for you, and how he has had mercy on you.' So the man went away and began to tell in the Decapolis how much Jesus had done for him. And all the people were amazed."

The pastor took off his glasses and began to preach to the flock. His voice didn't sound like rolling thunder, but more like a gentle father speaking to children he loved. "That young man wanted to get in that boat and go with Jesus." He fixed his attention on a deaconess on the front row, who wore a large white hat covered with white and silver artificial flowers. He nodded and spoke to her conversationally. "After all the people the Lord called to leave their homes—Peter, Andrew, Matthew, John, Paul, and so many more—it seems like the Lord would have just eased on over in that boat and made room for that young man. Think of all he had been through. For years he had been so out of his mind, so out of control. Everyone—his family and the whole town—knew it."

Reverend Howard looked at the congregation and raised his arms in the air, so that the sleeves of his robe hung down in the shape of angel wings. Shirley smiled. It seemed that there were angels everywhere.

"Everyone knew it. People had given up on him. They called him crazy and demon-possessed. Nobody wanted to be around him." He lowered his arms. "It didn't make things any better that some of these same people saw the demons come out of the young man and jump into a herd of pigs when the Lord healed him. They saw all the pigs run into the water and drown." Reverend Howard raised an eyebrow and smiled. "To tell the truth, I'm not sure what I would think about inviting him to a barbecue at my house after all of that."

He rubbed one hand over his short-cut gray hair. "It had to be hard on that boy. You know how people are. For years people must have been saying to him, 'You need to get yourself straight.' Not thinking that it would ever really happen. They waited and waited for him to change. They gave up hope. They got comfortable with him being out of his mind and out of their lives.

"Then, suddenly, here comes Jesus! The boy is healed and whole, but those same people don't want him around—in fact, they seem to want the young man around even less than they did before he got healed." Shirley watched the pastor walk down the center aisle, walk closer to where she and Windy sat. He stopped and nodded at a man in the pew next to where he stood. "We're some funny folks."

"Amen to that, Rev," the man said.

"We want God to move, but when He does, we get scared and we call it the devil, or say it didn't happen." Reverend Howard shook his head. "We want any explanation except that God has the power to move, to change, to heal. Ain't that something?" He shrugged. "I can imagine how that young man felt." He raised his arms again. "Too much baggage. Too much history in that town and with his family." He pretended to jump off the bank into the water and to wade to the boat. "I can just feel him getting excited about a clean start with some new people that believe and understand what happened to him." Reverend Howard's voice rose.

The man in the pew next to where the pastor stood rose to his feet and cheered. "All *right* now! Preach, brother! Teach us the Word!" His wife's hand tugged at the end of his suit coat, and the man sat down.

Reverend Howard nodded at the man and kept preaching. "But—" he looked around the room—"the Lord said, 'No!'" The pastor shook his head. "I bet that young man's heart jumped in his throat. 'Go back home,' the Lord said. Bless that boy's heart."

Reverend Howard lowered his head, walked back to the rostrum, and put on his glasses. He lifted his head. "Most times we think it takes so much courage to be like Peter, Abraham, or Paul, and go to a foreign land we never heard of." He waved one arm. "We can just see ourselves on some great mission, can't we?"

He lowered his arm and searched the congregation with his eyes. "The Lord told us to spread the good news in Jerusalem, Judea, Samaria, and the world." Shirley shivered when the pastor's eyes passed through and over her. "Sometimes, though, the world is the easy part. The world doesn't know our history. If the world doesn't love us, at least they don't hate us or know our past. The world doesn't know us—we've got a clean slate. We don't have ruined, hopeless relationships with the world. The world looks alive and full of possibilities." His voice rose and seemed to wrap around each syllable. "It's the people at home who call us names, who hurt us, who don't believe in us, who want us to always be the broken person that we were. Sometimes it's the relationships at home in our community—in our Judeas—that look dead. We look at all the broken relationships facing us, all the people we've hurt—it seems so much more exciting to sail the seven seas!"

Silence rushed in to fill the vacuum when Reverend Howard removed his glasses and wiped them on the hem of his robe. He nodded, and Shirley felt that his eyes were focused directly on her. "Sometimes the one who believes in us the least…is us." He tapped his eyeglasses on his chest. "Sometimes the most difficult place to find a new beginning, to offer new life, is right at home with ourselves—in our Jerusalem places. It's hard to give ourselves a chance, to believe that we can start again. Sometimes the thing that takes the most courage is doing the work we have to do at home."

Shirley rose quietly, slipped from her pew, and out the door.

After the sermon, Reverend Howard looked out over the congregation. "I know the service is over, but I've held back the benediction because we have something unusual planned. Everyone involved needs to move quickly."

Some people began to rise from their seats.

"So it would help if the rest of you will stay seated. We'll be able to move *expeditiously!*" Reverend Howard said the word with dramatic flourish. He smiled and nodded. "I promise you, you'll be glad you stayed."

Mother Johnson rose and, holding Mika and Lex's hands, tiptoed out the back door leading from the sanctuary to the rear fellowship area.

"Trust me."

Some young women carrying baskets filled with flowers and ribbons looped bouquets of pale white tulips and green tinged snowballs tied with maroon grosgrain ribbon over the ends of the pews. Men, women, and children turned in their seats and whispered to one another, while two young men carried candelabra with thick, cream-colored candles to the front of the church. Then they quickly unrolled a bolt of what looked to be a thick, velvety, cream-colored carpet.

Reverend Howard looked out at the congregation. Hats were bobbing, the room was all abuzz. He nodded when Mother Johnson walked back in the sanctuary and began to walk toward the front doors. He looked at the woman standing just inside the front doors and then nodded at the empty piano bench.

A large, elderly white woman daintily huffed up the aisle. She was all smiles, and the flowers on her cobalt blue-and-white dress and her blue-and-white hat bobbed up and down. A puff of blond hair peeked from underneath. The occasional pale blue in the hat matched her eyes.

Reverend Howard looked at the congregation. It was hard not to laugh at the smiles he saw on their faces. He overheard one woman say, "Ain't that the lady that runs the Dairy Queen? What's she doing here?"

The Dairy Queen lady settled onto the piano bench like a hen on a nest. After she struck the opening chords, the door flew open. In marched a choir, hands folded, each member walking slowly and with great solemnity as they sang. Miss Mildred seemed to be fighting a grin as she led the group of fifteen or so blue-and-white robed people who marched up front and into the empty choir stand.

Reverend Howard hoped his face didn't betray his amusement. The woman who'd spoken previously looked as though she was about to bust. She jumped to her feet, then waved her arms and looked around the room. "What are these white folks doing in here? They don't never come in here!" She lost her very large red hat as someone jerked her back to her seat. The pastor covered his mouth as he looked over the people in the church. He smiled warmly at a beautiful woman dressed in a silvery, sea-mist green dress. He'd never met her before, but it was no doubt that she was Shirley's mother.

When the Dairy Queen lady began to play the wedding march, Pastor Howard moved the fulcrum to the side and took his place in the pulpit. Two of the young women who'd placed the flowers on the pews held the doors open. Mika walked in the door wearing a pale, sage-colored dress with layers of ruffled lace that began just above her hips. She wore matching fingerless lace gloves and a large matching lace bow in her hair. With slow, graceful movements, she dropped handfuls of flower petals that drifted almost like snowflakes to the creamy carpet on the floor. Lex, close beside her, stepped from foot to foot, as though he was trying to find a beat in the music the Dairy Queen lady played. He held the pillow and rings pressed close to his cream-colored suit and maroon tie. He smiled and waved when he passed by the pew on which his grandmother sat.

Windy walked in next, followed closely by Leviticus Lamentations Jones. Reverend Howard could not help but smile. It had been years since he had seen the old man in church—maybe twenty years or more—but it was good to see him on this day. The two of them joined Mika and Lex at the altar.

Tony Taylor walked through the door, dressed in a black tuxedo, taupe shirt, and a maroon tie that matched Lex's. The lady who had lost her hat jumped to her feet again and hollered. "I *knew* it! I *knew* it! I told you it was gone be a wedding. I *told* you those two was gone get married!" She lost her hat again when she was jerked back to her seat.

Tony smiled and nodded at the pastor and then at Leviticus.

The doors closed after Mother Johnson walked through, with Shirley on her arm. It had been years since Pastor Howard had seen Mother look so good. The ivory silk dress she wore was beautiful against her mahogany skin. Her gray hair gently framed her face. He nodded at her, then turned his focus to Shirley. Her skin glowed against the empire-waisted, antique-white taffeta dress that appeared to have iridescent ripples of green similar to the color of the snowball flowers she held. Out of the large snowballs peaked white tulips, accented with one single tulip that matched the maroon-colored ribbon that held the bouquet. Flowers that mimicked the snowballs wreathed Shirley's head.

A sigh escaped Tony's lips when she finally came to stand beside him. "You look beautiful."

Reverend Howard smiled at Shirley and then looked out over the congregation. He looked back at the wedding party in front of him. "Who gives this woman in matrimony?"

Mother Johnson seemed to blush and turn toward Shirley's mother, who rose. "We do," they said in unison. Just then, the doors banged open.

"Stop the bus! Hold the phone!" It was Ma Dear. "I been waiting all this time for a church wedding. You *know* you can't do this without me!" She dragged her husband Ely down the aisle. White tulle drifted—no stirred and swished—all around her. Ely smiled to beat the band as he almost ran to keep up with Ma Dear's charge for the altar.

Reverend Howard threw back his head and laughed out loud. "I'm sorry, Ma Dear. I just got a little excited. It's not every day a preacher gets the privilege of marrying two lovely women." He looked at his watch and smiled. "I'd say we've all waited long enough for this wedding." He nodded at Shirley and Tony. "And these two, I believe, have a honeymoon flight that they have to catch."

"Us, too!" Lex crowed. "Me and Mika are going on the honeymoon, too! We're going on a cruise!" Mika bumped him with her elbow, but it didn't stop him. "And then when we get back we're moving to—"

"Lex!" For just a moment, it seemed to the pastor that Shirley stopped being a bride and went back to being mother.

"Sorry, Mommy! I'm excited!"

Ma Dear giggled and batted her eyes at her husband then turned her head. "I'm with you, Lex. We've been waiting too long for this, if you ask me!" She looked back at Reverend Howard and then at the wedding party. "All right, everyone. Let's get this show on the road!"

The pastor reached in his pocket for a handkerchief and wiped his eyes. "Amen," he chuckled. He wasn't the only one laughing. "Let the church say, 'Amen!'"

Dear Readers,

Here is the ending, the completion of Shirley's story that I promised you. Many times the most difficult journey we face is the journey back home—either the journey of self-exploration or the journey to the place of unfinished business. When we have changed and been blessed, it's often easier to walk forward in our new lives and leave the old rubbish behind. We struggle as we wonder how those who knew us then will accept us now.

We wonder if the people or the old situations will be the same. We don't want to go back, and there are plenty of logical reasons not to go there.

It may be that some people don't have to go back, but if these words are tugging at your heart, then you possibly have such a journey before you. There are old friends, family, lifestyles, or even old enemies that need to see the new you.

Others of you have been afraid to change, to be all that your spirit longs to be, because you are afraid of what people or what your past will say. We have become satisfied with enduring, we're afraid to hope for anything more. We're afraid to hope for joy.

Fear not.

I want to encourage you to embrace the journey ahead of you. Don't let unfinished business defeat you. Be assured that God has a good plan for you. The journey that awaits you is part of that good plan. Don't waste your time or energy imagining the worse. What lies ahead may look impossible, but God loves you. You may be from a hopeless place or a downtrodden past. Know that He loves you and He only has good plans for you—"plans to prosper you and not to harm you, plans to give you hope and a future" (Jeremiah 29:11, NIV).

What God has planned for you is more than you could ever think or imagine. I am not simply sharing Scripture with you. I'm sharing what I know, what I have experienced. Surrendering to God's plan has changed my life in ways I never could have imagined. I have joy and blessings I didn't even know to ask for, and not because I am perfect with a spotless past, but because God is good and merciful and He takes pleasure in restoring those of us who are lost and broken.

Step boldly into what God has for you. While you step, breathe in joy. In fact, hold your head up and sing a song. Expect the best. God is the God of the whole universe and He is determined to give you the best life you will allow. No matter how long it takes, no matter how many angels He has to dispatch, God is determined to give you a happy ending. Don't expect anything less.

Sharon Ewell Foster

sharonewelfoster@aol.com

Multnomah Publishers®

The publisher and author would love to hear your comments about this book. *Please contact us at:*
www.multnomah.net/sharonfoster

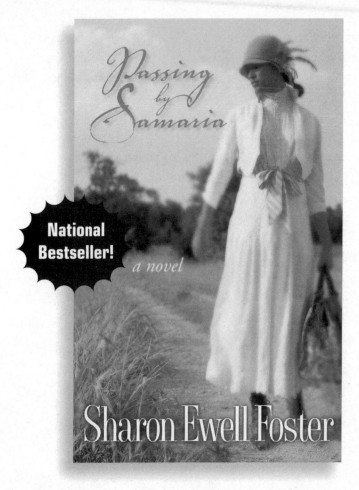

National Bestseller!

Passing by Samaria

a novel

Sharon Ewell Foster

Fleeing danger in her beloved Mississippi homeland, a young African-American woman seeks new life, love, truth, and joy in romantic turn-of-the-century Chicago.
ISBN 1-57673-615-6